ANDREA B. LAMOUREUX

SEPHEUS

BOOK THREE OF
THE ELEMENTAL DIARIES

Cover Art @ Fotolia
Cover Design: Art4Artists www.art4artists.com.au
Map: John Renehan
Formatting: Integrity Formatting

For Sarah
Even though we are blood, I'd still choose you to be my friend.

N

W · E

S

Ventosa

Terra

Solis

Lottenheim

Gwon

Ambedar   Carabroke

Aquila

The Vitreus Sea

The Kingdoms of
SARANTOA

Raised to be a torturer, I never imagined I'd one day be called upon to be a hero. I'd been taught to care for nothing and no one. Love meant pain. Love was weakness. Darkness resides in all of us, but the light that drove it back in most people's hearts had been absent in mine. Or so I thought, until someone showed me even the smallest of sparks can ignite in the dark.

I wasn't always a good man, and my story's not for the faint of heart.

CHAPTER 1

I TURNED MY back on my father and the woman tied to the wheel with a gag in her mouth to fetch the vial of green liquid as ordered.

I still felt pity at the sight of the victim's pleading eyes. No, not victims I had to remind myself... suspects. Suspects wanted for crimes against the crown.

I clutched the glass vial in my hand. It was as cold and hard as my father's heart. The woman, whose brown hair was plastered to her forehead with sweat, cried through the gag in her mouth.

My father, keeping his voice low, said into her ear, "Are you ready to confess to your crime?"

The woman nodded frantically, so my father took the gag out of her mouth, but she didn't confess as she'd promised. They usually didn't.

"I didn't do it! I love my king and queen! Please!" Her tears made muddy streaks down her cheeks. Her expensive, lace gown, once the colour of pink roses, was now soiled. She'd been down there for over seven sunrises—in my father's torture chamber, the place where he earned enough coin to live comfortably.

My father cringed at the woman's shrill cries and stuffed the wool ball back into her mouth. He held his palm out for me and I placed the glass vial in it. He uncorked the stopper and said to the woman who was one of Queen Nicola's handmaidens, "You're making me do this. This is *your* fault." He held the vial up to her face and slowly poured the contents down her cheek. The skin the sickly green liquid touched began to bubble and bleed. Her screams were so loud I thought they might make me deaf. The smell of burning flesh was a scent I'd never get used to, would never forget. As her melting cheek filled the chamber with the smell of cooked meat and blood I was thrown into a memory.

Ten springs ago, I was six... six! I watched as my father dragged a sharp blade down a man's back. The obese man was chained face first, to the wall in the torture chamber. Old blood had stained the wall a dark shade of burgundy. New blood was falling to the floor like a crimson rain shower.

"All right! All right, stop! I did it," the man confessed, his numerus chins smooshed against the wall as my father flayed his back like a piece of meat. "I killed the mother and her child! Please stop!" he wailed.

I stared at my father with wide eyes... saw the cruel smile on his lips. "There's a place waiting for you in Mnyama," he said. He drove the knife into the man's butchered back, pulling downward so blood poured from the gap between the back of his ribs.

My father handed me the knife he'd just used to kill the murderer. "Find a rag and clean that up while I deal with the body."

I blinked once at him, but then I took the knife and scrambled to find a rag while he unshackled the body. Blood, endless amounts of blood.

Those, and other similar memories are the first I can recall of my life. My father had brought me along only to watch him work before. But that time, he'd made me help him. It's funny, the awful things one can get used to when raised around such horrors. "*For the good of the kingdom,*" my father always said.

I wasn't so sure this woman was guilty. She certainly didn't appear so, tied helplessly to that giant, iron wheel. I supposed she could have been the one who inadvertently killed the chef while trying to poison the king. Usually the suspects confessed by now though.

The woman turned her pained gaze on me, her one cheek now ruined. I stared blankly at her. I knew better than to show empathy...to even *feel* empathy.

I'd once taken a wild rabbit as a pet. It wasn't afraid of me like an animal should be with a human. So I'd brought it to my room and fed it some left over vegetables from supper. When my father found it, he stuck his dagger through its fluffy, white body. "*Everything you love will die,*" he'd told me. It was a hard lesson to learn, but I'd learned it that night. After I was done grieving the loss of my new pet, I told myself I could never show care for a living being again. To do so would only cause pain for me and that being.

"I know you did it, filthy wench. A number of others saw you leaving the kitchens that night. Confess!" Spittle sprayed from my father's lips, which were hidden within his bushy, brown and grey beard. His long brown hair had come loose from its tie at the sides of his face. He never cared about neatness. It made him all the more intimidating… gave him a roughness most knew not to cross.

The woman shook violently as he grabbed an iron spike and a hammer off one of the shelves on the wall.

He placed the spike on her abdomen but paused. He turned to me and held out the spike and hammer. "It's time you learned, boy."

I couldn't speak so I started to shake my head, but my father pressed closer and scowled at me. He was shorter than the average man, but his sturdiness told everyone he wasn't one to be messed with. His build made up for his lack of height. In his dark brown eyes I saw expectancy… expectancy that I would comply as I always did. I took a deep breath and accepted the items from him.

I stepped up to the woman. Her sad eyes only made me want to wipe the look off her face. *She thinks you're weak. Prove her wrong.* It was my father's voice inside my head.

I placed the spike to her chest. "Not there, you'll kill her," my father ordered.

He didn't want her dead. The king hadn't given him leave to end her life as he sometimes did with criminals.

I moved the spike lower. My hands shook uncontrollably. I tried to clear my mind. I wanted… no, I *needed* to make my father proud.

"We don't have all day. Move. I'll do it." My father shoved me aside with his burly body, taking the spike and hammer from my hands.

I never knew my mother. When I'd asked about her, my father had said she had been some serving wench he'd coupled with a few times. She died giving birth to me, and her friend found my father and gave me to him, his burden to keep.

Cedric Lequerc had never been a loving parent. He did, however, show pride towards me once in a while.

I would succeed the next time a confession waited to be pried from a criminal's lips.

The woman's high pitched shriek tore me from my thoughts. My father had removed the gag again, and the spike he'd taken from me poked out of her bare forearm. Sticky, crimson blood wept from the wound and down her arm.

"*Forgiiiive me!*" she screamed. "*I did it! I did it! I was me!*" A confession… finally. They almost always confessed.

"And who gave you the poison?" my father asked, his tone bored.

She hesitated, taking quick, loud gulps of air. "Elfron."

My father's brows rose. "The healer?"

"Yes."

"Your confession has been heard. You will be executed at the king's pleasure," my father recited the words he spoke after every confession.

The woman was no longer our responsibility. She'd likely be hung in front of the court within a few days.

We left her to seek out one of Terra's guards. It didn't take long to find one. Higher numbers of them had been stationed around the kingdom, day and night, since the uprising against the regents had started five springs ago.

The guards all looked the same to me in their uniforms; chainmail with a green tunic over top, and Terra's symbol of two gold leaves embroidered on the chest.

"The handmaiden confessed. Take her to the dungeon and bring me Elfron the healer."

"Yes, sir, right away." The guard wasted no time. All of Terra knew my father worked for King Corbin. Anything he asked for was crown business.

"Let me get his confession," I pleaded while we waited by the torture chamber not far from the palace. "I can do it."

My father began to shake his head. He didn't trust me with the responsibility. And why should he after I'd just failed him?

"I need to start somewhere."

"You think a sad, old man is the right place to start?" he challenged.

"Maybe not, but it shouldn't matter who it is if they're guilty."

It seemed like he wasn't going to answer, but then he said, "So be it. I'll give you one more chance. Remember, this is for the good of the kingdom. Fail and you fail not only me, but all of Terra."

I wondered if he said those words for my benefit or to ease his own conscience—if he even had one. I didn't believe he actually did.

We didn't wait long before the guard brought the old healer to us.

The poor man was already trembling. Did I feel sorry for him? I felt sorry he'd made such a dire mistake in selling poison to a stupid woman who'd used it to try to kill our king and queen.

"Do I need to tie you up, or will you tell me it was you who sold poison to one of the queen's handmaidens?" Sometimes suspects confessed without having to be tortured. Sometimes the sight of the blood stained walls and cruel devices were enough to urge the suspect to spill everything to us.

But this man wasn't going to be so easy to crack, "I—I don't know what you're talking about."

I grabbed one of his twig-like arms. My father grabbed the other. Forcing him down onto the table on one side of the chamber was easy. He struggled as we tied his arms and legs down, but he was no match for our strength and youth. My father and I kept our bodies in good condition. We had to, considering the work we did.

Once he was constricted, I took a sharp dagger and flashed it in front of his face... a tactic to scare him before touching him. "Did you sell poison to a young woman recently?"

Silence.

"Did you know she would use it to try to kill the king and queen?"

Still, he didn't speak. He just stared at me with hateful, dark brown eyes.

"All right then. I guess we're doing this the hard way." I could feel my father's eyes on me. This was my moment. I couldn't think, couldn't hesitate.

I moved closer to the table and placed a dagger between two of the healer's fingers. Slowly, I made a small slice on the patch of tan skin. It was like cutting into an apple.

The man screamed. I moved on to the next finger.

It took two more cuts before he confessed. "It was me! I sold her the poison." He said the last part quietly, ashamed to speak the words. His crinkled face was scrunched up in pain. "I didn't know what she wanted to use it for. I needed the coin."

"Why do you even have poison? You're supposed to heal people, not kill them," my father questioned from behind. I never forgot his presence even for one moment. As he stepped closer to us, the scar bisecting his one eyebrow stood out stark white against his beige skin. He'd received the scar from one of his suspects before I was born. His mistake, he told me.

"I didn't have it—not at first. I knew how to make it. When she requested it, I told her I could concoct it for her. When I asked who it was meant for, she told me no one of importance. I would've never sold it to her if I knew it was meant for King Corbin and Queen Nicola. I'm not stupid." His eyes dared me to argue the point.

"So you're not part of the uprising," I stated.

"As I said, I'm not stupid." He actually looked offended. I believed him.

"Your confession has been heard. Your sentence will be the king's decision," my father said.

We untied the old man with only a wisp of white hair left on his shiny head and took him to the guard to be taken to the dungeon.

"You don't think King Corbin wishes him executed?" I asked my father.

"Healers are respected. Likely, he'll live out the rest of his existence in the dungeon, maimed but alive until death comes for him. The people will be happy enough to see the handmaiden hanged."

He was right. There were few healers and their skills were necessary. King Corbin couldn't make a habit out of killing them.

I waited for praise from my father, but it never came. All he said was, "You're lucky. You had it easy with him. Don't think it'll always be so." My father was a hard man to please. Though I was disappointed I had not won his pride that day, I was used to his lack of affection.

After arriving at the simple home we shared in Terra, the kingdom of earth, my father announced he had to meet with King Corbin to discuss the confessions.

I never went with him when he saw the king. I was of no importance to our rulers. I would change that someday soon.

CHAPTER 2

I WAS FALLING through an endless pit of darkness, trying to scream for help, but no sound would come. A bright green vine shot through the darkness and wrapped around my ankle. It glowed against the black nothingness like a lifeline. And then another vine latched onto my wrist. A moment of panic had me thrashing. These vines could rip me apart. I was about to attempt to scream again when more vines appeared. More and more of the green strands appeared until I was cradled by the thick, otherworldly plants and carried up out of the pit... out of the darkness.

I jolted awake with a gasp. I took in the simple room, noting the bare walls and beige curtains. I was in my bedroom. A speck of green on the wooden floor caught my attention. I rolled off the firm mattress to inspect it. Just as I suspected, a small green vine was peeking out from between two floor boards. I plucked the vine out and tossed it under my bed as I'd done many times before. Every time I dreamed of vines, I'd awake to find one growing in my room.

A memory came rushing back to me.

I was still a child when I'd had the nightmare about a wolf with a snake's head charging for me with wide open jaws. Black venom dripped from its curved yellow fangs. I couldn't move, paralyzed by my fear. It got so close I could smell its breath when vines wrapped around the creature's neck and pulled it back.

I woke to a vine with a closed bud growing along my floor.

"Father! Father, look!" I called.

Father's footsteps stomped across the house. He threw my door open. His body loomed in the space, blocking out the light from the main room. "What is it, boy?"

"Look. When I woke, it was here." I touched the bud and it opened, revealing a white flower. The flower was like a beacon in my dark room. I stared at it in wonder. "I think—I think I made it… somehow."

Father frowned and moved closer. I thought he would explain to me what had just happened… would tell me it was a miracle. But he crushed the flower beneath his leather boot and growled, "I hate magic. It's dangerous and unpredictable. If I ever see you practicing it again, I'll toss you out on the streets. Understand?"

"But I—"

"Understand?" His tone caused me to recoil.

I was about to tell him I didn't know how I did it, but he didn't want to hear anything from me except those two little words he loved. "Yes, Father."

I didn't dream about plant life of any kind for a long time after that morning. I told myself it was all one big coincidence… until it happened again a few springs ago. I remembered my father's words when I saw the vine and ripped it from my floor before he could see it. This was the fourth time I'd hid the truth from my father. What that truth was exactly, I didn't know. To believe I had magic was lunacy. Someone had to be playing a trick on me. But who? That was the question. I had no friends. The whole kingdom feared my father. I couldn't think of a single person who would dare break into our small home to play a trick on me.

A loud knock came from the front of the house and I shoved the memory away.

"Seph! Sepheus!" my father bellowed from his own bedroom.

"I've got it, Father!" I pulled a brown tunic and black trousers on and went to see who was at our door.

A messenger boy, dressed in an outfit that matched the limes on the tree outside my bedroom window, held out an envelope with an emerald green seal with the letters K and C stamped on it. In his other hand, he held a sack of what I assumed were more messages waiting to be delivered.

"From His Majesty, King Corbin." The boy announced formally.

I accepted the letter and was about to thank him, but he turned and marched off toward the next house before I had the chance to utter the words.

"Who was it?" my father asked from the main room just inside of our home's entrance.

"A messenger." I held the envelope out to him. "It's from King

Corbin."

"Read it to me."

I hesitated. I could barely read or write. My father had taught me the little I knew, but he didn't have the patience for teaching. He'd given up on me well before I had the skill developed. My cheeks warmed as I cracked open the wax seal and began to sound out the words. "Yeh—you ahh—reh innn—vet…invet—eed."

My father ripped the message from my hand with his big paw and read aloud. "You are invited to the Tree of Ends at high noon today. King Corbin."

Shame filled me when my father turned his mocking grin on me. Sometimes he enjoyed embarrassing me for his own entertainment.

"They're going to execute the handmaiden today. Fetch us some food. We don't want to be late to see the lady get what she deserves."

My father combed and tied his hair back neatly and dressed in some of his best black attire for the occasion. He enjoyed seeing his work finished at the Tree of Ends.

Terra was a kingdom surrounded by lush forest. Other than fruit and ornate trees, most grew outside of the kingdom's walls. The Tree of Ends was one of the only trees that hadn't been cleared away when the kingdom of earth was built by the first royals in this part of Sarantoa. The tree earned its name because it was used to hang criminals for executions. It had strong enough branches to hold a person's body without breaking. Many believed its bark gained its rusty colour from the blood of its victims. Most avoided the tree altogether, unless coming to witness an execution like the one we'd gathered around for on that day.

I gazed at the forest beyond the wide, stone palace. The forest itself was known to claim the lives of some of those who travelled through it. The first earth elemental used magic to ensure the climate would always benefit the forest, protecting the kingdom at its center. Besides poisonous plants, the forest was also home to various dangerous animals. The only thing separating us from those predators was a wall covered by centuries of moss. A few of those vicious animals had gotten inside the kingdom before. Their heads were mounted on walls to prove it… to make us remember what dwelled in that forest. A ruby red bird with long, fluttering tail feathers flying above squawked as if to say, "*Pay attention!*"

"One more chance! Child of Celestia." A priestess dressed in white robes said loud enough for us all to hear. "The goddess gives you one more chance to return to her. For the sake of your spirit, do what's right. Name your leader and you shall return to her in death."

Everyone waited silently, as still as the statue of Celestia erected in our kingdom's Temple. Even the handmaiden didn't blink. I thought she was going to speak a name when she finally closed her eyes and said so quiet I barely heard the words, "I don't know it."

The short priestess with golden-brown hair pursed her lips. "Then to Vesirus you shall go. May you be redeemed in you next life—if you have another one."

Vesirus. Our goddess Celestia's brother and exact opposite. She was light and he was darkness. If one lived a life of darkness, they would be sent to the dark world known as Mnyama to live with him. They'd eventually be reborn and be given one more chance to return to Celestia. If a person missed both their chances to return to the goddess, they'd be forever damned to stay in Mnyama. No one knew if a person was already living their second life or not. Not even the person in question.

I saw the handmaiden's throat move as she swallowed. She was still wearing the same soiled gown we'd tortured her in.

The priestess began babbling on again about Celestia. This was custom. The words were said at every execution. It was always about doing what's right in the eyes of the goddess. Other's eyes glazed over around the tree as she spoke the words we'd all heard thousands of times.

I smelled apple blossoms as a smooth arm brushed up against mine. That scent belonged to Claudia, the flirtatious brown-haired lady with soft curves... then again, most of the females of Terra fit that description just as most of the males were short and stocky. Of course there were a few exceptions, myself being one with my tall height. What made Claudia stand out were her big, hungry grey-green eyes and the way she swayed her hips. She had a confidence others her age lacked, others my own age.

She placed a small, tanned hand on my chest and rolled her eyes as she said lowly, "Executions can be so drab. How about a distraction to pass the time?" I didn't miss her wink.

I'd coupled with her once before at a party inside the palace.

Apparently she found those "drab" too.

I took her hand, pulling her through an archway and behind one of the palace walls surrounding the courtyard.

A deep giggle escaped her throat as I kissed the silky skin on her neck. She let the straps of her pastel purple gown fall even farther down her shoulders.

She didn't need any wooing. She was looking for a bit of fun.

I hiked up her skirts and took her hard against the wall. Her quick, deep breaths told me she enjoyed it, so did her roaming hands. It wasn't hard to sate my lust with so many women hungry for attention in Terra. The problem was keeping them from becoming clingy afterward. I didn't have time for courting. I usually only coupled with a woman once to keep her from getting too attached. I'd slipped up that day though, bored by the execution and still trying to forget my dream.

Claudia kept up with me and slipped her arm around my waist as I strode back to the Tree of Ends, and I realized I was paying for my mistake.

"That was fun," Claudia chirped, sidling closer as I tried to edge out of her arm.

"You should come to my home sometime. I make the most scrumptious cherry pies."

That was enough. I twisted out of her grasp and faced her. "Claudia, no. I can't see you again. This was a mistake."

Her grey-green eyes filled with tears and her bottom lip quivered, so dramatic. I didn't give her the chance to argue. I turned and headed straight for the Tree.

The handmaiden was still swinging from the thick branch. The executioner had just pushed her off the step beneath. Her eyes were lifeless and her lips had turned blueish. She hadn't died mercilessly from a broken neck like some, she'd suffocated.

King Corbin stood with his wife, his face unreadable. Tears streaked Queen Nicolas round, pink cheeks. This was one of her handmaidens, one of her closest friends… or so she'd thought.

I scanned the crowd surrounding the big tree until I spotted my father. He looked pleased. He had done his job well. When he noticed me, his eyes turned hard as stones. He'd noticed my absence.

"People of Terra," King Corbin began in his authoritative voice. "Have no fear. Those who go against the crown, against our *kingdom,* shall be punished. You are safe here. This I promise you. If you are true to us, true to *Celestia,* you are safe. Should you have any information—*any* suspicion about the traitors, you must bring it to my attention so I may further protect you and this kingdom from danger. These miscreants will get what they deserve!"

The crowd erupted with cheers, approving of their king's message.

I looked back to the spot where my father had been standing and found him gone. I couldn't spot him anywhere. So I went home by myself.

CHAPTER 3

THE WALLS OF my home were bare. My father didn't care for art or décor. We had only the necessities; a table for dining, chairs on which to sit and beds for slumbering. We had more than enough coin, but my father said we didn't need trinkets to show off our wealth. We had respect, which was worth more than all the paintings and jewels the kingdom had to offer.

Celestia only knew what my father was up to now. If it was to do with work, he would've informed me. He wanted me to be part of it. He wanted me to learn from him.

It felt strange to be out of his ever watchful stare. I could breathe easier, as if his presence was an endless weight bearing down upon my chest and it'd been lifted in his temporary absence. Unfortunately, it didn't last long. I heard the door open and his heavy footsteps cross the house. The weight fell again, suffocating me. My father was never quiet. He could never creep up on anyone, even if he wanted to. Then again, he never needed to be quiet… never needed to be sneaky. I swear he enjoyed knowing he struck fear in the hearts of others.

Father threw the headless chicken he'd carried inside on the table in front of me. Blood dripped from the hole in its neck and stained its white feathers. "Supper," he grunted.

It was my job to prepare and cook our meals. We could have afforded a small kitchen staff, but my father didn't want anyone knowing his business. Why have servants when you have a son?

I made a face at the bird before picking it up, careful not to get blood on my tunic. I carried it to the kitchen and got to work on plucking and gutting it.

We ate our meal of chicken and potatoes in silence. If my father was disappointed by my disappearance at the Tree of Ends, he didn't mention it.

I didn't dream of vines that night. My sleep was deep and dreamless, until a pounding on the front door shook me awake.

Groaning, I tossed a cloak over my night garments and answered the door before my father could yell at me to see who was calling on us.

A guard stood waiting with his arms crossed over the crest on his green tunic when I opened the door. "Where's your father?" he asked bluntly.

"I'm right here." My father stomped up behind me and pushed me aside.

"A letter was found in Louis Demonte's home this morning."

"A letter?" my father repeated, a line forming between his thick brows.

"Yes, an incriminating letter was found in his room by one of his maids. We've taken him to the torture chamber." The guard held a folded piece of paper out for my father.

My father unfolded the letter and read it silently to himself, his lips moving as his eyes scanned the parchment. "Demonte... I cannot believe it." My father shook his head, stuffing the letter in his pocket. I'd never seen him so shocked. "He's a noble. If they turn against us, we're in more shit than a pig in a pen."

"I believe that's why the king has given you leave to find your answers by whatever means necessary." The guard paused before adding, "There'll be no execution for Demonte." In case my father hadn't gotten the hint.

"I understand."

The guard left us alone. Demonte... the name was familiar.

No execution... whatever means necessary. The words echoed in my mind as I changed out of my night garments. *The king wants us to kill him.* Sometimes suspects died with us by accident. We pushed them too far, and their heart gave out—or we made them bleed so much they bled to death. We were hardly ever given leave to kill a suspect on purpose though. *King Corbin must not want this to get out.*

I jogged to catch up to my father, already making his way to the torture chamber.

Demonte awaited us, shackled to one of the blood splattered walls inside. Upon seeing us he began babbling like most suspects do. "Lequerc! It wasn't me! I'm not a traitor and you know it!"

Father waved his hand, mocking him. "That's what they all say." He dug into his pocket and pulled the now crinkled letter out. He held the parchment up to Demonte's face.

"I don't know where that came from!" Demonte's features twisted. He still wore his night garments, his shoulder-length brown hair uncombed.

"Thank you for the information, Demonte," my father read out loud. *"You are invaluable to our cause against the crown—"*

"NO! That isn't for me!"

My father went on, ignoring his denial, "Signed, *The Redeemers.*"

I almost gasped at the last two words. We knew the traitors called themselves The Redeemers. I supposed they'd named themselves that because they believed they were going to redeem Terra from the royals. We'd never gained anything written in their own words before. They were careful. They lurked in the shadows and rarely gave evidence of their existence unless caught. From what I'd learned in the torture chamber, most who were a part of The Redeemers didn't even know who the leader was. Those who risked their lives for the cause were at the bottom, the least of importance. They didn't care who made the decisions. They only wanted to aid in bringing down Terra's rulers.

King Corbin wasn't meant to be king. His brother, Lelund, was loved by the people. His spirit dwelled with Celestia now, due to an unfortunate incident. King Corbin was doing his best to run the kingdom. Yes, he'd spent his first couple of springs locked up in his grand palace, afraid to face his subjects. But he'd eventually gained the confidence it took to rule… to stand in front of his kingdom. And yes, he'd risen taxes to help pay for construction of the palace, but he wasn't the first king to have done so. The poor were upset because they couldn't see the benefit in having a palace fit to host Noctis de Celestia every four springs when we celebrated our goddess. If they were invited to attend, they'd feel differently. The celebration was a chance to show off a kingdom's success and fortune. If the palace crumbled, our kingdom would crumble along with it. It'd be a sign of weakness. It wasn't King Corbin's fault they were born poor.

Louis Demonte struggled against his shackles when my father stepped closer to him. "I would *never* betray my kingdom!" It was strange Demonte would betray the king. I didn't understand his motive, but the letter proved him guilty.

Father picked a rusty dagger up off a table and studied it. "Maybe you believe going against your king is what's best for your *kingdom,* hey?" He slid back to Demonte and ripped open the delicate, silk, white night shirt the lord wore and dragged the blade across his hair-speckled chest.

Demonte began blubbering incoherent nonsense.

The door to the chamber flung open and a young lady with golden-brown hair rushed to Demonte's side. "Don't hurt him! Please! Whatever you think he did, he's innocent."

Claudia... so *that* was why his name had sounded familiar. Louis Demonte was Claudia's father.

"Did you know about this letter he received from The Redeemers?" My father held up the piece of parchment for her. If she did, she was just as guilty as her father.

Claudia shrunk back. "What? No. I—that's impossible! My father is no traitor. Someone has framed him."

"Why would anyone want to frame your father?"

"I—I—"

"Well?" my father pressed.

"I don't know!" she cried.

My father smiled and turned back to Demonte. He made another slice in the noble's sweaty chest.

Claudia turned to me with pleading eyes. I didn't know what to say. I stared blankly back at her. What did she think I'd do? Come to her father's rescue? She really didn't know me at all.

Her eyes flashed with anger. "Stop this! My father is innocent."

My father watched me from the other side of Demonte, waiting for me to give in to Claudia... waiting for me to show weakness. I wouldn't give him the satisfaction.

I straightened my back and looked passed the pathetic sight of Claudia Demonte to my father as I said to her, "Louis Demonte is a traitor. He will suffer."

Claudia crumpled to the dirt floor as my father went back to work. Both her and her father's protests rang out each time my father made a cut. I didn't take my eyes off the scene, not once. I took whatever emotions I may have felt and pushed them somewhere deep inside myself.

When Demonte's chest and arms were covered in long bleeding cuts, the colour drained from his face. My father made one more cut along his neck, deeper than the rest. Blood fell from the wound like a scarlet waterfall as the noble slumped. Only the chains kept him up right. His eyes turned glassy. I knew that look. I'd seen it many times within the eyes of criminals. Lord Demonte was dead.

We left Claudia alone to mourn over her father's body. I felt proud of myself for showing my father strength.

"I suppose even those born of high blood can become traitors," I said to my father on the way to the palace. My father had asked me to come with him to see the king this time, a sure sign he was proud of me as well.

"Perhaps."

I stopped walking. "What do you mean 'perhaps'?"

"I mean perhaps he was a traitor, perhaps he wasn't." He kept walking as if I hadn't stopped.

I had to run to catch up to him. "You mean that letter wasn't for him?"

His silence was my answer.

Hot anger washed over me. "You did this. You framed him! What about 'for the good of the kingdom'?"

"It was for the good of the kingdom. I needed to see if you're strong enough to handle the job. You were getting too attached to the daughter." So he did care I had disappeared with Claudia at the Tree of Ends.

I couldn't believe him. He'd just tortured and killed an *innocent* lord. "I told Claudia I was done with her. You didn't have to do this."

"Relationships cause problems for people like us. I hope you've learned your lesson."

I thought quickly as we neared one of the palace's back entrances. He couldn't get away with this. "I'm telling King Corbin what you did."

My father laughed, a malicious, cold sound. And then turned and throttled me. His grip tight enough it almost cut off my breath. "You will tell no one. And *if* you do, you'll wish you were never born. No one will believe you. I help protect this kingdom. What do you do?"

I believed him. My father had earned his place. He was a valuable asset to the king... a friend even. And my father *would* make my life even more miserable than it already was if I challenged him. "Go see King Corbin yourself." I choked the words out.

My father released me. I coughed and rubbed my neck where I could still feel his fingers imprinted on my skin. I strode back down the pathway to our home and marched straight to my bedroom, slamming the door behind me.

CHAPTER 4

I GOT OVER my anger quickly. Claudia and her father meant nothing to me. I had shown strength. Even if it was a lie, I had passed my father's test.

As for Claudia, I barely saw her after Demonte's death. She was too busy taking care of her little sister now that they were orphans. I found out from the whispers of gossiping courtiers their mother had left them when Claudia was still a child. When I did run into her, she eyed me with loathing and disgust. I brushed her off like the insignificant fly she was. And I never told anyone my father had planted that letter.

I peered up at the cherry tree in one of Terra's orchards. The only way anyone could tell what season fell on Terra was by the cycle of the orchard trees—that or by counting the full moons. The temperature was always warm, except in summer when it was stifling hot. The barren fruit trees told me winter was currently upon us. The rest of Sarantoa would be cursed with bouts of rain or snow right about now. I had never seen snow. I could barely imagine a land so cold the rain fell frozen from the sky. I shivered as I pictured myself being pelted with pieces of ice.

I wished it was summer, hot as it may be. I'd have given almost anything for a fresh cherry at that moment. As if the tree I stood beneath could read my mind, the impossible happened; it began to bloom. Pink flowers erupted from the branches and transformed into the small, garnet fruit. I couldn't believe my eyes. I had to pluck a piece of the fruit off a branch and pop it into my mouth to convince myself what I'd witnessed was real.

I had always blamed the vines growing in my bedroom on pure coincidence. Now, I was sure I had some sort of earth magic running through my veins. But how? And why? I knew I couldn't go to my father about this. He hated magic. There were a few who were said to be witches in the kingdom, but I didn't trust them. I didn't trust anybody, really. Besides, the witches were outcasts. I didn't want to be seen associating with them.

I grabbed a handful of cherries and left the orchard. I hoped the tree would go into slumber again before anyone saw it and started asking questions. *No one will know it was you,* I told myself.

If anyone had noticed the tree full of fruit, they didn't say anything. I stayed clear of the orchards after sating my craving for cherries.

At some point during the winter, my seventeenth birthday had passed. I never knew the exact day of my birth. My father hadn't kept track and had said it was foolish to celebrate such a thing. I counted each winter to keep track of my age. It was important to me, even if it wasn't celebrated.

A few people disappeared before winter turned to blooming spring. We hadn't found their bodies or any suspects. King Corbin had the kingdom meet in the courtyard one full moon away from Noctis de Celestia. Terra was to host the celebration that spring. Whispers had spread about Noctis being cancelled due to the unsafety of the kingdom. King Corbin was about to put a stop to those rumours.

"Good people of Terra," the king dressed in green velvet robes boomed beside his queen from the raised platform at the center of the courtyard. "Some of you believe Noctis de Celestia will be cancelled this spring. I am here to tell you this is not true. It is important we honour our goddess, especially during these difficult times."

A few murmurs of approval ran throughout the courtyard surrounding the rulers.

"I know some of you have lost," King Corbin continued with sympathy, running his thick fingers through his wavy brown hair. "I am sorry for those losses you have suffered, but we will *not* show weakness to these traitors. We will not yield!"

Cheers rang from the crowd. It seemed everyone was in agreement with him on that matter.

"Terra isn't safe! You're risking us all!" a woman dressed in a puffy pink gown cried out.

Maybe not everyone.

Two guards moved to grab hold of her arms.

King Corbin turned his eyes to the noble woman. "I know your son has disappeared, and I'm truly sorry. If you or anyone else does not wish to attend the celebration, you won't be judged by me or by the goddess. Celestia understands your pain. But for those who wish to stand strong, join me in showing this kingdom—all the kingdoms of Sarantoa—that strength."

The crowd roared. Lords and ladies waved their arms in the air.

The woman shrugged the soldiers off and left the group of gathered courtiers. One more joined her—a man whose wife had recently disappeared. Everyone else stayed and applauded the king.

Queen Nicola stood proudly beside her husband in a matching green velvet gown with white roses embroidered on the bodice. She was a young queen, but stood beside King Corbin in every decision he made. Her unwavering support a rock he could lean on. Most people loved her for her kindness. The Redeemers accused her of being weak and unfit to rule. If she cared what others thought of her, she never showed it in public.

"The theme of this spring's Noctis is animals of the earth. Do your best to impress me with your costumes," King Corbin said. "I bid you all farewell until then." He then descended the steps of the platform and departed down the carpeted lane back to the palace with Queen Nicola at his side, dismissing us all.

Immediately ladies and lords began discussing outfit ideas, claiming the animal they would portray before someone else stole their idea. Others kept their ideas secret.

"King Corbin loves his theatrics," my father scoffed from beside me.

"Are we taking part?" I asked him.

"We have to. King's wishes," he grumbled, leaving me behind to ponder what type of animal I wanted to be.

I clasped my silver brooch shut to hold my grey cape in place over my brown doublet with silver buttons. I'd purchased grey breeches to match. My father had given me enough coin to find something suitable for the night of our goddess. The mask I pulled over my face was a beautiful piece of silver and grey art made by Evette D'etiou, the kingdom's renowned seamstress. My father put less effort—and coin—into his own outfit.

He came out of his room wearing a black cloak and a raven mask with a long, shiny black beak. I was sure he'd scare all the women away in his ensemble. He never cared about impressing anyone. I had never even seen him flirt with a woman.

The courtyard was filled with carriages from other kingdoms. Each was painted a different colour and had different emblems upon their doors, depending on which family the carriage belonged to. Everyone of importance from across Sarantoa was invited to join Terra on this night.

We climbed the wide stone steps up to the palace's main entrance. Vines climbed the walls and spiraled around the bars of the windows framing the golden filigree door, which was opened by a pair of guards dressed in their finest green livery. Their boots and sword hilts had been polished until they gleamed against the glimmering torchlight.

When we stepped into the great hall, the herald recognized our faces and remembered our names without having to ask like he would of the guests. "Cedric Lequerc of Terra and his son Sepheus Lequerc." A few turned their masked faces to us. Those who didn't know us went back to their idle conversations. Those who did averted their eyes, their fear of my father a tangible thing as we swept passed.

The regents of Solis, Aquila and Ventosa sat together in splendor at a table near the front of the hall. Their high-backed wood chairs reminded me of miniature thrones. The rest of us sat on benches, of course. Two seats at the regents' table remained empty for King Corbin and Queen Nicola. They would be the last to enter as custom dictated.

The elderly queen of Solis wore the mask of a red dragon—odd considering dragons hadn't been spotted for centuries. She spoke with animated hands as the queen of Ventosa listened intently from behind her snow owl mask made up of pearls and white feathers.

The hall's floor was green marble swirled with white. The white walls were painted with golden filigree, much like the doors to the entrance of the palace. Various types of flowering plants with draping branches stood in clay pots around the hall. All of the tables were draped in emerald and gold linens and covered in golden dishware and tapered white candles. The domed ceiling was my favourite part of the great hall. It depicted paintings of vines and animals in a symmetric style. At the center of the design, an iron and gold chandelier hung, lit with dozens of tiny candles. The flames shifted with the movement of the hall's occupants.

The people who filled the space before me all wore elaborate costumes of different species of animals that made mine seem plain and boring. All were competing for King Corbin's approval. A lady dressed as a speckled cat pranced by with a man in bright colours only a parrot could claim. My father, who hadn't wanted to draw attention to himself, failed to do so. He stood out stark against the rainbow of colours in his dark costume of death. He growled at a servant passing by with a tray of Sanguis. The servant hurried away, the glass goblets rattling a little on the tray he cradled.

I picked a grape off a tray from another servant, tossed it into my mouth and went to find better company. A cute fawn crossed my path. I smiled at her. She smiled back until she realized who was behind the mask. She turned her back on me and found another man to flirt with. Obviously she knew who I was and what I did for work.

"Sanguis for the wolf?" A servant wearing a simple brown and white uniform asked.

I accepted the tiny goblet of the sacred drink named after the blood of our goddess. It was only enjoyed on Noctis. I finished the sweet, fizzing liquid in one gulp and frowned at the empty goblet, setting it on a table. I'd never been one to indulge in the pleasures of drinking. My father didn't keep wine or ale… or any kind of spirit in our house. He'd said it 'only dulled the senses and made one stupid.' I found two more goblets of Sanguis and downed them. Last Noctis had been my first, and my father never let me out of his sight. This Noctis I was going to enjoy not being supervised.

After my fourth goblet of the dark red drink, my senses indeed dulled. I shoved some cheese into my mouth and was about to find a place to sit when the herald announced Terra's king and queen.

Everyone halted their conversations to stop and stare at the kingly lion and his lioness. King Corbin's gold silk robes trimmed with cream fur draped over his short, bulky form. He adjusted the lion-shaped mask edged with gold filigree and emeralds on his face. Queen Nicola's costume was made to compliment his. Her dress was the same colour as her husband's robes, her mask the feminine version of the king's. A gold choker with emerald and topaz gemstones rested against her bronze neck, blinking like stars in an endless night sky. King Corbin's hair was fluffed and styled to resemble a lion's mane. His queen's was pulled back off her face. The pair walked painfully slow, with heads held high, to their seat at their table, allowing all to relish...or envy their presence.

I found an empty spot beside a brassy-haired rabbit woman from Solis who was already chattering with a man dressed as a stag with towering antlers beside her. I didn't have to wait long for King Corbin to begin his speech, fortunately.

"People of Sarantoa, Terra thanks you for journeying here to our kingdom to celebrate this night with us. May each of you live a healthy and bountiful life these next seasons. Our goddess, Celestia, smiles upon us. Happy Noctis!" Short and to the point.

"Happy Noctis!" Everyone shouted in unison then we downed goblets of Sanguis, which had been placed before us by servants during the king's speech.

Trays holding bowls of hot, steaming soup with warm, soft bread were brought out first. Once our bowls were mostly scraped clean, we were served carved up roast with a rich, creamy sauce. We finished our meal off with pudding and tarts baked by the best bakers Terra had to offer. Any left-overs would be given to the palace staff.

The effects of the Sanguis were wearing off due to my gluttony. Musicians had taken up a tune with a quick, choppy beat. I stood by a tray of Sanguis, watching the animals dance with each other. My father had planted himself by our king and queen, always ready to serve and protect, even though he was no soldier. Still, he had what most others didn't—the king's ear.

"Arg. I wish there was something other to get drunk on than this sickly sweet Sanguis," a feminine voice complained.

I turned my head toward the lilting voice. It belonged to a woman with dark brown hair and the mask of a lynx. The tanned skin on her bare arms told me she most likely hailed from Terra.

"I might know where we can find something else to indulge on." My lips curved up mischievously.

"You do? You must take me there." Her forehead inclined over her black, cat-like mask.

I glanced in my father's direction. He and King Corbin were in deep conversation. I was invisible to everyone except the lynx-woman. "Follow me, my lady." I led her from the hall.

We stumbled down the corridors covered with sage coloured carpets and lit dimly with a few torches set in brackets along each wall.

I brought us to a set of stairs leading down to the kitchens. We had to cover our mouths to silence our childish giggles to avoid being discovered by the staff. After we passed the kitchens and the larder, I snatched a torch off the wall and unlatched a wood door. I allowed the lynx-woman to enter before me, pretending to be a gentleman.

"The wine cellar," the woman exclaimed, turning around to take in the many casks around the fair sized, cool room. "Marvelous!"

My lips twitched. "We'll surely find something here that suits your tastes." I pulled the lid off one of the wooden casks and cupped my hands to drink from it. I scrunched up my face at the bitter taste. "I'm not sure this is good wine."

The woman slurped and moaned. "Oh, yes. This is much better."

I couldn't help but laugh at the pleasure in her voice. I pulled my mask up. "How refreshing. You're so different than the others."

She slurped more wine out of her cupped palms and then licked them clean. *Lynx indeed,* I thought. She was so strange, but for some reason, I liked it.

I tried more of the wine. It was still bitter, but the sense of warmth from within it gave me was welcome.

"So tell me," the lynx-woman in a black and silver gown that didn't leave much to the imagination began, "How do you know your way around the palace so well? Do you live here?"

"Not *in* the palace exactly, but near. My father... he's close with King Corbin so I've spent a lot of time inside these walls." The wine caused the words to fall easily from my lips. I stepped closer. I wanted to know who this mysterious woman was.

"How interesting."

We were so close I could feel the breath from her painted ruby red lips as she tilted her head up. "Is it?" I reached to pull off the mask covering the top half of her face, but a scream from the kitchen tore me back to reality.

The moment I turned my attention away from the lynx woman, I felt a sharp point jab into the skin between my ribs. I looked down to find her holding a simple dagger with a short, flat blade to my side. She knew exactly who I was.

My next move was a result of two things; I noticed the way her hand shook—she didn't want to hurt me. And the wine had given me more courage than usual. Or perhaps it made me more foolish. I used my forearm to knock the blade from her hand. She gasped, not expecting my reaction as the dagger clanged to the floor. Before she could try to retaliate, I shoved her back against the stacked casks of wine. Her head hit one of the casks with a *thunk* and she fell to the floor. Red wine dripped on her from a broken cask like blood gushing from a deep wound.

"*Filthy traitor!*" I spat at her unconscious body.

I sprinted toward the kitchen and found a man wearing the mask of a snake yanking a dagger from a cook's chest. It all seemed to happen in slow motion… more effects of the wine. Burgundy stained the cook's clean, white uniform like a blooming flower. His eyes were already lifeless.

A couple of servants ducked behind cupboards or under tables. I moved closer to the snake-man, ready for a fight. But instead of fighting, he shrank away and then bolted from the scene. I ran after him, meeting a pair of guards in the corridor. There were no carpets in the lower levels of the palace. The walls and floor were made of stone.

"Wine cellar," I huffed at the guards, slowing a little to get my message across. "The lynx-woman inside is a traitor."

The pair of guards glanced at each other gravely and nodded. "We're on it," one of them assured me.

Satisfied, I took off to catch up to the snake-man. I could still hear his footsteps echoing from down the corridor. He couldn't be far.

It was so dark. Barely any torches were lit in that part of the palace at this time of night. I spotted movement up ahead and picked up my speed. The wine had slowed my senses, but the whole ordeal was sobering me up.

The snake-man shoved the door to the servants' back entrance open and was heading for the Temple. If he thought I wouldn't hurt him in a place of our goddess, he was sorely mistaken.

Citizens who weren't invited to the palace and were waiting for their turn to thank the goddess inside the temple gawked in horror at the man who sprinted past them. He disappeared through the pair of large wooden doors with peaked tops and into the Temple with pointy columns and stained glass windows.

"Out!" I ordered the priestess who'd been shaken by the killer's sudden appearance as I entered the Temple.

The grubby, poor woman who'd been praying on the floor screamed at the sight of us. I didn't have to tell her to leave. She rushed from the Temple, still in bare feet and the robe the priestess had lent her to pray in.

The snake-man stopped at the bottom of the giant statue of Celestia, who waited with both palms pointing down and facing out as if welcoming her human children to embrace her. The man's bright green and silver mask had come half off his face. His russet-brown hair was rumpled. His tunic and cloak had spots of the cook's blood on them.

"You would dishonour the goddess, by drawing blood in her Temple?" the man challenged between breaths, gripping the bloody dagger he'd pulled from the cook's chest.

I stalked closer and pulled my own dagger from my belt. It was much more ornate than his. One of the only gifts my father had ever given me. He'd given it to me on my tenth spring, deeming me a man. "Celestia doesn't mind when it comes to *traitors*. Besides, I don't plan to hurt you—yet."

The snake-man slunk back until his back was pressed up against the white statue. I thought he might surrender, but then his eyes turned hateful and he gritted out the words, "King Corbin can't save you." He took his own blade and ran it across his neck. Blood poured from the gaping wound and he fell back against the beautiful goddess as though she'd accept him. His life had already bled from him by the time I crouched down and checked his heart for a beat. *That didn't go as I'd planned.*

Someone cleared their throat. I hadn't noticed anyone had entered. I rose from the snake man's body and found my father standing at the door. King Corbin was with him. Both their faces were grim.

"I—I'm sorry, Your Majesty... Father. I was going to arrest him, but he killed himself."

"He must have held important information he didn't want us knowing," King Corbin commented.

"You should've stopped him," my father growled.

"I tried."

My father didn't look convinced. How could he have so little faith in me after everything we'd been through?

"No one finds out about this. Go back to the hall. I'll have someone clean this mess up." King Corbin's gaze landed on the blood at the goddess's feet. His face hardened with disgust before he spun, a swirl of gold and emerald, and left us.

My father grabbed my arm and pulled me out of the Temple. "You reek of wine," he scolded.

"I was celebrating our dear goddess."

"We don't get that luxury. Don't be foolish. You disappoint me once again, boy."

Anger bubbled up from inside me. "I'll deal with the woman! I'll prove to you I'm no fool."

I thought he'd argue, but he simply sighed. "Not tonight. In the morning, she's your responsibility."

Resolve replaced anger. In the morning, she'd pay for making me look like a fool.

CHAPTER 5

THE LYNX-WOMAN no longer wore her mask. She was, however, still in the elegant black gown from the previous night.

I'd risen before the sky was fully light. My head ached from the wine. The fun I'd had for those few moments wasn't worth the trouble or the pain. I'd make her pay for what she'd done. She was one of them… one of the traitors. No wonder she hadn't wanted to take off her mask. I stared into her fiery hazel eyes. She wasn't so pretty behind the mask; an average face on a wretched soul. Her dark hair hung in knots down her back like tangled ropes, evidence of her struggle with the guards. Her painted red lips were chapped with dehydration, but still they curved slightly up at the corners in a taunting manner from where she sat bound to an iron chair.

I circled her, slowly, tapping my dagger against the flat of my palm. Oh, I was going to make her pay *dearly* for what she'd done. And I was going to *enjoy* it.

"Why?" I asked, stopping to crouch down so I was at her level.

The woman simply shrugged. "You were stupid enough to follow a stranger away from watchful eyes."

I grabbed one of her fingers, she couldn't resist with her wrists tied to the arms of the chair, and carefully slid my blade under one of her neatly filed finger nails. A gasp caught in her throat, but she didn't scream.

I took my blade over to the fire I'd lit when I arrived at the torture chamber and stuck it in the hungry flames. Satisfied the blade was searing hot, I grabbed a fistful of the traitor's hair, wrenched her head forward and placed the scalding hot blade on the back of her neck. This time, she let out a howl of pain.

I took the blade away from her skin, leaving it red and blistering, and let go of her hair. "*Who* do you work for?"

Her raspy breathing was her only answer. She was a tough one. I turned my back to fetch a tool I'd seen my father use to remove teeth from suspects. It wasn't hard to find on the table scattered with the rest of the horrible devices used for extracting information.

The woman realized what I meant to do and began to pull against her restraints. If her eyes were weapons, I'd have been dead right then and there. "I don't know," she hissed.

I set my jaw and gritted out, "How do you not know?"

"Few know the name or face of the one who leads us. We're given messages—tasks to complete. I've said too much." She pressed her lips together, locking answers away once more.

"Who gives you these tasks? How do you receive the messages?"

She moulded her lips into that mocking smile again, so I put my hands around her face and forced her jaw open. My finger ended up in her mouth and she bit down hard, causing drops of blood to form on my knuckle. I backhanded her across the face. She laughed so I did it again. She laughed louder the second time, like a mad woman. I threw the tool across the chamber. It hit the wall with a metallic *clang*.

"Terra is unsafe while King Corbin sits on his throne spending his people's coin. The killing will only stop when the king abolishes his throne, or he's dead. No one can stop us, especially not a boy like you." Her lips formed a pleased smirk. That word… the one my father used when he was disappointed in me, I *hated* it.

"I'm. Not. A. Boy!" A flash of green caught my eye. It had erupted from the dirt floor and was growing quickly toward the woman. The vine was thick and mean with sharp thorns. I let out a laugh as she squirmed in the chair when it curled around her calf and twined upward.

"What is this? Are you doing this?" The smile was gone from her lips. Panic rang clear in her voice.

I could do nothing but watch as the vine slowly wrapped itself around her body and then encircled her long, slim neck.

"Stop! Stop this at once! You *need* me." Her eyes widened as the vine tightened, cutting off her breath. She tried to scream, but no sound came out.

I hated her... hated how foolish she'd made me look, how she'd made me feel. I couldn't let her win. She had to pay.

Her eyes bulged, showing the whites around the hazel irises. Red trickled from the line of green around her neck and down her tan skin. Her head slumped to the side. Dead, I realized she was dead. And I had killed her—with my *magic*.

This wasn't right. This wasn't supposed to happen. I backed up, running into a table and knocking sharp tools to the floor. I'd *killed* her. She was guilty, but I wasn't supposed to kill the traitor. That was up to King Corbin to decide. I'd have to answer for my mistake.

I ripped the vines off the woman's body. They disintegrated like ash in my hands. The marks on her neck were the only evidence of the way her life had ended. No one would know it was magic vines that'd killed her.

I had to get out of there. I had to explain my mistake to King Corbin before my father found out. If I could fix this on my own, maybe I wouldn't be a complete failure. I was already imagining the disappointment in my father's hard, brown eyes.

I left the corpse strapped to the chair and bolted for the palace, shutting the door to the torture chamber behind me.

I paced the throne room inside the palace. The matching thrones of wood and gold with arms made to look like branches sat empty upon the dais. Heavy green curtains hung over the gold framed windows, blocking out the morning sunlight.

King Corbin entered the throne room with bleary eyes. The gold crown with wide points sat crooked on his freshly combed hair. That sun had barely risen, and last night's celebrations would have led to a late slumber. The tall, willowy chamberlain, Jacque Leblond, was in tow. He wore a wig of wavy brown hair, each strand placed perfectly. But out of all his features, his long, curved nose stuck out the most. He followed the king around like a shadow.

King Corbin didn't bother turning to him as he said to the man behind him, "Leave us, Chamberlain."

Leblond, in his usual sage velvet coat with gold buttons, bowed stiffly. "Yes, Your Majesty."

Alone with the king, I bowed deeply, crossing both arms in front of my chest… the terra custom. "Apologies, Your Majesty, if I woke you." I assumed Queen Nicola was still asleep because she didn't accompany her husband to receive me.

King Corbin waved a hand. "What's so important that you demanded to see me so early on this day?" He plopped down on his throne, his pale green and bronze robes crumpling around him.

Right to the point then. No need to be afraid. I squared my shoulders and met the king's gold-green stare. "I made a mistake, Your Majesty. I was—getting answers from the traitor woman from last night and accidently—um well, I accidently killed her." I didn't know if the sick feeling in my stomach was from the wine or from my confession… probably both.

"I see." King Corbin adjusted himself in his seat. I waited for him to continue. He scratched his silver and tawny beard.

"She did tell me she didn't know who the leader is. Only that she received tasks in the form of messages."

"Who gave her the messages?"

I looked at Queen Nicola's empty throne. "She wouldn't tell me." I placed my gaze back on my king. "I apologize—" I began.

The king cut me off. "Listen. Torturing people, it is a type of art. It takes a special kind of person to be able to do it well. Am I wrong?"

"No, Your Majesty." Was he trying to say I wasn't the right person for the job? Worry began to seep into my bones. My father's trade was all I knew. I *had* to be good at it.

"I'd like to offer you an alternative. Your father would argue my point, but I believe you would be better suited as a soldier in my personal guard."

"A soldier, Your Majesty?" This was unexpected. I'd never even considered taking up a sword.

King Corbin cleared his throat and said, "Yes, you've just shown your ability to kill. I could use a man with your intelligence in my army. Someone to help Constable Bouvant lead my personal guard in this war against the traitors who call themselves The Redeemers." He spoke the traitors title in a mocking tone. "What say you?"

I lost my tongue for a moment. He was offering me a role alongside Constable Bouvant, a gallant man driven by the cause against the traitors. Would he accept me as an asset? And yet, who was I to refuse my king? My father wasn't going to like this, but perhaps I *would* make a good soldier. A wave of excitement washed over me. "Y—yes, Your Majesty. I accept your offer."

"Good," replied the burly king with a firm nod. "I'll inform Constable Bouvant. Be at the training grounds at midday." He pressed his hands against the arms of his throne, ready to rise.

I bowed again. "Your Majesty."

I was dismissed.

Excitement and dread mixed together on my way home to tell my father about the conversation I'd just had with our king.

"I knew you'd screw up." My father's voice startled me as I quietly crept inside my home. He'd been waiting for my return. He stood with his arms crossed over his chest, feet spread apart.

"Good day to you too, Father."

"Don't be smug. You killed the woman without an order to do so. You should've waited for me to watch over you. What did you strangle her with?" His eyes were endless pits of darkness. I'd been afraid of him once, but no longer.

"A rope." The answer came easily. "Don't worry. I've already informed the king of my mistake. He's given me a position with his personal guard instead... says I'm more suited for soldierly work." Our eyes locked. He couldn't argue against the king, but I saw the rage burning within him.

"You shouldn't have bothered King Corbin. You're *my* responsibility!" He turned away and flexed his hands. "You'll make an even poorer soldier. Don't come begging me for your position back when you fail."

It was my turn to rage. "That's all I am to you? Your *responsibility?*"

"Get out." He pointed at the door.

I was so angry, I was shaking. "Don't worry, I'm leaving. Who'd want to remain here with such an unloving *father?*"

I could tell he winced at the word 'father' even with his back turned to me.

I didn't need him or his poor hospitality anymore. I was a soldier now.

CHAPTER 6

CONSTABLE BOUVANT MET me with a group of the king's most trusted soldiers, who introduced themselves to me at the training grounds.

"We're glad to have you fighting with us." The weathered but tough constable slapped me on the back. "As long as you remember *I'm* in charge."

"Yes, of course, sir."

"Good, now stand before us and swear on Celestia you will remain loyal to us, your new family, and to your kingdom, until death or your release from service. You will fight and risk your own life for the safety of The Guard and this kingdom."

Pairs of eyes watched me, waiting for their new comrade to make the unbreakable oath they'd each made themselves.

I was already loyal to my kingdom. I was ready to fight and kill and die for Terra. I hadn't proved a worthy torturer. I promised myself I'd be a worthy soldier. I nodded. "I swear on Celestia I will remain loyal to this army… to this kingdom, until my dying day. I will fight and I will die protecting Terra and its people."

Approval stared back at me on the faces of my comrades as they each slapped their own chests with their right hand, a sign of respect.

"Your first duty," the constable said, "is to learn how to properly fight with a sword." He chucked a wooden sword at me.

I caught it. "You'd have me use a child's toy?" I asked incredulously.

"I have no knowledge of your experience. We all start at the bottom."

"Fine," I muttered. This morning I was using daggers and magic, now I was forced to use a weapon made of wood.

"Gerard, you train with Sepheus," the constable handed another wooden sword to a soldier with straight brown hair, which was long enough it had to be tied back off his face.

"Yes, sir," the soldier replied.

"Call me Seph," I said to my opponent.

He cocked his head to the side and gave me a big, yellow-toothed grin. "And you can call me Ger." He smashed his play-sword against mine, almost knocking it out of my hands.

I scowled at him for not giving me the chance to get ready and swung back. I lost my balance and fell face first to the ground. I spit out a mouthful of dirt and pushed myself back up.

Ger laughed, though not cruelly like my father would've. He didn't move to strike again until I had my feet under me.

I blocked his next attack. I wasn't completely useless with a sword. My father *had* taught me how to use every weapon… he just hadn't focused much on sword fighting.

We circled each other, striking and parrying, trying to force the other into a position that would have him dead in real life.

Ger bested me every time. It was obvious I wasn't ready to fight with a real blade. I wanted to prove my worth so badly, but it ended up being my downfall. I fought with too much emotion.

Constable Bouvant called for us to halt when I was beaten, bruised and gasping for air.

Ger lowered his sword and held out his calloused hand. I glared at his outstretched arm but he kept his hand open until I shook it. "You put up a good fight. It was your first day. Don't be too hard on yourself." His smile caused the skin around his eyes to crinkle in the corners.

I couldn't tell if he was mocking me or not so I shrugged and turned my back on him.

"We meet again tomorrow, same time. Go get yourselves a good meal and some ale," Constable Bouvant said to all of us.

I didn't know how to tell him I didn't have a home *or* coin to pay for a meal. I hadn't thought that far ahead when I'd let my father kick me out. I didn't even know where I'd be spending the night.

My thoughts were interrupted by a heavy arm slung across my shoulders. "Coming with us?" It was Ger. Apparently he wasn't offended by my dismissal of his praise. "We always go to The Watering Hole after training."

"No I—" I tried to think of an excuse, but Ger interrupted me.

"Nonsense. You're coming. Ale's on me this time."

I couldn't argue with that. I didn't really want the ale after last night's events, but perhaps I could nab some food while I was there. My empty stomach agreed.

The tavern was dimly lit, with no windows, only candles and torches for light. Serving wenches wearing beige and dark green poured ale and carried food to low, square tables around the tavern, bosoms almost spilling out as they leaned forward to flirt with their customers.

The guards at our table laughed and knocked cups of ale together. I slowly sipped the foamy, pale gold liquid. I didn't know how to act. Groups had never been my forte. Hell, *people* had never been my forte.

Ger indicated the empty space on the table before me, chewing on the drumstick of a roasted chicken loudly. "Aren't you starving? We trained hard today."

I hoped my silence would make him leave me alone, but he pressed further. "What's wrong? Worried about getting fat?"

The other guards laughed. A man sitting across from me, who had to be twice my age, pulled a serious face. "You need to keep up your strength, lad."

My eyes met his. I saw concern there so I explained, "I have no coin." The words were barely above a whisper.

"Speak again." He leaned forward.

"I said, I have no coin," I bit out louder.

The table went silent.

"But your father is paid well, is he not?" Ger asked beside me.

"My father tossed me out. Look, I don't want to talk about it."

The guards all glanced at one another. "No matter. You're part of The Guard now. You'll be paid and given a room at the palace. Here." Ger handed me his other drumstick. "Share with us tonight."

The guards nodded and pushed their metal plates to the centre of the table.

I would've refused from embarrassment if I wasn't so damn hungry. I didn't know how to thank them. I'd never been shown such kindness. I nodded curtly.

"We're your brothers now." Ger patted my shoulder.

I scowled at his hand. He sure enjoyed touching me.

Someone cracked a jest, and the whole table laughed. I was glad the attention had been taken off me. I devoured the shared food and licked my fingers clean when the plates were empty.

Without my knowing, some of the guards told Constable Bouvant about the situation with my father. The constable passed the message along to King Corbin, and I was given a bedchamber in the soldiers' quarters on one of the lower levels of the palace. A pouch of coin waited for me on the table beside my bed, a bed big enough only for one body. I sat down on the mattress and took in the small, plain bedchamber. I wasn't used to luxury so it was perfect, much better than sleeping in the barn with the horses.

The following days were much the same. We'd rise early, polish our leather practice armour and meet at the training grounds by midday. We shared a meal and ale afterwards. I grew used to the routine, even began to enjoy my time with my comrades. Ger became my first friend. He was patient with me, but he pushed me to do my best. He told me stories of when he was my age. His own father was a retired knight who lived in a manor outside of Terra.

Eventually, the constable deemed me worthy enough to use a real sword. He gifted me with a blade of my own, a simple longsword with a deadly sharp blade. He told me he was proud of me. I'd tried not to care what others thought of me after my father had kicked me out, but I couldn't help but feel a sense of pride at his praise.

My father avoided me like the plague. It was as though he were pretending I'd never existed. I was sure he wished it to be true. It didn't bother me anymore, what he thought. I had my brothers. I had a purpose to serve and protect my kingdom, which I hadn't felt when I'd been torturing.

I took my pleasure with one of the serving wenches late one night. Tess, a new wench with a bodacious body and curly, dark hair had been undressing me with her big, brown eyes since she saw me.

Her top lip curled as I pinned her against a wall in the kitchen of

The Watering Hole after the other staff and customers had cleared out for the night. "Such a strong man, you are," she breathed. As I buried my face in her neck, she added, "Too bad even you can't stop The Redeemers."

I pushed away from her and caught my bearings. *"Traitor,"* I sneered.

She put a hand to her bare chest. "No, not I. But I hear whispers." She bent forward and pulled her dress back up to cover her body.

I narrowed my eyes at her. "Go on."

She busied herself with the buttons on the front of her serving dress, taking her time to answer. "I'd look to the slums if I were you."

Those words were all I needed. I had my beige tunic and black breeches back on before she glanced up.

"Going so soon?" she pouted.

"I have work to do."

I flew from the tavern back to the soldiers' quarters.

I pounded on the door to Ger's room. He opened it wearing nothing but a blanket.

"Put some clothes on. We're going to the slums."

He gave me a bleary-eyed stare and asked, "Why would we do that?"

Impatient, I went to his chest of clothes and dug out a pair of breeches and an old tunic. "I believe we may find some traitors there."

Ger smirked. "Don't you think we've checked there? I'm sure there are traitors in the slums. Traitors are everywhere. We just haven't had any luck finding them unless they want to be found."

"Have you tried disguising yourself as one of them?" I took the bottoms of the breeches and tore them a little.

"Hey! What are you—"

I'm making us look like one of *them.*" I indicated my own torn up clothing from under my cloak, which I'd rolled through the dirt.

"Oh." He took the tunic and helped me make his clothes appear more worn. He grinned. "No need to comb my hair then."

I laughed and roughed up his hair even more.

We both wore our hoods up. We'd streaked dirt across our faces, but we wanted to be sure we wouldn't be recognized.

Buildings became more worn the closer we got to the slums. The smell of urine swirled through the air. Loud conversations and yelling echoed out through the windows and doors of tiny, cramped taverns. I almost stepped on an old woman sleeping in one of the alleyways as we searched and listened for anything suspicious. Only the unfortunate dwelled here. One had to be rough to survive in the slums. Though I kept a pair of daggers hidden beneath my cloak, walking through the shithole of Terra still made me apprehensive. Maybe it was stupid to listen to the words of a tavern-wench. Ger ambled along beside me carelessly like he'd been there dozens of times. Maybe he knew we'd find nothing. Maybe he was just humouring me to prove there was nothing to be found in the slums.

I was about to suggest we go home when I saw someone disappear into an old, abandoned shop. I frowned and headed in the direction of the crumbling stone building. Moss claimed part of its decaying walls. The wood around the frame of the door was half-rotted. Whoever once held business there was long gone.

"Did you see something?" Ger had to lengthen his stride to catch up to me.

"Someone went inside there." I didn't bother slowing to answer.

"It's probably just some vagrant living there until someone else comes along to boot them out."

"No, look. It's more than that." A flicker of light shone through the broken window. The closer we got, the clearer I could hear voices from within.

"So maybe it's a group of vagrants then," Ger offered.

"Let's check it out."

Ger shrugged and stepped up to the rotting door and opened it. "After you, my lady."

I stepped inside and was met by thick, stuffy air. A group of about a dozen and a half filthy slum rats stood near the back of the room. They all faced a man wearing a black cloak. His hood was drawn, and his mouth and nose were covered by red material. Only his dark, gleaming eyes showed.

"What do we have here?" Ger said lowly enough only I could hear as he brushed against my side.

I stopped before the crowd. A middle-aged woman with matted hair and a tattered dress, which I couldn't even tell the colour of, scowled over her shoulder at us.

"Shh, quiet," I warned over my shoulder as I inched closer to listen to what the robed man was saying.

A young couple came in and joined the group.

"No one should have to live like this. But you are not alone. I'm here to help you." He sounded a bit familiar, but his voice was gravelly—like he was trying to disguise it.

A few nodded their chins at his words. *Could this be the leader we've been searching for?*

"Your lives are worth more than this. Your *deaths* will be worth more. You have come tonight for a reason. I urge you to join us in the fight against the useless king who sits, stuffing his face on his golden throne while you all rot here in the slums."

"Yeah!" A bunch of voices rose up in agreement.

"Let me lead you. I will make sure you are treated fairly once King Corbin is crushed. With me, *you* will rise," the cloaked man rasped to the crowd.

"Traitor," I said under my breath and made to move.

Ger gripped my arm. "Not here." He kept his voice low while the robed man continued to gain cheers from the audience with his words.

I shook his hand off and glared at him.

"There's too many of them against only two of us. Let's go. We will get back up." He stepped backwards.

"Death to King Corbin! Death to Queen Nicola! Death to the Dirva's," a young woman began to chant. She couldn't be more than my age. An even younger girl stood at her side in a dress that was too nice to belong in the slums. I took in their round cheeks and wavy brown hair… sisters.

Though the older sister was more worn and less curvy than the last time I'd seen her, I recognized her instantly when I spied the side of her face… Claudia.

I didn't wait for Ger. I slunk to the door and slipped out before she could see me.

Ger caught up moments later. "You look like you've just seen a ghost."

"I have. Let's find Constable Bouvant."

The Constable was built like a rock, and though kind-hearted, he'd gained his position for a reason. He wasn't someone I'd want to mess with. I was reminded of that fact when we'd woken him up and told him our information.

He took no pity on the guards who'd been asleep when he all but broke their doors down and tore them from their beds to get them ready and moving quicker than I'd thought possible.

Ger and I kept our disguises on, but strapped our swords to our waists. Garnering frowns from drunks stumbling home for the night, we led the others to the old shop where we'd witnessed the gathering of what appeared to be new recruits for The Redeemers.

I pondered Claudia's appearance there. A lady of the court fallen to the slums. She was one of *them*. My father had done that... *I* had let it happen. I didn't understand. Her father had been a wealthy man. His wealth would've gone to her and her sister. How could she have possibly spent it all already?

One of my comrades kicked in the now locked door. Wood splintered where it was rotted. He shoved his shoulder through the rest of the way and we followed him into the empty shop. The smell of burned wax was the only evidence anyone had been there.

"You should've brought reinforcements," the gruff guard with a long beard spat, turning to Ger. "I don't expect much of the new one, but you should know better."

Ger opened his mouth to argue, but I stepped between them. "We wouldn't have learned anything if there were more of us. They would've spotted us and ran."

"That wasn't your decision to make." Spittle flew from the soldier's angry lips.

I stepped closer so I could look down at him. "I was trying to *help*."

"Enough!" Constable Bouvant shoved us apart. "Reynard is right. This wasn't your call to make, Sepheus. You have done well in finding the leader, though I doubt they'll ever meet here again. Next time, come to me with your plans."

I tore my gaze from Reynard and bowed my head to the constable. "Yes, sir."

"Good, now I want an account of what you saw as soon as we get back to the palace. Faces, what was said... anything you can remember."

"Of course."

Constable Bouvant gave Ger a calculating look. "Meet me in my quarters, both of you." He led the way out of the empty shop.

Ger and I stayed near the back of the group. We'd had enough attention for the night. I was lost in my own thoughts when a hand tugged on my sleeve. "So it was you I saw running for the door," declared a voice I knew all too well.

"Claudia, what are you doing here?" I scanned the area. Her little sister was nowhere in sight.

"I don't believe my father was a traitor. The king shouldn't have either." Her voice shook.

The others had begun to notice I'd fallen behind. I turned away from her. "Get out of here."

"Not before I do this," she shrilled, stabbing me under my armpit with a short blade.

Pain flowered from where the blade still stuck in my side. Slowly, carefully, I pulled it from my body and let it fall to the ground.

Her jaw was open, her eyes wide. It was like she couldn't believe what she'd just done. She was about to bolt, but I was quicker. I lunged at her and we fell to the ground. I heard Ger shout for help as I reached for the blade, still covered in my own blood, and shoved it into her chest. It wasn't a move I was proud of. It was fueled by rage... by panic, a killing blow. We'd needed her alive. I'd let my emotions get the best of me. The memory of her playful pout before we'd taken pleasure in each other before everything went wrong flashed in my mind.

A single tear escaped from the corner of her eye as I crouched beside her. Her breath came in rasps. I'd hit a lung. The rest of the world disappeared. I didn't even see my comrades crowded around us.

"Take care of my sister," she breathed. And then the light in her eyes went out like a snuffed out flame. She was gone.

I dropped the blood-coated knife on the ground.

Ger placed a rough hand on my shoulder. "I'm sorry."

"Get off!" I pulled away from his hand.

The others stared with judging eyes. I faced them all. "She was a traitor. Find her sister. Do what you will with her."

I walked away from their accusing eyes. They let me go.

CHAPTER 7

NO ONE QUESTIONED me about Claudia after her death. I did my best to forget her. Her death had made something twist inside my chest. She was turned into a traitor because of my father's lie.

Her sister was found and questioned by Constable Bouvant. His methods of questioning were slightly kinder than my father's. The girl knew nothing except they'd been living in the slums since Claudia had secretly married a lord who threw them out shortly after he'd taken possession of her wealth and estate. The young girl was sent to live with an old widow who took in children who'd been lost to the world... children with disturbed minds who needed someone to keep them in line.

We'd gone back to the slums a number of times to see if we could catch any word of where The Redeemer's leader had gone, or what their next move might be, but our luck had run out. Constable Bouvant came up with a plan; a plan which would lead us into the forest to scour for traitors. They had to be hiding somewhere.

Flowers beginning to bloom through the thick trees gazed up at me from on top of my chestnut mare. We clomped along the mossy forest, watching for any signs of people, watching for any sort of danger—a vicious animal who'd love to eat us for dinner. Keep moving, the key to staying out of danger. The damp air clung to our skin, made heavy by the spring rain. As the season turned into summer, the air would grow thicker and stifling hot, even under the shade of the trees. It was like the sun poured its heat into the forest to be trapped within the branches of those tall trees.

I didn't have much hope for this quest we were on. The forest around Terra was vast. The traitors could be anywhere. I wondered if any of them had met up with sharp-toothed animals or poisonous insects. Maybe nature was picking them off... doing our job for us.

The forest thinned and we came across a farm owned by an elderly couple. They invited us inside their small home and offered us tea. They were no traitors. Not with their curved backs and brittle bones.

Exhausted from our travels and in low spirits from our failure, we ventured back through the forest. Constable Bouvant wasn't ready to give up. He had us travel back to the palace a different route than the way we'd come. He was skilled in navigation. I was grateful someone knew where we were going. I'd have never found my way home from where we'd ventured. He promised to show me his map and teach me how to navigate one day.

The sun burned molten orange through the trees. My mount's withers quivered, trying to stop the black flies from feasting on her blood. A painful cry came from the front of our group. Elly, one of our female guards, clutched her arm where an arrow protruded through it. I peered up into the large leafed trees as another arrow loosened. My mount shook her head. Even she could feel the fear in the air, the promise of death.

"Forward! Hurry!" Constable Bouvant ordered.

A handful of our soldiers carried bows and arrows. They aimed for the trees. I squeezed my heels into my horse's sides to keep up with the rest.

Deer skin tents were erected through the trees. Movement caught my eye. Just over a dozen men and women scrambled for weapons.

I leaped from my mare's back, drawing my sword. I charged for a giant of a man with a weathered face and long, scraggily hair. He wielded a sword larger than mine. The nicks in the blade told me mine was of better craftsmanship. I charged at him with iron force. My strength stunned him, and he stepped back to try and regain control. It only took two strikes before I knocked his blade from his hand and shoved mine through his throat. Red sprayed my face like the wet paint of the newly renovated palace of Terra.

A warrior of a woman lunged toward me with her sword raised, her rusty-brown hair braided back from her sun bronzed face. Her eyes hardened as she licked her cracked lips. The face of every suspect… every *traitor* I'd met, flashed in my mind.

I ducked as she swung.

She was the queen's handmaiden. *She* was the lynx-woman who'd taunted me. She was *Claudia,* who I'd killed with her own blade. Justice? What justice? There was only death; as far as I could see.

I slashed my blade at the warrior. She'd anticipated my move. She dodged and came up on my right side with a swing. Pain stung my right shoulder as my leather armour split, skin torn beneath it. I ignored the searing sensation.

"Who is your leader?" I managed between breaths.

She only cocked her head to the side and smiled, taking another swing.

I blocked her and kicked her in the shin so hard she shrieked and almost dropped her sword. She tried to recover. Too late. I'd already buried my blade in her stomach. She slunk to the ground. Thick crimson covered my hands.

I moved on to the next traitor, and the next. Their faces blurred together. I didn't consider trying to experiment with my magic. I didn't need it. I found killing with a blade much more satisfying.

I stood over a young man, close to my age, my sword pressed against his cheek beside the cut I'd already made. I'd disarmed him easily. He squeezed his eyes shut, his whole body trembling.

"Tell me the name of your leader." The tone in my voice was so cold it was like it belonged to someone else.

"Enough." I recognized the voice beside me.

It wasn't enough. This man was a traitor. I was about to drag the edge of my sword across his face, but my weapon was knocked from my grasp.

"I said, enough!" Constable Bouvant repeated.

"He's a traitor." I snapped at the man who'd taken me under his wing, the man who'd given me a chance.

"So we take him to your father—to Cedric! We are not torturers! For goddess sake." The Constable wiped his mouth. His shoulders sagged. "Come."

I glared once more at the young man on the ground and picked up my weapon.

Bloody bodies, dead or dying, were scattered on the ground around the tents. A couple of them belonged to our side. Archers lay shot beneath the trees. The aims from our soldiers had met their marks.

The man whose cheek I'd cut was now on Constable Bouvant's horse, riding in front of him with bound wrists.

Ger clapped me on the back. "Well done. You're a natural. I've never seen a soldier take down so many enemies their first time during a fight. We're lucky to have you with us."

My other comrades beamed at me in approval.

"Thanks." I didn't know what else to say. I'd never been given such praise. Killing was easier than I'd imagined. Watching my father do it, time after time, I'd never understood how he could be so detached. Now, I did. It was simple. The guilty deserved to die, and it was an honour to serve my king.

We came to a bubbling waterfall, pouring into the stream running through the forest on our way back to Terra. Mist clouded around the fall, casting dewy prisms through the air.

We used the water from the stream to wash most of the blood off ourselves and refill our water skins. I hadn't said a word since we'd left the Redeemers' camp. I splashed cool, clear water in my face and wiped the blood, which had dried, from my hands. I'd have to address the wound in my side when I got back to the palace. It wasn't deep. The leather armour had done its job.

Elly, whose arm had been wrapped with a piece of materiel from her tunic, placed her water skin in our captive's hands and told him to drink. It was more kindness than he deserved.

"I'm sure your father will be able to get information from him," Ger offered.

I was sure he was right, but I didn't like being reminded about the man who'd tossed me out. I'd tried my best to forget him. I shrugged Ger's words off.

"What's got you in such a mood?"

"I'm not in a mood," I countered.

"Could have fooled me." Ger hauled himself up out of the stream, doing his best not to stumble on the sharp rocks.

A flash of bright orange caught my attention behind him. "Ger—"

"You know. You're an asset to this army, but sometimes you can just be an ass." He laughed at his own play on words as he tugged the boots he'd left on the bank back on.

The orange moved toward him.

"Ger," I warned again. "Don't move."

"Wha—?"

A deep growl rumbled from a ginormous, solid orange cat's chest. Tygrons, we called them. My usually loose and relaxed friend stiffened like a marble statue. The whites in his eyes grew large.

The cat with fangs sharp enough to rip out any man's innards in one bite prowled closer. It stopped directly in front of me and fixed its golden eyes on my gaze. I could not look away.

Ger whimpered as the ferocious feline sniffed the air audibly.

"Shhhh." I put my hand forward as though telling both my friend and the tygron to stay calm. "It's okay. We're going to leave now. Slowly."

The cat's eyes were still on me. It licked its lips but didn't move. *You will not harm us. You will let us go.*

As if it understood, it lay down on the damp earth edging the stream.

I beckoned to Ger. "Come here, but don't make any sudden movements."

"Any sudden movements?! How in the Dark Lord's name—"

The big feline growled lowly. A warning. It didn't like loud noises. "Shh! Quiet."

He clamped his mouth shut and, as slowly as his panic would allow him, he made his way to me. I nodded at the beast with pointy ears and claws bigger than daggers and mouthed, *"Thank you."*

Some of the others had seen us and went back to inform everyone else of the danger. Reynard stood with an arrow aimed at the tygron.

"No!" I stepped in his way. "She left us alone. Let's go."

He kept his arrow cocked for a moment longer before relenting. We were all far enough away now from the majestic beast to mount our horses and ride away peacefully.

I don't know why, but I'd felt some connection with the animal. I could've sworn it understood my thoughts. *Ridiculous,* I told myself. It had probably eaten recently and wasn't hungry. Pure coincidence. It made more sense.

We rode back to the palace without any further incidents. I had my wound cleaned and dressed with a healing salve and then wrapped in bandages.

CHAPTER 8

THE FOLLOWING DAY, I rode a white mare around the perimeter of the kingdom scouting for traitors. The horse I'd ridden the previous day deserved a break. Terra had a big stable with tons of horses to choose from. There was no reason to make the chestnut work after the previous day.

Bright, colourful birds soared through the clear blue sky. The air was fragrant with blooming wild flowers. I enjoyed the solitude, even if the memory of Claudia still haunted me. I kept telling myself killing her was the right thing to do. She'd been a traitor when my blade had stolen her life.

Regardless of my slip up with the young man at the end of the fight, Constable Bouvant told me I'd done well yesterday. It was easier to extinguish an enemy than to get answers from them. Maybe one day my father would be proud of me too. I almost laughed out loud at the thought. He'd never forgive me for leaving his side, never mind be *proud* of me.

I stopped my horse at the sound of branches breaking and the thundering of hooves on the soft earth. "Whoooa, girl." I freed my sword from its scabbard and waited.

A bay horse carrying a petite young woman came crashing to a halt before us as she yanked on its reins. The horse's coat beneath its saddle was dark with sweat, a sign she'd been ridden hard.

The young woman eyed my sword and wiped her brow. "You can put that thing away, soldier. I've come to join you."

I kept my sword unsheathed. "State your name and business, and perhaps I will."

"My name is Blaise D'meras, and I've already told you my business." The sun's rays hit her brown hair, bringing out highlights of red and gold. She'd tied it back, but it'd come half undone in her haste.

"You wish to be a soldier?" I half-laughed and put my blade away. This woman was no threat. Crazy maybe, but threatening? No.

"Aye, I do." Her amber eyes burned. "Is that a problem?"

"You're a lady. You're not fit to fight as a soldier," I explained, about to edge my horse forward and suggest she be on her way.

"You're wrong," she bristled, reaching down to her calf. From beneath her worn, ivory skirts, she pulled out a dagger. Maybe I'd been wrong. Maybe she was a threat.

But then she took the small, dull blade and began sawing off her hair.

I opened my mouth to speak, but decided to wait until she was finished.

Once it was completely hacked off from the place where the piece of cloth tying it back had been, she tossed the loose hair on the ground. "Now I don't look like a *lady*. Do I?"

I pressed my lips together then said, "That's not what I meant. But yes, you still look like a lady."

She fumed. "That's not fair."

"What I meant was, you're too young... too delicate. We have women in our Guard and in our army, but they're warriors. You're no warrior."

"We'll see about that," she challenged. I didn't expect what came next. She flung her arm back and threw the dagger through the air. It arched perfectly and came down to hit a black bird sitting on a branch. The bird fell to the ground with a *squawk*.

I dismounted and retrieved the dagger from the bird's body. Its black feathers shone an iridescent green. I wiped the blood off the blade on my breeches and handed it back to her. "Impressive, but was that really necessary?"

"You made it so." Her chin lifted. "The bird's life is on your conscience." She didn't know me at all.

"All right, you've got my attention."

Her amber eyes lit up like an inferno. "I don't need your approval. Take me to King Corbin. He will know who I am and agree to let me serve him."

I scoffed. Was this some sort of trick? "Why are you so bent on becoming a soldier? Are you bored of playing dress up and drinking tea?" I questioned her.

Her triangular-shaped face turned away as if she had to gather herself. She looked back over her horse's ears and said, "The Redeemers, they murdered both my parents. It's my right to end them."

I considered her words. "I'm sorry for your loss. A lot of others feel the same way, but getting yourself killed isn't going to fix anything."

"You should have more faith in me. We've just met, so I'll give you that. I don't care if I die. As long as I take some of those traitors with me my life will mean something."

I couldn't argue with that. If she wanted to die, who was I to stop her? "Fine. If you show me you know how to use a sword, I will help you see the king, but make a fool of me and I'll kill you myself."

"Fine."

After we handed our horses over to a stable boy, I took her to the training grounds and found her a sword, a real one, not a wooden one like I'd been given. If she wanted to fight with us, she was going to have to show she could handle it. We couldn't afford to have any weak spots in our army.

I started out by taking it easy on Blaise. My mistake. She knocked my sword out of her way with a grunt and feigned a killing blow. She smirked. "You call yourself a soldier?"

I picked the sword up off the packed dirt, trampled by seasons of soldiers' feet. "I was going easy on you."

"Don't"

So be it. If she wanted me to make a fool out of her, I would.

I blocked her next hit and countered. She evaded my strike and came at me with a routine of hits and parries. Our moves became a rhythm, and I almost felt myself enjoying our dance... almost.

My lungs burned. My face flushed from the blood pounding through my veins. I was winded by the time I finally spun and knocked her sword from her grasp. "Enough!" I bent forward to catch my breath, placing my hands on my knees. Blaise grinned, her chest rising and falling as she regained her own breath.

Someone clapped from behind us. I turned to find Ger walking toward us. I didn't know how long he'd been watching.

Blaise swung her sword once and buried its tip into the ground. "I told you I can fight. You should see me with an arrow."

"Fine. You've proven your point."

"The lady has skill." Ger beamed at the fierce little warrior woman.

We both scowled at him.

Ger put his hands up, a sign of surrender. "I've come to inform you the king's invited The Guard to dine with him. He wants to thank us for taking down the group of traitors yesterday."

"I'll be there as soon as I clean up," I told him.

"Who is she?" Ger asked me, nodding toward Blaise.

"Don't speak of *she* as if she's not standing right here." Blaise put a hand on her hip. "My name is Blaise D'meras. I'm your new comrade."

Ger chuckled. "That's funny. Seph, I'll meet you in the great hall. Don't be late."

Blaise watched him go. "I don't like him."

"He grows on you, unfortunately." I slid my sword into the scabbard on my hip and pulled the one Blaise had been using out of the ground and handed it to her. "You may keep this one. You'll have to sleep in the stables for tonight. I'll request an audience with the king for you tomorrow. We'll see if he truly knows who you are and if he trusts you enough to appoint you as part of The Guard."

"Wait, no. I'm coming with you. I will speak with King Corbin at supper."

I shook my head. Who did this woman think she was? "It's not polite to invite yourself to dine with the king."

"He won't mind. Believe me. He knew my parents," she said, following me to the palace.

I tried to ignore her, hoping she'd give up and go away, but she was persistent. She stared in wonder as we entered the palace through the doors of the soldiers' quarters. The official crest of Terra, two golden leaves painted on an emerald green background, hung on one wall.

We passed a few soldiers on their way to their rooms. They gawked at the small, fiery woman nearly jogging in order to keep up with my long strides.

There weren't many windows in the soldiers' quarters, so torches were kept lit along the walls of the corridors day and night. The floors were bare stone, unlike the green-carpeted upper levels. It was much cooler down there though, a reprieve from the blistering heat of summer.

When we reached the door to my room, I turned to shut the door, leaving Blaise in the corridor, but she darted into my room beneath my arm quicker than a hare. She headed straight for the wooden chest sitting by my bed and pulled out two pieces of clothing. "Mind if I borrow these?" She held up a white tunic and a pair of dark brown breeches.

I regarded her incredulously. "Yes."

She twisted her finger. "Turn around." Apparently my answer didn't matter.

I didn't comply, so she shrugged and began undoing the buttons down the front of her worn ivory dress.

"Goddess, woman!" I turned my back to her and closed my eyes. "You can't come to dinner. What about that don't you understand?"

"Okay, how do I look?"

Anything, she didn't understand anything.

I twisted back around, slowly, taking in her appearance. The tunic was like a pillowed cloud around her small form. And the pants, they were baggy and much too long. "Like a boy," I told her truthfully.

She smirked. "I'm coming to dinner. My dress is too filthy to wear in front of royalty."

Unbelievable.

"I give up," I said, going to find my own outfit to wear for the night. "Do what you want. You're not my responsibility. If King Corbin throws you out on your ass, don't look at me." I settled on a grey tunic and my best black breeches. I had better clothes at my father's, but I wasn't going back to retrieve them.

Blaise busied herself with shuffling through some books on my table while I dressed myself. I had taken them from the palace's library to try to teach myself to read better. I'd given up after a few attempts. I didn't have the patience to learn.

Fully clothed again, I turned back and found her running her fingers over the mahogany table. She studied the marks I'd dug in the wood the night Claudia had died... the night I'd killed her.

Noticing me watching her, she scanned my face. "What happened here?"

"Nothing." I pushed her aside and placed a book over the spot. "They were there when I moved into this room."

I saw a thousand thoughts in her face, which she didn't voice. She settled on, "If you say so."

Goddess, she was infuriating.

I ascended the stairs to the great hall with Blaise in tow. Maybe if I stopped talking to her she'd leave me alone.

I heard her gasp as we entered the hall through the tall doors. She gazed up at the colourfully painted ceiling as though it were a sky full of stars. The green marble floor had been polished so well, it glimmered like the facet of a diamond.

Most of King Corbin's personal guard, Constable Bouvant included, already sat at the long, bronze linen covered table in the centre of the hall. The iron and gold chandelier hung over the table, its candlelight casting a glow over the gold edged dishes and candelabras.

A looming, black shape at one side of the table caught my eye... my father. *What is he doing here?*

He sat in his usual bulky black robes beside Chamberlain Leblond. The chamberlain fiddled with his gold fork as he awaited his king. Neither man had been known for keeping good conversation.

I took a seat beside Ger and Elly, leaving Blaise no choice but to sit across from us.

"What is she doing here?" Ger nudged me, but the king and queen's entrance saved me from having to answer.

Everyone stood and faced the king and queen. Both rulers were draped in rich green silk and topped with proud golden crowns.

King Corbin reached his seat at the center of the long table. "Be seated," his voice boomed.

We obeyed.

Queen Nicola wiggled her small, rounded nose at the food the servants brought out. "Smells delicious! We are honoured to share this meal with you all tonight."

"Indeed," the king agreed. "Because of you, my guards, we have finally made progress against The Redeemers." The king dipped his soft bread into the bowl of beef soup placed before him. Thick broth dribbled down his beard.

"We only wish we'd have found more of them, Your Majesty," Constable Bouvant offered. He was wearing a rust-coloured doublet with silver buttons. I wasn't used to seeing him wear anything but his uniform. It was strange to see him gussied up.

"Yes, well, they're sneaky bastards, but I have faith you'll snuff each of them out." King Corbin pierced the table with his eating knife for theatrics, gaining a few laughs.

I didn't laugh, neither did my father. I watched from the corner of my eye as he scowled at his food, wearing his usual sour expression.

Queen Nicola's plump lips curved upward. "I see we have a new guest here tonight." Her eyes set on Blaise.

Blaise looked to me. I suddenly found my soup very interesting. She was on her own. I'd told her not to come.

"Yes," Blaise cleared her throat. "Excuse me, Your Majesties. Pardon me for my boldness in joining you tonight. I am Blaise D'meras. You knew my father."

The king and queen both raised their brows, but it was King Corbin who asked, "D'meras. Was your father Dozier D'meras?"

Her mouth twitched and her eyes darkened as she answered, "Yes, he was."

"Your father was a good man. He's the reason my army has quality weapons," King Corbin told her. "He was a talented blacksmith. I'm sorry for your loss, of him and your mother. I knew they had a daughter, but I believed you'd been killed too. Tell me, how did you escape?"

Blaise took a long sip of the wine we'd been poured, wine I left untouched. She answered, "The Redeemers, two men, came to our house while we slept. I heard them enter. My father went to see who'd intruded. I hid in my wardrobe while they fought. I knew he was dead when my mother screamed. I couldn't stand to leave her to face them alone. I came out of my room just as one of the men slit her throat. They didn't notice me." Her hand tightened on her fork as she continued, as if remembering the exact motion she'd made. "I had the dagger I kept on me at all times. I leaped on the closest man's back and stuck it through his neck. His friend, the one who'd killed my mother came at me. I threw the dagger. It struck him in the eye. I never miss my target. My father created weapons. He taught me how to use them.

"I left my home to come here and ask to join The Guard. I want to kill the traitors responsible for my parents' deaths. Their lives were taken because they worked for you, Your Majesty." She bowed her head, releasing her fork.

The hall was silent. I swear I could hear the king's breaths. Her words hung in the air like a heavy burden.

King Corbin closed his eyes. "My condolences, daughter of Terra." The tension in the hall melted with his words. The king opened his eyes, resolve shone in their hazel depths. "You will have vengeance. We all will. I would be pleased to have you in my guard." He pointedly looked at Constable Bouvant who nodded in agreement. And that was that. Blaise was now a member of The Guard.

Plates of cooked vegetables and slabs of glazed lamb were brought out. My mouth watered at the aromas filling the hall.

We dug in to our meal in silence, until Chamberlain Leblond asked in his soft, almost feminine voice, "What of the Redeemer boy who was captured yesterday? Were you able to get answers from him, Cedric?"

I paused chewing, waiting for my father's answer.

"No." My father turned his unforgiving gaze on me. "He's just a boy who wanted to defy his parents. He didn't understand what he was doing. His father should've kept a better eye on him instead of letting him runaway to become something he's not."

I fumed at those last words. It was obvious he was speaking to me... *about me.*

Blaise noticed my clenched jaw. "Perhaps you should taste the wine," she advised.

"I. Don't. Drink. Wine," I ground out.

"At least you learned one of the things I taught you," my father grumbled.

I pushed myself back from the table and rose. "Excuse me, Your Majesties, but I'd like to take my leave now." I bowed deeply, remembering to be respectful.

"You are excused," the king said, unable to keep the amusement from his tone.

I didn't give anyone else the chance to speak. I marched from the great hall without a glance back. I hated how much my father affected me. I wasn't going to stay and take his ridicule though.

Footsteps scuffed from behind. I paused. Blaise caught up to me. "I see where you get your moodiness from now," she mused.

"Go away." I started back down the corridor leading to the stairs that would take me to my room.

Still, she followed.

When I reached my room, I opened my door and faced her, making sure to block her from entering this time. "Find someone else to bother, Blaise. I'm in no mood for company."

"You can't shut everyone out because you feel sorry for yourself."

Our eyes locked. I took a step closer. "Perhaps you're right. Perhaps I need a—*distraction.*" I let my gaze roam over her lean figure and watched her shrink back. My face twisted with disgust. "Then again, maybe not."

I slammed the door in her face before she could utter another word.

CHAPTER 9

I SLEPT UNTIL midday. I missed my shift, but I didn't care. I stretched and rolled over in my bed. My feet hung off the end of the mattress, a downfall of being tall.

A loud pounding on my door had me sitting up straight.

Constable Bouvant didn't wait for me to answer before entering. The seasoned man with steely grey hair and an unshaven face tore the blankets off me. "I know your father's a cold-hearted bastard, but that's no reason to sulk in here all day and miss your shift."

I groaned, tilting my head against the cheaply-made wooden headboard. "I know, I'm sorry. I let him get to me."

"You're lucky Ger offered to take your shift. You'll take his tonight. Don't think you're getting out of this," he said sternly.

"Yes, sir." His eyes softened, and I wished he were my father instead of Cedric.

"You should've told me about Blaise."

I placed my feet on the cool, hard floor and got up to don my leather armour. "I planned to, but she didn't give me a chance before she invited herself to dinner to ask the king to be his soldier."

"Try harder next time. Her father served the king well. He seems fond of her. You're both lucky. There could've been repercussions for bringing an uninvited guest to dine with the king."

"My thoughts exactly," I said on a sigh.

"Pardon?"

"I understand," I replied louder. "I'll do better next time."

"Good. Now, get cleaned up." He scrunched up his face. "It reeks in here."

I tucked my face into my arm and smelled. I grimaced. He was right. I needed a bath.

On my way to drop off some of my clothing with the laundress, I ran into Blaise. She'd found a tunic and breeches that actually fit her. The white and brown fabric hugged her body in a flattering way. Her figure wasn't boyish at all. She'd strapped a bow and a quiver full of arrows to her back. "Prick," she spat as we passed each other.

I smiled widely and continued on my way. It seemed I offended her the night before. *Good. Maybe she'll leave me alone.*

After the laundress promised she'd have my clothes clean and back in my room the next day, I washed myself in the creek running through the eastern side of Terra.

I'd barely finished washing up when a frantic tolling sounded from the bell tower, my cue something was amiss. I rushed from the water to find out what was going on, almost slipping along the way. The soles of my boots had muck on them from the banks of the creek.

My comrades were charging for the gates, swords ready. Archers climbed into the bushy trees. I thought I spotted Blaise among them. Ready or not, she was now a soldier... part of The Guard responsible for wiping out The Redeemers.

At the gates, men and women fought their way inside, shoving and cutting through our soldiers.

I dove into the chaos with the sword I'd always kept by my side. A battle cry escaped my lips as animal instinct took over. Kill or be killed. Slash, parry, strike, spin, a brutal dance of blood and guts. I welcomed the blood washing over me like a cleansing rain.

A man with one eye cornered me. It could have been coincidence. Or he could've been the man Blaise had stabbed in the eye.

I moved to trip the unskilled brigand, not paying attention to the opening he'd left me.

He froze before I reached him, his face a picture of shock. He toppled to his knees and fell face forward into the dirt. A sturdy arrow with vivid emerald and ruby covert feathers stuck out of his back. Slick crimson seeped around the arrow's shaft.

I scanned the trees. I didn't see her, but I heard Blaise holler,

"That's for my parents!"

I spat out a gob of blood and sought my next prey. A young woman with no hair snarled at me; she was practically foaming at the mouth like a feral animal. Red blood splattered her face like war paint.

I smiled.

I advanced on her with a series of strikes.

She parried every blow, crying out like a lunatic each time. Her wild eyes flashed... inhumane.

She twisted and hit my sword with her wider blade so hard I felt the reverberations all the way up my arms.

Too slow, my recovery was too slow.

She slid her blade up, slicing my chest with the tip of her sharp steel.

I grunted. Dark spots danced in my vision. I couldn't afford to make mistakes.

I ducked and swung at her stomach, gouging her. She yelped and covered the gushing wound with her arm. She tilted her head to the side and laughed as though she welcomed the pain. Goddess, this woman was insane.

She stomped down hard on my foot. The pain, worse than the cut on my chest, blinded me.

I blinked to clear my vision as her foot met my hip, sending me crashing to the ground, my sword knocked from my grip as my jaw met dirt.

She flew through the air with a glee-filled scream, her weapon aimed for the kill.

Time slowed. My fingers met the hilt of my sword. I regained my grip and pointed the blade skyward as I pushed myself up, catching her beneath the jaw. I drew the blade up, finishing the kill.

Blood poured down on me and gurgled from her mouth. Her once wild eyes turned lifeless. Just like the eyes of every other traitor I'd watched die.

I retrieved my weapon and continued ending any traitor who crossed my path.

Dark crimson puddled on the ground. The metallic scent of blood filled my nose. This group was larger than the one we'd attacked in the forest, much larger. Friend and foe fell around me.

King Corbin rode on his white stallion, cutting down Redeemers with his infamous battle axe. I didn't know when he'd joined the battle. He was no coward, hiding behind his palace walls while his soldiers fought to save his kingdom.

While there were dozens of Redeemers, and they'd had the advantage of surprise, we still had the numbers.

A few stragglers got away, running from the kingdom like rats running from water. Those who couldn't escape took their own lives. No one wanted to be questioned… tortured.

Arrows jutted from many of the bodies splayed across the ground. I was sure a large sum of those arrows belonged to Blaise. She was a good shot, but I didn't dare tell her so when I spotted her speaking with some of the other archers afterward. Instead, I said, "I see you found some clothes that fit." She didn't need her ego stroked. She was annoying enough as it was.

"No thanks to you," she hissed. "Elly was kind enough to give me some of hers and let me sleep on her floor."

"How nice for you. I'm ravenous after executing so many Redeemers. I'll be at The Watering Hole if anyone's looking for me."

"No one will be," she assured me in a sing-song voice and went back to her conversation.

I bit my lip to keep from smiling and went to find my first meal of the day, late as it was.

On my way to the tavern, Ger intercepted me. "Hey! Constable Bouvant wants us all to meet him at the training grounds."

I sighed. "I'm half starved. I haven't eaten today."

He clenched his fists so hard his knuckles turned bone-white. "That's your own damn fault! You can fill your stomach after this."

I'd never seen Ger so angry. I guessed he wasn't too happy about covering for me.

We hurried to the training grounds without another word.

"Now that we're all here," the constable started shortly after I'd joined my comrades at the training grounds. "I need to get to the bottom of *how* those traitors got inside the kingdom. Ger and Faron, you were on perimeter duty. What did you see?"

Ger answered first. "Pierre was dead at the gates and Redeemers were already partway through when I made it around there. Fabien was nowhere to be found." Pierre and Fabien were on gate duty when we were attacked.

"And you, Faron? What do you have to say about all of this?" The constable turned his unrelenting green stare on the giant soldier who I was supposed to be on duty with.

Faron straightened his back, as much as he could, and answered in his thick, deep voice. "I had made it around to the gate just in time to see Pierre fall. I didn't see Fabien."

Constable Bouvant tapped a calloused hand on the pommel of his sword, circling The Guard. "Does *anyone* know where Fabien is?" A blue vein popped out of his neck where the skin sagged with age as he scanned our faces.

Everyone shook their heads or muttered, "No, sir."

"Shit!" the constable raged, causing a few to start. "If any of you see or hear of him, you come tell me—immediately! We have let a traitor fool us. Are anymore of you confused about where your allegiance lies? Because I'm telling you, if I find out anyone else here is a traitor, I will personally end your life! Is that clear?" He was so worked up, blood rushed to redden his tanned face. His chest rose and fell with each breath.

"Yes, sir," all of us answered in unison.

"Pardon?" he shouted.

"Yes, sir!" we repeated, shouting our answer.

"Good. You're dismissed. Get your wounds looked after. I better not hear of any infections from any of you. I want an extra two men on perimeter duty from now on."

Ger turned his face at me.

"Can I eat after I see a healer?" I asked Constable Bouvant. I knew he'd want me on duty since I'd missed my shift.

"Fine, but you're pulling a double shift after that. No more impertinence will be tolerated."

"Yes, sir."

The constable was about to stalk off, but he turned back and searched the crowd. He pointed at Blaise. "Good job today. I want you on duty with Seph. He found you, so he can teach you."

"If I did so well, why am I being punished?" she commented low enough he couldn't hear her.

I was sure *I* was the one being punished.

After a healer's apprentice tended to my wounds, Blaise followed me to The Watering Hole.

She kept her burning gaze on my bowl of thick stew while I ate. I pretended she wasn't there and enjoyed every bite of my meal, taking my time.

When the serving wench I'd dallied with came around, bosom pushed high against a teal corset, Blaise asked her for a mug of ale. She downed the foamy pale liquid quickly and slammed it down. "I needed that."

I sniffed. "Alcohol isn't the answer."

"Maybe for you it's not. I know how to handle my ale. And what's it to you, anyways?" She smoldered from her wooden stool across the table from me.

"You're right. I don't care what you do. Just remember to keep your wits with you. We're about to be on duty."

"I wouldn't be if it weren't for you. And I'll be fine, thank you."

She was almost cute when she was so furious... *almost*.

When I tired of wasting both our time, I paid the serving wench enough coin for my food.

The wench held out her hand, waiting for Blaise to place the coin in it for the ale she'd drunk.

Blaise slid her gaze to me, shame written in her eyes.

A smile pulled on my lips as I realized she didn't have any coin yet and she had to rely on me to pay. I waited a moment longer, to see her squirm a bit, before I plunked another coin into the waiting hand.

"Thank you," she mumbled.

I shrugged off her gratitude and headed for the exit.

We had two horses readied at the stables and met the other two guards on duty outside of Terra's looming stone walls.

"I'll take the north side," I told the others.

"I'll take the south," Blaise cut in before one of the others could answer. "I'd like to be as far from him as possible." She pointed her chin at me.

The average-sized soldier with oily light brown hair chuckled to the other one. "These two could use a tumble in the bedchamber I think."

Blaise shot him a look that would cause any normal person to wither.

"I'll take the east side," he smiled at her, leaving the west for his older comrade, the man with two chins and almost no neck.

"Ride back and forth along your side. Yell if you spot anything suspicious," I explained to Blaise. There was nothing to teach about being on perimeter duty. It was a boring job most of the time.

I didn't see her for the rest of the night. Once I'd finished my double shift, she'd retired to the palace already, probably gossiping away with Elly in her room. Celestia had mercy on me, for once.

I heard movement from behind my room's closed door when I approached it in the corridor. I unsheathed my sword and prepared to attack as I flung the door open.

I froze, my sword mid-air, as my gaze fell on the black robed man slouched on my stool. "Father?" He hadn't even flinched. "What are you doing here?" I demanded, putting my weapon away. Shock gave way to annoyance. He had no right to come into my room uninvited.

He didn't speak. He studied a spot on the floor. It was then the flashes of steel poking out from the sleeves of his robes caught my eye. I went to him and pulled one of his sleeves back. He growled a warning.

The steel was a splint, strapped to each arm to keep it from moving. "Who did this?" I asked, carefully putting his sleeve back in place. "Who broke your arms?"

"Traitors. Who else?" he hissed.

I couldn't help but laugh. He'd thrown me out like I'd meant nothing to him. And now... *now* he needed me? This was preposterous. Celestia was toying with me. "Where are they now?"

"Dead. Two of them. They knew what I do, who I am. They disarmed me. One held me down while the other broke my arms. They would've eventually killed me if one of your comrades hadn't come."

I silently wished they would've just killed him. "What now?" I asked.

He shifted uncomfortably. "I know we haven't been getting along, but there's no one else who can do my job while I heal."

I couldn't believe it. He wanted me to become Terra's temporary torturer. I ground my teeth together. "You said I'm not fit to torture."

"You're not."

I had to bite my tongue to keep from injuring him further. "I'm sure the king can find someone else—"

"The *king* was the one who sent me here." He winced as he tried to adjust his seat.

"I suppose you'll need me to care for you too?" My mouth tugged up a little. I knew he'd loath his helplessness.

"I don't need anyone to take care of me." He rose from the stool to leave.

"And how are you going to feed yourself without the use of your arms?"

"Shut your mouth!" he snarled. He stared at the iron handle on the door as if willing it to open with his mind. I didn't know how he'd gotten in. He must have bullied someone into opening the door for him.

"Fine, hire a servant to aid you while you heal."

He still faced the door as he said, "You know how I feel about servants and their prying ears."

I let him stare at the door handle a little longer, until he said, "Sepheus…"

I opened the door and followed him outside.

Once I got him to bed, I stared up at the ceiling in the room I'd grown up in. *I'm a good soldier,* I told myself. I'd made friends for the first time in my life. I didn't want to give that up to do the one thing I'd always failed at. Maybe now that I'd killed a handful of men and women I'd be better. Taking life would be easier. I'd just have to hold back until I got the answers we needed. Restraint was tougher than killing. Perhaps this was my chance to prove to my father I had what it took. I wasn't thrilled about having to take care of him as though he were my child instead of the other way around. A small part of me loved him enough not to let him starve to death. Even though I believed he deserved to suffer for tossing me out with nothing but the clothes on my back. Celestia had seen what he'd done and had judged him for it.

The next few days were trying. I spent most of my time caring for the man I swore hated me. Not only did I have to cook for him and feed him, I had to cloth him, bathe him and assist him with any other menial task he couldn't do himself. My life had never been worse. I wished he'd let me hire a servant. Stubborn ass. He probably enjoyed watching me suffer with him.

"Eat your oats," I ordered.

He clamped his mouth shut like a child.

"You need to keep up your strength so you can get better." I had the urge to dump the bowl of cooling oats over his head. "So I can go back to soldiering," I added.

"You think you're a good soldier?"

I was able to get a spoonful in when he opened his mouth to speak. "I am a good soldier."

"King Corbin took pity on you when he gave you that position because you were a shitty torturer." He chewed on the oats in his mouth and then continued. "You're a *decent* soldier. Don't fool yourself."

I set the spoon down. "Fine. I'll go practice becoming a better soldier. You can take care of yourself for the rest of the day. It doesn't matter what you think if you're dead."

"Wait," he began, but I was already out the door.

CHAPTER 10

I FUMED AT the fact that the traitors who'd broken my father's arms were already dead. I wanted to be the one to make them pay for the position they'd put me in, for taking me away from The Guard.

A captured traitor, a man with long, thin, greasy hair watched me from where he was restrained. His thin, dark lips reminded me of worms. He breathed heavily when I brought a tool used for breaking bones to his face. "If you don't tell me who your leader is, I'm going to break you like your friends broke my father."

The man clucked his tongue. "Poor boy. Has no one to take care of him now?"

"I don't need anyone." My voice shook with rage.

His mad laugh echoed off the walls, taunting me.

I swung the club against his arm, over and over, until I heard a *crack!*

The man howled in pain.

When he was able to speak again, he rasped, "I—I don't know who our leader is."

I believed him. None of the lowlifes knew who they followed. "Useless." I slammed the club into his face until it resembled a crushed tomato. I dropped the heavy, iron club on the floor and stalked out of the chamber.

I didn't care that I'd killed him. He was a waste of space. King Corbin wouldn't even notice his absence in the dungeons. I'd discovered a number of traitors had been caught during the attack and disarmed before they could end their own lives. What was one against many?

On my way to my old room in the palace to fetch some of my necessities, I ran into Blaise in the soldiers' quarters. She squinted against the torchlight burning along the walls. "Seph? We've been worried—well, *Ger* has been worried. What happened to you? Constable Bouvant told us you're no longer part of The Guard."

I paused and studied her face; her amber eyes shone bright, reflecting the flames. Her perfect peach lips parted. She had on a slightly wrinkled dark green tunic and tight black breeches with knee-high boots. Why did she care? I brushed her words off. "I've taken over my father's position as Terra's torturer."

Confusion crossed her face. "But you're a good soldier."

"A decent one," I echoed my father's words.

"We need you to help us eliminate The Redeemers."

"I am. I torture them." It was my turn to be confused. "Why do you care?"

"I—I don't. I simply want justice for my parents' lives. I saw you during the attack. We need your fighting skills if we're to prevail."

Such kind words. I chuckled. "Did the constable put you up to this?"

She tucked a short piece of golden-brown hair behind her ear. "No. You're skilled at crushing traitors though. Anything to help us defeat them…"

I leaned in closer to her and said lowly, "I'm still on your side, darling."

She crossed her arms and bristled. "There's blood on your tunic."

I glanced down and she walked away. "Tell Ger I'm fine," I called after her. She waved me off with a hand.

Worried one moment, angry the next. Blaise was the most temperamental female I'd met. Perhaps I should've told Ger what had happened. The next time I saw him, I'd tell him. He'd only been kind to me, and he put up with my moodiness. He deserved to know the details.

But I didn't see my friend, or any of my other comrades, for a long time. When I wasn't taking care of my miserable father, I locked myself in the torture chamber, seeking answers I never found.

I tired of all the creative ways I could think of to use the tools to extract information from my suspects. I hadn't used my power since I'd killed the lynx-woman. It was unpredictable, as my father had warned, but maybe if I practiced I could learn to control it better. It could become a weapon I could depend upon if I could hone it.

A woman who'd posed as a maid to gain information for her leader stood shackled to a wall inside my chamber of horrors. Yes, I called it *my* chamber now.

Spring had given away to the sweltering heat of summer, and then summer had transformed into autumn, turning the forest around the kingdom into a land of rubies and caramel. Dying blooms were evidence winter would soon grace us with her presence. I preferred the cooler days of winter in Terra. It was a relief from the unrelenting heat most of the other seasons brought. The most rain fell during winter and spring, bringing blankets of mist to the land each morning.

My father healed well enough to take care of himself, but I still attempted to torture answers from his suspects.

Dampness, thanks to the dewy weather, stuck to my skin as I ran a finger across an older woman's plump, freckled cheek. Silver peppered her dull brown hair, which had come unbound.

"Such a shame you were caught, Avingale," I mused as the woman shuddered.

She kept her mouth shut, but I saw tears shining in her brown eyes. Eyes so similar to the ones of my other victims, open wide and franticly darting from side to side.

"I tire of my usual methods, Avingale," I repeated her name, enjoying the personal touch. "Perhaps I'll try something new today. What do you say?"

She whimpered. She had no idea what I could do to her.

I imagined a vine growing from the earth as I curled a finger.

She kicked out a leg and tried to move to one side, the movement catching my attention.

A thick vine rose up from the ground. It reached for her. Her chained wrists kept her from straying far. The vine found her thick ankle and twisted around it. Her whimpers turned to wails as it moved up her leg like a slithering snake. I realized she probably thought it *was* a snake. A laugh rose up from my chest. "I'm just getting started. Tell me who you report your information to."

"I don't report to anyone!" she squealed.

I made a fist and the vine tightened around her leg. My power was easier to control than I'd imagined. It felt natural, felt *good*.

"You were caught sneaking around the queen's chambers when she was with her ladies. I know you're a Redeemer. Who are you helping?"

"He doesn't need my help!" She clamped her mouth shut, realizing her mistake.

"So it's a he, is it?"

She bit her lip so hard blood smeared it like carmine. "I don't know anything else. I never saw a face. Please!" she begged.

The vine edged up higher, creeping over her torn skirts.

"You will tell me everything you know. Or you will wish for death, but trust me, I won't kill you. Not yet. You're going to feel everything I do to you."

"He's someone higher up than I! I don't know his name or face. Please. I left my information in a letter inside an unused guest chamber's wardrobe. That's all I know."

Satisfied, though a little disappointed I didn't get to keep playing with my power, I let my hold on my magic go and the vine disintegrated in a cloud of dust. "Your life is in the king's hands now. You will be executed at his pleasure." I spoke the words I'd so often heard my father use.

The woman sagged against her chains, a blubbering mess of sweat and tears.

I sought an audience with King Corbin and was escorted to the throne room where he sat beside his queen. A furry white cat slumbered in Queen Nicola's lap as they listened to my new information.

King Corbin sipped wine from his golden chalice. The emeralds on his jeweled fingers reflected the light from the windows like tiny green mirrors. "So you believe The Redeemers leader to be one of our own? Living here in the palace?"

"Yes, Your Majesty," I replied, meeting his eyes.

He took a deep drink.

Queen Nicola had stopped stroking her feline pet. She wore a rich umber, velvet cloak trimmed with gold thread. "That's madness," she commented.

"How can this be? Are you implying I don't know my own people?" the king accused, his usually soft voice rising a few notes.

"I'm not suggesting Your Majesties don't know your own people." I dropped my gaze to the floor. Music drifted from somewhere beyond the closed door. "I'm only advising you be careful. Don't trust anyone. The leader is a man. We know that. I will try to narrow down a list of suspects."

King Corbin sat deeper in his seat and breathed deeply. "You're work is appreciated. You've gained us information which has brought us closer to finding the leader of our enemies. We thank you for your service to the crown. You are dismissed."

I bowed and turned to leave.

"Wait." Queen Nicola stopped me. The cat had jumped from her lap and now rubbed up against her legs. "How did you encourage the woman to speak? What did you do different this time?"

I pondered my answer. I didn't feel comfortable revealing my power to her and the king. So I said, "This woman cracked easier than the rest have, but I believe our new knowledge will help persuade others to follow her example."

The queen accepted my answer. "Good."

I used my power from then on with my suspects, knowing I *could* control it. I blindfolded each of them before I began with my magic. The tactic worked well as they believed the vines to be snakes slithering up their bodies instead of vines. This ensured no one would find out about my special *skills*.

One time, the cloth I'd tied around a man's eyes came lose and he witnessed my lie. I cut out his tongue to ensure he couldn't tattle to his guards.

A sense of pride filled me. I was getting the job done, and I was doing it my own way. I could never tell my father I'd been using magic to do his job. He'd never understand.

Unfortunately, after the spy posing as a maid told me about her secret letters to an important man within the palace, no one else gave me any useful information. King Corbin let her live, confined to one of the towers, hoping others would see they'd be shown mercy if they only helped us. It didn't work. And her letters had revealed nothing except that she'd told her leader she needed more time.

Suspect after suspect I tried to scare and squeeze the truth from them. I lost count of how many I'd nearly strangled to death with vines. As much as I enjoyed strengthening my use of magic, I was running out of patience.

No other groups of Redeemers attacked the kingdom, but I knew they still existed both outside and inside of the palace walls. Until we figured out who led them, there'd always be more. There would always be new traitors to recruit. It wasn't hard to find people who believed they'd been wronged by the crown. Everyone who wasn't royalty was jealous of the riches... the power that came with their blood. Everyone remembered the gracious King Lelund and his beautiful queen, Vivienne. It wasn't King Corbin's fault Queen Vivienne had lost her mind and killed her husband. No, he hadn't trained to be a king his entire life like his brother had, but he still had a right to the throne.

I stood back and watched as a young man struggled while my vines cut off his air. He was a cup-bearer. Surely he heard whispers echoing throughout the palace. I'd asked for anyone who'd come to the palace with nothing and looking to earn coin to be brought to me for questioning. If anyone were to be a traitor, it would most likely be people like him.

When his face turned a deep plum colour and liquid ran down his leg, I released the vine and ripped the blindfold off his face. So close to the kiss of death he was. I had to be careful. I'd gotten away with that first kill. I didn't know if I could do it again. Especially since this man wasn't proven a traitor yet.

"You will remain imprisoned in the dungeons until you're found innocent," I informed him.

"But how can that happen?" he choked out, craning his neck to try to spot the 'snake' that had almost strangled him to death. The vines had temporarily ruined his pretty voice.

"I don't know. Not my problem." I went to find a guard to take him back to the dungeons, where he'd probably live out the rest of his life.

I spotted a small lad with shaggy brown hair and a feminine build on duty. He faced me upon hearing my footsteps. Not a lad, Blaise stared back at me. Her hair had begun to grow out, but wasn't long enough to be tied back or braided yet. Ger was with her. I hadn't spoken with him since I'd left The Guard. He laughed at something she'd said but stopped when he saw me.

"The cup-bearer in the torture chamber needs to be taken back to the dungeons," I informed both of them.

Both watched me in silence until Ger finally said, "Good day to you too, Sepheus."

I drew closer to him. "You haven't bothered to come speak to me since I left. What do you expect?"

Ger inclined his head, clearly shocked by my statement. "*You* were the one who left. You didn't even bother to tell me why. I had to hear it from Constable Bouvant. Some friend you are."

"Let's not fight," Blaise interjected. She wore Terra's official uniform, her and Ger both did.

"I had to take care of my father! I didn't have time to worry about you," I hissed at the man who'd been my one true friend, ignoring her.

"Maybe if you didn't have so much self-pity, you'd realize you're not the only person in this realm."

"Stop it!" Blaise yelled, raising her arms. Twin daggers glinted off each arm, strapped down with leather straps. "You're acting like girls."

I tore my gaze from Ger to look at her. Her eyes held accusation. She was siding with him. They'd probably grown close since my absence, became friends even.

"Sorry for interrupting you while on duty. Take care of the cup-bearer." I turned to leave them.

"Seph, wait," I heard Ger call, but I kept walking.

I returned home to find my father awaiting me. He set down the goblet of wine he'd been drinking and beckoned me to sit across from him. He'd taken up drinking to help alleviate the pain in his arms. "Sit. We need to talk," he rumbled.

I hung up my dark grey cloak and took a seat, folding my arms on the table.

"I want to let you know I appreciate the help you've given me these last few seasons since my injuries. I wouldn't have survived without you." He stared at his hands. This was difficult for him.

I nodded slightly and shifted in my seat. "Thank you." Silver light flashed through the window. Thunder shook the house shortly after.

He stretched his back, finally meeting my eyes. "I grow wary of my uselessness. I'm taking my position back."

My jaw slackened. This couldn't be. I still hadn't found the leader of The Redeemers.

"You can remain as my assistant if you wish, but you must follow my orders," he continued.

I opened my mouth to argue, but a knock interrupted me. My father stayed seated regardless of his working arms.

I opened the door and found Blaise on the other side, drenched in rainwater. "Are you going to make me stand out here and continue to be drenched, or are you going to let me inside?"

I gaped at her but opened the door wider to allow her entrance. "What are you doing here?"

"May I have a word?" Her gaze flicked to my father.

"As you wish." I led her to the drawing room, which contained two cream coloured loungers and a stool. I offered her the stool.

She had the audacity to look offended.

"You're sopping wet."

She relented, adjusting her scabbard as she sat and wiped the water dripping from her hair off her forehead. "I think you should return to The Guard," she informed me bluntly.

"Do you?" I raised one eyebrow. "And why would I do that?"

Her eyes scanned my face. "Because you don't look well."

I gave her a half-laugh and ran my hands down the tops of my thighs. Who did this woman think she was?

"All this torturing, it hasn't done you well. Look at you. You've lost weight, you stink like a boar and I can barely make out your face beneath that unkempt hair and unshaven beard. You've lost yourself."

"Ha! Who are you to judge me? These things—*my appearance*—doesn't matter. What matters is catching the traitors' leader! And I'm this close," I made a small space between my finger and my thumb to show her, "to figuring out who they are."

She slumped in the stool, her sopping uniform dripping onto the floor. "You can still find him as a guard."

"I—" I began to retort. But what was the point? My father wanted his position back, and I didn't want to be anyone's assistant. So instead I asked, "Do I really look that bad?"

She wrinkled her nose. "Yes."

"I suppose I better clean myself up before I seek out the constable."

A pleasant look crossed her features. She left the stool and held out her hand. I shook it and she said, "It's good to have you back, comrade."

On her way out the door, she paused. "Ger will be happy to hear you're back too."

I offered a small smile, and she disappeared back out into the rain, probably to inform him of the news.

CHAPTER 11

I THREW DOWN my cards and slid a silver coin across the table to Ger. It was the second one he'd won from me. He and I were back to normal. There was no sense holding grudges when we were both at fault.

Ger tapped his foot and gathered the hand-painted cards into a neat stack. "We need to keep an eye on the chamberlain."

I rested my chin on my fist and watched him shuffle the deck. "Why?"

"Blaise doesn't trust him. She says he seems suspicious... will never meet her eye when she's on duty inside the palace and always hurries from her sight. And when she asked him where he was going the other night, he told her to mind her own business."

"Maybe wherever he was going was confidential," I answered. "Jacque Leblond has always been an odd man. He's been friends with the king since before he took the throne. I doubt he'd betray him."

After counting out the cards, Ger pointed out, "There's still a chance she's right."

"I'll keep it in mind." I took my cards off the table and commented, "You and she have grown close."

"Blaise is—she's like my little sister. We bonded in your absence. She's a fierce fighter."

I scowled at the cards I held, another awful hand. "I know she is."

Ger won that round too. I won the one after and decided to quit on a good note.

The next evening, I snuck into Chamberlain Leblond's chambers while he was busy with the king and queen.

I adjusted the hood of my dark green cloak to ensure my face stayed hidden within its shadow. I leafed through the parchments on his desk. Most of which appeared to be letters of business. My eyes drifted over the words of one. *His Maj—Majesty wishes to...* I couldn't decipher the next word. I was a terrible spy. I really needed to learn how to read better.

I shoved the letter back into the middle of the stack where I'd found it and continued on into his bedchamber. I ruffled through his wardrobe full of identical sage velvet coats and clean beige breeches. Hung on iron hooks along the wall were half a dozen of the wavy brown wigs he always wore. His white and gold covered bed was neatly made. Nothing out of the ordinary.

I left his chambers and a flash of sage down the corridor drew my attention. The tall, willowy figure drifted quickly down the stairs to the next floor. Leblond. I followed him but kept enough distance to remain unseen.

The chamberlain exited the palace with nonchalance. Perhaps he was going for an evening stroll. Then again...

I kept far enough back that he didn't notice me. When he arrived at the stables a horse and carriage were waiting for him. A bit late to be travelling, but he could have easily been following the king's orders. He handed a heavy purse to the driver. Too heavy. My gut twisted.

The carriage rolled off.

I hollered for the stable boy, but he was nowhere in sight. I quickly bridled a horse and trotted bareback after Leblond who was still in view.

I had to be careful. If he saw me I'd have to explain myself. And if he was guilty, I'd have a harder time catching him once he guessed my suspicions.

His driver kept a steady pace north until the forest opened up to the well-built manor house belonging to a noble, Lord Monair. I'd passed his picturesque home before but had never spoken to the wealthy man with an unfairly pretty wife who'd bore him two sons. When I was a child, Monair had worked for the king as his secretary.

I waited for the chamberlain to exit the carriage and disappear into the enormous manor before I tied my horse to a post and approached the driver.

He almost fell off his seat when I jumped up beside him. He didn't have time to react before I hit him with the pommel of my sword, knocking him out cold.

I managed to stuff him in the hollowed out passengers seat meant for storing luggage.

I crept around to the back of the manor where a balcony jutted out from one of its walls. I climbed up, grinding my teeth as my muscles worked to pull my weight.

Voices drifted out through the open window. I crouched low and snuck forward to hear better.

"He gave your position to his friend," Leblond's voice pointed out. "And he gave your land, the land meant for one of your *sons,* to the queen's brother. If that isn't enough to motivate you to join our cause, nothing is."

Right. The king had given Lord Monair's position to our current secretary. I'd never known the reason why.

A shuffling, and then another man's voice offered, "We do agree the king is selfish and should be called out for some of his actions. We just aren't sure we're comfortable following—er—the Dark Lord." *Vesirus?* Leblond was a follower of *Vesirus?*

"What has Celestia done for you?" No one answered so the chamberlain continued, "The Dark Lord has come to me—"

"You've *seen* him?" a different voice exclaimed.

"No, I haven't seen him. I've heard him. He whispers to me in the darkness of night. He promises glory for all of his followers. The world as we know it will be forever changed. All we have to do is weaken the kingdom from within." He was mad, completely and utterly mad.

"And do your followers know of this? That what they do is in the name of the Dark Lord?" the man who'd agreed about King Corbin's selfishness asked.

"Not yet, but they will. Once I have your alliances."

I'd heard enough. I scrambled down from the balcony and rushed back to the carriage to wait for Leblond. One against three was poor odds regardless of the advantage of surprise. Once the chamberlain was in chains, the rest would be easy.

A groaning came from beneath the seat when I climbed back into the carriage. I opened the seat and clocked the driver on the side of the head again to ensure he stayed down. I didn't care if he'd never fully recover from the injury. He'd aided the enemy, the *leader* of The Redeemers.

I drew the curtain in the carriage closed and waited with my sword readied.

Footsteps crunched on the soft earth outside the carriage. I braced myself, giddy as a child with a mouthful of cake.

"Benoit? Benoit, where are you? Bloody useless driver," Leblond muttered. His bony hand clasped the teal curtain and slid it aside. "Benoit?"

"Don't move." The chamberlain's face paled as the point of my sword met his throat. "I heard everything. I'm taking you to King Corbin. I will relish in watching you hang."

Jacque Leblond held his hands in the air. He swallowed. "I don't know what you're talking about."

"Get in the driver's seat." I indicated with a tilt of my head. "You're going to drive us back to the palace."

"Where—where's Benoit?"

"Get in the driver's seat!" I shouted.

He listened, moving slowly to the front of the carriage. I kept my blade pointed at him as I sat beside him. He glanced down at the reins. "I've never driven."

"It can't be that hard. Pick up the reins and tap them across the horse's back."

Leblond stared at me until I pressed my sword against the side of his neck. He slapped the reins against the horse and clucked. "Come on, horse!"

The well-trained horse walked forward.

When we reached the post I'd tied my mount to, I said, "Stop. Pull back on the reins."

He did as I asked, though he pulled a little hard and the horse tossed its head in the air. The carriage halted.

"Get up." I took his slim arm and steered him off the carriage toward the horse tied to the post. "Untie him."

Chamberlain Leblond glared at me as his fingers worked to untie the reins from the post.

"Good, now tie him to the back of the carriage."

He wrapped the reins around the bar on the back of the carriage. As he finished off the knot, his hand shot down and drew the sabre dangling from his waist.

Wrong move.

As soon as the blade was free from its scabbard, I knocked it from his grip.

He bent to retrieve it and I gouged his shoulder.

"Ow! Celestia's tits!" He covered the wound with his hand. Blood seeped through his fingers.

I picked his sword up and pointed both weapons at him. "Get back in the carriage." I wasn't about to let my prey get away. I had been waiting for this moment since The Redeemers had become a problem. He was mine.

Clouds covered the silvery stars like a blanket. Nightingales twittered songs for love and joy as we wound down the road to the palace. I hummed along to their tune with a smile on my face.

Elly frowned in confusion as we rolled through the gates. She left the other guard on gate duty to question me. "Seph? What's the meaning of this?"

"I've caught The Redeemers' leader," I announced, turning my smile on my prisoner.

"Leblond? Truly?"

"Yes. Will you fetch one of the stable boys to take care of the horses?" I had the chamberlain exit the carriage in front of me. He'd kept his mouth shut after I'd stabbed him. The blood on his shoulder had begun to thicken and crust.

Elly nodded. "Of course."

She returned shortly after with a young lad with a mop of hair who led the horses away. More guards followed her.

"I'll alert the king," one of my comrades offered.

"Tell him I'm taking him to the torture chamber," I told him.

Leblond stiffened. "This is a mistake."

I ignored him.

"We could take him if you want to fetch your father," Elly suggested.

"No, I don't trust anyone else with him." Hurt flashed across her face, but I didn't care. Anyone could've been working with him. *Anyone.*

She sighed but accepted my answer. "All right. I'll fetch your father."

Another guard said, "I'll go inform the constable."

"Thank you. And tell him Lord Monair and Lord…" I searched my memory for the name of the lord who'd lost his property to the queen's brother. "Belrose are involved."

By the time I had the struggling chamberlain chained inside the torture chamber both King Corbin and my father had joined us, ready to hear his confession.

"Help me put him on the rack," my father said to me.

King Corbin crossed his satin covered arms and spoke to his chamberlain. "I don't understand, Jacque. Why would you betray me?"

Leblond only stared at the king with hate-filled eyes as we forced him onto one of the worst torture devices and strapped his arms and legs down.

A fist pounded on the chamber door. My father looked at me.

I opened the door and found Elly dangling a black cloak and a red scarf in each hand. "We found these in his chambers beneath his mattress," she explained.

I took the items from her and closed the door in her face. She didn't need to see what happened next.

I shoved the cloak and scarf in Jacque Leblond's face. "We have our proof. You may as well save yourself the torture and tell us everything."

The traitor's leader tried to spit in my face and failed. Saliva slid down his own cheek instead.

I shrugged.

My father cranked the wheel, stretching his arms and legs farther out on the rack.

"Tell me everything and your death will be quick," the king urged. His usual bronzed face had turned a shade lighter.

Leblond twisted his neck to stare back at King Corbin. His pressed his lips together so tightly they turned white.

My father turned the crank a couple more rotations.

A groan rose from the traitor's throat. Sweat coated his face.

"Still don't feel like talking?" my father goaded.

"We know Lord Monair and Lord Belrose are involved," I put in.

Leblond, eyes still on the king, laughed. "You don't know anything."

A couple more cranks.

The chamberlain shook as his wrists and ankles strained. He howled.

"Keep turning," King Corbin ordered my father.

The device turned, stretching its victim's arms and legs further and further. He screamed so loud my ears rang. A sickening pop told me his shoulders and hips had just dislocated.

Leblond's eyes bulged. His teeth gritted together so hard I thought they might break. "You killed her," he ground out, his voice high with pain.

"Who?" the king prodded.

"Lucille, my daughter."

The king threw up his hands. "I thought we were past this. It's not my fault Lucille killed herself. She was morose."

"She wouldn't have been if you'd have let her marry the man she loved instead of using her like some pawn." The flood gate had burst. Leblond couldn't keep the words from spilling. "I'm not the only one you've wronged for your own selfish needs."

"She was the daughter of my chamberlain. I couldn't have her marry some poor slug." And there it was. The seed that had sowed all of that rage. "You and your friends will hang at dawn." King Corbin turned away. Finished with the man he'd once thought a friend.

"It doesn't matter," Leblond flung at him. "Vesirus will tear this kingdom apart."

The king paused by the door and chuckled. "You're mad." He stepped outside and yelped.

My father and I rushed to King Corbin's side.

A stable boy, dressed in all black, held onto the dagger sticking into the king's ribs; a fatal wound if he'd have hit any higher.

He released the blade's unpolished handle and took off.

I was faster. I gained on him as he headed for the slums.

Almost close enough to grab him, I pulled my own dagger out from my belt and threw it with precision.

The blade stuck into the back of the young lad's head, and he toppled forward.

He lay sprawled face down on the ground as I walked up and put my boot on his neck. I bent down and wrenched my dagger free from his skull.

So close, he'd been so close to assassinating the king.

I turned the body over and stared down at the face of the stable boy. "Traitor," I murmured as I slung him over my shoulder and carried him back to be buried with the rest of his kind in an unmarked grave.

CHAPTER 12

T HE LAST STARS were blinking out of the sky as Ger and I dragged Leblond through the soil to the Tree of Ends. Others had already gathered around the enormous leafless tree. It was one of the only trees that lost its leaves in the winter. Its leaves turned red like the colour of its victims before dropping. I stared up at the ominous shape standing out like a skeletal silhouette against the lightening sky. Spring would soon grace us with her presence, bringing buds to even the most horrifying tree.

Leblond's face was the colour of ashes falling after an inferno. He couldn't struggle and made no complaint as we lifted him onto the platform beneath the tree's thickest branch.

Lords Monair and Belrose already kneeled on that same platform awaiting their dark fates. Repercussions for conspiring against the king.

A priestess, with flowing sable hair dressed in billowing, white robes, glided to the side of the platform to wait for the king and queen's arrival.

My father squinted against the golden sun ascending through the tall trees as King Corbin and Queen Nicola approached, hand in hand and flanked by their attendants. The pair dressed in elaborate robes of green and white, the thick material hiding the wound from the night before. They moved slowly, for the king's benefit. Otherwise, he kept his face blank, no evidence of pain. He hadn't made the attempt on his life public. It would be a sign of weakness to admit the enemy had come so close to ending him. No, King Corbin wouldn't let anyone

SEPHEUS

doubt his strength. He'd see this execution through before he went back to the bedrest his healer had surely ordered from him.

When the rulers stopped, facing the tree, their subjects bowed or curtsied.

"Begin," King Corbin bade the priestess.

She obeyed. "Jacque Leblond, you may confess your transgressions to Celestia now."

Leblond's eyes moved over the crowd as he spoke. "I, Jacque Leblond, am responsible for the deaths of many. I have betrayed my king."

The priestess turned, believing he was finished his confession.

"But my king betrayed me," he went on. "He's betrayed all of you. He and anyone who follows him will suffer. Vesirus has promised this."

Gasps of horror fell from mouths surrounding the Tree.

"Madness!" someone shouted.

Another threw a rotten potato at his face.

The king stepped up on the platform behind the traitors as whispers wove through the crowd. "Anyone who continues to follow this man's example deems themselves a follower of the Dark Lord and will be annihilated and sent to Mnyama."

Unease erupted throughout the king's people. Courtiers turned to one another with suspicious glances. Afraid their neighbours may be a follower of Vesirus.

"Get on with it," King Corbin said to the priestess with distaste.

She bowed her head and then continued while Ger and I placed the rope hanging from the branch around Leblond's neck.

She repeated the same rights of death for the other two lords. One of them cried and begged to be spared. His words fell on deaf ears. The other hurled all over himself and the boards he kneeled upon. A woman wailed from the edge of the platform.

Four other guards, two for each lord, pushed them forward and positioned ropes around their necks too.

Blaise watched with her arms folded, a fire burning in her eyes. She was finally getting what she wanted; revenge for her parents' deaths. I didn't believe it would make her feel any better, but perhaps she'd be able to move on.

The priestess looked up at the three men and spoke the next words loud enough to carry over the whole crowd. "To Vesirus you shall go!"

Ger and I shoved Leblond off the platform with his friends.

Lord Monair's neck snapped at his fall while Lord Belrose clawed at the rope before stilling.

Leblond dangled in the air, choking for a few moments longer before his face turned purple and he stiffened. When his body slackened and drool dribbled out the corners of his mouth, we knew he'd never draw another breath.

The crowd erupted in cheers, fists raised in the air. "Rot in Mnyama," someone hollered.

"That was the most interesting execution I've been to," I admitted to Ger, stepping off the platform.

He shook his head. "I need a good cup of ale after that one."

"That's always your answer."

He grinned widely at me and teased, "It's a good answer. Come on. You can have your usual cup of water."

I chuckled. For the first time since I could remember, I felt relaxed. My relationship with my father was the best it had been. There would likely be no great danger to the kingdom for a while since Leblond admitted he was a follower of Vesirus and was now dead. And I had people I could call friends. I was almost able to forget the power within my veins. I hadn't told anyone about it. It was bad enough I was the son of a torturer. Having magic would only cause others to fear me more. I didn't even understand why I had this power. Witches' magic was usually passed down through their blood. As far as I knew, no one in my bloodline had any magic. Then again, my father refused to share much about my family.

I was soaking a piece of bread in my leek soup when Constable Bouvant slid into a chair beside us.

"I'm proud of you both, Blaise too," the constable announced, pulling the chair closer to the square table. "So are the king and queen. Queen Nicola has announced she will be throwing a ball in a fortnight to celebrate."

"I think there are still Redeemers who will act against the crown," Ger said into his cup of ale.

"It's possible," the constable agreed. "But they won't be any match for us unless they find a new leader. And word has spread about

Leblond's dealings with Vesirus. Most fear to go down that dark path. Should anymore traitors arise, we will do our best to find and stop them before they can gain the upper hand."

"Do you think there's any truth to Leblond's warning? Would Vesirus really come here and try to destroy our kingdom?" I asked through a mouthful of bread.

The constable let out a laugh. "No, Leblond was taking one last jab at King Corbin. Don't believe the words of a traitor."

"We should search the forests anyway. See if there are any Redeemers attempting to regroup."

"Good thinking, Sepheus. I couldn't agree more." Constable Bouvant cracked a smile and pushed himself off his seat. "Tomorrow we ride. Enjoy the rest of your night off."

As soon as he left, Ger grumbled, "You made more work for us."

I pushed my empty bowl away. "He was already planning it. There's always more work to be done."

He sighed dramatically.

I laughed. "Lazy ass."

I was right about Blaise. She wasn't at peace after Leblond's execution. She rode near the front of the group of soldiers as fierce as ever the next day on our mission to seek out remaining Redeemers.

When we spotted a group of about a dozen people gathering under the cover of thick trees, she shrieked like a cat who'd gotten its tail stepped on and shot a woman with an arrow from atop her horse.

"Blaise!" Constable Bouvant shouted in warning.

She either didn't hear him, or she didn't care. She nocked another arrow and let it fly, impaling a young boy through the back of his neck.

"*Blaise!*" the constable yelled louder, kicking his horse to catch up with her.

Blaise dismounted from her horse and drew her sword.

With two dead, the rest of the group had begun to scatter, crying out with fear.

We surrounded them, but they were unarmed and stared at us wide-eyed, like a herd of frightened animals.

"State your reason for gathering out here in the middle of the woods," Constable Bouvant demanded, holding his horse still.

"We were mourning the loss of our friends. We meant no harm," a hunch-backed man came forward.

"Our leader is dead, many of our friends imprisoned. We can do you no harm." A frail woman moved beside the man. Her sun bleached hair was cropped short.

"No harm? Your group is the reason my parents are dead!" Blaise snarled at the woman and raised her sword.

"Many people are dead," the hunched man countered. "We are unarmed, as you can see."

"I don't care." She pressed the point of her sword to the woman's chest.

"Blaise," Constable Bouvant warned.

I recognized the darkness in her. I knew what that darkness felt like. It was so easy to be pulled into its cold embrace. So much *easier.*

I dismounted my horse and put a hand over the hand holding her sword. "Not like this. You will only give them reason to spill more of our kingdom's blood. They can be dealt with in other ways." *Let them suffer in the bowels of the palace,* I tried to tell her with my eyes.

She glared at me but lowered her sword.

"Groups are not allowed to gather outside of court. You are all to remain within the kingdom's walls. If any of you disobey, you will be executed on sight," Constable Bouvant told them and then added, "King's orders."

"Fine," the man bit out. "We will come back with you, but bring the bodies back too. They deserve a proper burial. They did no wrong."

Constable Bouvant lifted his brows at the man. "They were Redeemers. They'll be a feast for the crows."

The man stepped closer to the constable. Each of us drew our weapons.

The weaponless man backed off.

"Tie their hands. We'll lead them to Terra like mules," the constable ordered us. "Ignore me again and you'll find yourself in the dungeon with your enemies," he said to Blaise.

Though a fire still smoldered in her amber eyes, she replied, "Yes, sir."

I rode near the back, beside Blaise, our enemies trailing on our return home. "Maybe you should take a break from all of this," I said to her as our horses slowed to step over a fallen log. "Leblond is dead, and the path you're on leads to nothing but misery."

She stared straight through her horse's ears. "That's funny coming from you."

"You don't want to be like me, trust me."

"At least we agree on one thing," she said bitterly.

I was silent a moment, then offered, "I never congratulated you. If it weren't for your keen sense of distrust, who knows when we would've caught Leblond. You should give yourself a break." I didn't know why I was trying to make her feel better. She usually annoyed me, but now... now she was one of us, a soldier of Terra.

"My parents never got a break." She finally looked at me, but tears shone in her fiery eyes. Then her mouth curved up a little in the corners. "Don't fool yourself. You would've never caught Leblond without me."

"Someone has a big ego."

She puffed out a half-laugh and edged her horse in front of mine.

When we got back, we took the Redeemers we'd captured to the dungeons to live out the rest of their miserable lives.

We continued to search the forest the following days until Queen Nicola's celebration. Blaise had insisted on coming each time. She kept to herself and abided Constable Bouvant's commands. We didn't find any other Redeemers. If any hadn't been scared enough by Leblond's proclamation of his devotion to Vesirus to give up their cause, they remained hidden from our eyes.

I did up the last golden button on my sea green doublet and smoothed my hair with my palms. I'd even shined my leather, knee-high boots for the occasion. While I never loved celebrations, I knew the importance of making a good appearance before the court. I used a rag to quickly polish the hilt of my sword and left my room for the great hall.

The usual courtiers pranced around in their outrageous outfits of silk and lace, pretending to be interested in each other's prattle. My father studied me for a moment before turning back to his conversation with Constable Bouvant. I hoped my name hadn't fallen from either of their lips.

I disappeared into the crowd and emerged on the other side, hoping they'd forget about me, and almost bumped into Blaise.

"Watch it," she scolded, holding her goblet of wine out to avoid spilling its contents.

I barely recognized her in the chartreuse and ivory gown she wore. Her brown hair shimmered red from the candlelight beaming down from the chandelier. It curled just below her ears. My gaze was drawn to the jade earrings dangling against her slender neck. I wondered what it'd be like to kiss that delicate beige skin. I cleared my throat, "Good evening, Blaise. I've never seen you look so... womanly."

"You're so rude," she shot.

"You aren't the most polite person I've met."

She gave me a gesture that would have most ladies tutting, point proven.

She breathed loudly out her nose and faced the crowd. She tasted her wine and then said, "I hate parties."

I accepted a piece of soft cheese from a servant's tray. "I do too, but I believe this one is being thrown in our honour. The queen would have us put to death if we didn't show our faces."

Musicians played a fast paced tune. Blaise had to raise her voice to be heard above the flute, drum and tambourine. "She doesn't scare me. Care to dance?" She finished her wine and held out her hand.

I'd never danced before. My father said it was a useless skill, so I'd never learned. I shook my head and backed away. "I don't dance."

"Don't be foolish." She stretched her arm out further.

But I was already out of reach. "Not tonight."

Our comrade, Reynard, came just in time to sweep her onto the dancefloor with the throng of other glittering courtiers. He'd shaved his face bare for the occasion and put on a fine doublet of white and gold. Blaise all but swooned over his fresh appearance. I watched her as she laughed and blushed at something he said. He held her close, one hand upon her tiny waist. "Just friends," I muttered to myself. Friends didn't dance like that. I imagined *my* hand on her waist... *my* comment making her blush. I was being foolish. I didn't wish to be embarrassed by my inability to move elegantly across a dancefloor, a skill most knew. I shouldn't have cared she was having fun with someone other than me. I needed a distraction.

I searched the room and found a young lady of average height with luscious curves standing near a corner, alone. She would do just fine.

I took a swig of water and marched up beside her. "No one to dance with?" I let my gaze run down the length of her body.

She smiled playfully. "Are you offering?"

I met her soft brown eyes. "No, but I thought perhaps you'd like company."

She ran her fingers through her dark curls. "Good, because I don't like dancing."

I leaned in and brushed my finger along her jaw. "How about we entertain ourselves another way." It'd been a long time since I'd had fun with a lady.

I swore I heard Blaise laugh from across the dancefloor. I leaned in for a kiss, to stop myself from thinking about how delightful that laugh sounded—and how furious it made me feel that I wasn't the cause of it.

I ended the kiss and was about to suggest we find some place more private, not so far as the wine cellar. No, I'd learned my lesson with the lynx-woman. I could easily find an empty corridor to fully enjoy her in. But when I opened my eyes, it wasn't some random woman staring back at me, it was Claudia.

I stumbled back, knocking goblets filled with wine from a servant's silver tray.

"What the Mnyama!" the servant dressed in all back snapped.

"What's wrong with you?" the woman I'd been kissing asked, clearly offended. Her face was her own again. "You look like you've just seen a ghost."

"I have," I muttered and strode back through the dancers. *Damn Claudia, will you haunt me until the end of my days?*

"There you are," King Corbin exclaimed. He was radiant. The only sign of his wound was the stiffness with which he moved. He had the best healers the kingdom had to offer. "I have a surprise for you."

"Your Majesty." I bowed to the king dressed in silky gold and silver. Queen Nicola joined him and smiled warmly down at me.

"Attention!" King Corbin shouted, clapping his hands.

The musicians noticed and stopped playing. Conversations halted. The whole hall faced their king and queen.

"First of all," King Corbin started. "Thank you all for joining us to celebrate our victory against The Redeemers. Second, it is with great sadness I inform you of the death of Queen Jelena of Solis. She was a just ruler and will not be forgotten by any of the four kingdoms of

Sarantoa."

Many of the courtiers murmured, but then the king added, "She is to be succeeded by her granddaughter, Queen Adelaide. Terra stands with Queen Adelaide as her friend as we did her grandmother. Long live Queen Adelaide!"

"Long live Queen Adelaide!" the hall roared as goblets were raised.

Once the crowd quieted, King Corbin continued, putting a hand on my shoulder. "We have one more thing to celebrate tonight. With pleasure, I am going to knight Sepheus Lequerc. He has shown great bravery. He was the one responsible for catching Leblond, the man who tried to tear this kingdom apart in the name of the Dark Lord."

More cheers of approval.

I felt the blood leave my face. He'd caught me off guard. Claudia laughed in my mind, *You? A knight? You'll be the least honourable knight in history.* I ground my teeth and told her to shut up.

"Come," King Corbin beckoned me with his open hand. "Kneel."

The room spun, a thousand eyes watched me. Their faces blurred together. I did as I was ordered and focused on the marble floor.

"Do you promise to continue to serve your kingdom and its rulers until the end of your days?" King Corbin began the ceremony.

"I do," I answered, keeping my head bowed. I was grateful I didn't have to face the eyes of so many upon me. It was bad enough I could feel them.

"And do you accept this offer of knighthood, given to you by your king and queen?"

"I do."

I felt the flat of a sword's blade press to my shoulders, one then the other.

"I hereby knight you Sir Sepheus Lequerc. Arise."

As I lifted my head, applause filled the hall. I slowly got to my feet, feeling more than a little nauseous. I swallowed hard. *Not here. Do not get sick in front of your king and queen.* I sucked back a few deep breaths and managed to smile at the king and queen. "Thank you, Your Majesties."

"We are honoured to have you in our kingdom. Congratulations," Queen Nicola cooed, gratitude shining on her face. "Let the dancing commence!" She clapped her hands together and the musicians took up another light tune.

My father gave me a tilt of his chin but offered no words, as to be expected.

"A knight, hey?" Ger put his arm around my shoulders, startling me. Where was Blaise?

"It seems so," I replied, ducking out of his arm. "You and Blaise deserve it as much as I."

He waved a large hand. "Don't worry about me. I was knighted long ago for saving the queen."

I frowned at him. "I never knew."

A well-groomed Ger shrugged his shoulders. "I thought it was obvious."

"What about Blaise? She was the one who first suspected Leblond."

"You don't get knighted over a lucky hunch," Ger chuckled.

"Good point."

As though she'd known we were talking about her, Blaise approached us. "Congratulations, Seph." Did her voice hold a bitter note? She offered a hand.

I wanted to tell her she deserved to be knighted as much as I. I wanted to tell her how beautiful she looked in that gown. But the words wouldn't come. So instead I said, "I think I've had enough excitement for one night."

I didn't wait for either of them to object. Air. I needed air. My stomach still rolled.

I flung the main doors to the palace open. I managed to descend the stairs before I bent over and hurled on a patch of dirt. Wiping my mouth on the back of my hand, I planted my feet and gazed up at the starless sky. Would I be able to live up to my new position? Was I truly an honourable man? Claudia obviously didn't think so. But why did I care what a dead girl thought? I'd saved my kingdom. I needed to forget about her once and for all.

I was about to venture back to my room for the night when movement behind the shrubs along a wall of the palace caught my eye. I crept closer and found a hunched old woman, wearing a black cloak, the hood raised to hide her face. A piece of silver hair poked out by her sharp chin.

"Shh." She raised a finger to her lips. "Sepheus I—"

Before she could finish, a pair of lovers stumbled out of the palace giggling, drunk on wine and each other.

I turned back to where the old woman had been, but she was gone. My brow furrowed. *What a strange night.*

Maybe she'd seen me knighted and wanted to ask some sort of favour. I put her from my mind and re-entered the palace.

Surely tomorrow everything would be normal. Surely my tired mind was only playing jests on me.

CHAPTER 13

HE SCENT OF fresh rain danced through the air as I ambled along to the market. Sunshine urged new petals to bud on the flora dotting the lush green grass. Spring had officially opened her arms to Terra, the days lasting longer with each sunrise. I had the day off from soldierly duties. It was too nice to stay inside, and I couldn't recall the last time I'd been to visit the merchant's tents full of items begging to be purchased. Cherry blossoms lined the path leading to one of the busiest places in Terra.

Delicious aromas of spices and incense invaded my nostrils. I strolled casually past tents filled with all sorts of wonderful, glimmering items. An old woman bartered with a seamstress over a piece of rose coloured fabric, while a merchant filled a pouch with cinnamon to hand to a customer. One could spend all day simply observing the activities of others at the place full of bustle.

I stopped before a weathered man, who I'd have guessed to be in his fifth decade, selling jewellery.

He set down his polishing rag and a silver chain to greet me. "A necklace for your lady?"

I shook my head, glancing at the sparkling necklaces laid out on the piece of midnight blue velvet. "I have no lady." But then a piece of jade, round with symbols etched on its surface stole my attention. It matched the earrings Blaise had worn to the ball perfectly.

"A beautiful piece," the merchant commented, picking it up so I could have a closer look. "It's an amulet of protection. It brings its wearer luck anytime they're faced with danger.

"How much?" I was sure Blaise would laugh in my face and tell me she didn't need an amulet to protect her. Maybe I wouldn't tell her what it was meant for. Maybe I'd just tell her it was a peace offering. I didn't believe it would truly bring her good luck anyway. I was sure it was a tactic to convince gullible customers to purchase. Still, I liked the way it looked.

"Two gold coins."

I slipped my hand into my leather pouch and dug out the gold. I handed the coins to him, and he dangled the amulet for me to take. I placed it inside the pouch with the rest of my coins.

"A pleasure doing business with you, sir," he said with a bright, crooked-toothed smile.

I wandered around the rest of the market, squeezing through hordes of people. I had to side step a few times to avoid children who weren't watching where they were going. One trod on my foot and, when I growled at the young boy, he ran away calling for his mother. I didn't buy any other items.

When the sun began descending through the leafy trees, I left the market for home. My mind was lost on thoughts of Blaise and how flattering she'd looked at the ball. The image of her in that gown was burned into my mind.

A bony hand gripped the upper part of my arm, pulling me back to reality. The old woman I'd seen outside the ball peered at me from beneath her deep black hood. Her cloak hung off her like ominous black smoke. Her golden eyes bore into mine as though she could read my thoughts. She reminded me of the witches I'd witnessed people rush away from.

"What do you want?" I asked her, an icy edge creeping into my tone.

"I know who you are." Her voice was rough and harsh, a sound which would haunt my memory forever.

I pulled my arm from her grasp and snapped. "No, you don't. Stop following me."

She pointed a gnarly finger tipped with a long yellowed nail at me. "The boy born into bloodshed has a darkened heart."

"Born into bloodshed? You have the wrong person." She probably knew I was the son of Cedric Lequerc. Of course the son of a torturer would be born into bloodshed. I wasn't about to reveal anything about my life to her though.

I backed away, but she whispered eerie words in a language I didn't understand and I found I couldn't move.

I could see her smile from within her hood. "You have magic like I, yes?"

"No," I denied. "So you *are* a witch."

"Shh," she hushed me, watching a pair of ladies pass by. "I'm more than a witch. I'm family… blood."

My mind whirled at those last words. Could she be telling the truth? My father hadn't told me about anyone in my family other than my mother, and I *did* have magic. Maybe I'd inherited it from this old witch. I took a step back and realized I could move again. The spell had worn off. A weak spell.

"Come to my cottage tomorrow, east of this kingdom. Follow Willowing Creek until you reach a clearing. Keep going until you see my old carcass of a cottage. I will tell you everything there, son of Cedric."

"You know my father," I stated. Could I trust this witch? It could be a trap.

"I know Cedric, and I know you."

"Why not just tell me now? Why try to lure me to your home?" I questioned.

I imagined she was pursing her thin lips from beneath her hood. She jerked toward a trio of men ambling by, sharing in some jest. "Too many prying ears here," she rasped.

I stayed silent for a moment, thoughtful. I needed to know who she really was and what she wanted. I wouldn't go unarmed. She was only an old woman after all. If she really wanted to harm me with magic… well, I had magic too. "All right, witch, I'll come find you."

She smiled again, and I caught a glimpse of narrow, pointy teeth.

I left her to go fill my stomach.

I played with the shiny silver chain of the amulet that night in my room. The exquisite piece of green jade reminded me of a lake I'd once seen in the forest. Surely Blaise would appreciate such remarkable craftsmanship. Any other lady would swoon over such a gift. Blaise wasn't like other ladies though. Maybe I would tell her it was a token of good luck. Surely a warrior could appreciate such a symbol.

I dropped the amulet back into my leather pouch. Tomorrow, after I visited the witch, I'd give Blaise her gift. It would be a new beginning for us. Friendship. Did I hope we might eventually become more? It was something I wasn't ready to admit. Even to myself.

I followed Willowing Creek east as the witch had instructed. The map reading Constable Bouvant had taught me paid off. I stopped and took in a breath of fresh air as the forest opened up to a field of long grass rippling in the wind. In the near distance, lay a small, wooden cottage with a porch at the front. Weeds pushed their way up around the small home, claiming the territory as theirs. Grasshoppers and birds sang duets to the rising yellow sun.

I stepped up onto the porch, careful not to tread on any of the rotten boards. I knocked loudly, using the iron door-knocker shaped like the head of some sort of demonic creature.

The floor from within the cottage creaked before the door opened widely, revealing the old witch.

Her tanned face crinkled like crumpled parchment as she smiled at me. Her lips pale and thin made her pointy teeth look even longer. But her eyes… her eyes were sharp, like two golden pools filled with wisdom. Her smile was meant to be warm. Others would have found it menacing.

"Welcome to my home, my grandson," the witch said, making enough space for me to enter.

I stepped inside, that last word echoing in my mind. *Grandson.*

She offered me a seat in a rickety old chair and handed me a mug of something dark reddish-brown. I sniffed the mug's contents and winced. It smelled strong. I didn't trust her enough to believe it wasn't poisoned. The shelf in a corner of the room held containers which I imagined were full of potions, poultices and poisons.

"It's safe to drink, I promise," she assured me as though she'd read my mind. When I still didn't take a sip, she took it from me and tasted it herself. "See."

"Point proven." I accepted the mug back and asked, "Sorry, did you call me grandson?"

She sat across from me and folded her wrinkled hands. She wasn't wearing that awful cloak today. Instead, she'd dressed herself in a loose white dress, yellowed in places with age. The hollows of her cheeks were sunken, and the thin skin under her eyes made it appear as though she had twin purple bruises. Her golden eyes held a kindness as she confirmed, "I did."

I took a sip of the drink and immediately spat it out with a cough. "Oh! That's horrible." I set the mug down and pushed it away. "What *is* that?"

She chuckled. "It's only wine. I make it myself."

"It's strong."

"That's what I like about it." She smacked her palm on the table between us and cackled.

I shivered; the taste of alcohol still strong on my tongue. "We are unalike in that sense at least. So, tell me, are you my father's mother?"

She put her chin in her hand and replied, "No. I'm your mother's mother. You're father isn't really your father—"

"That's madness!" I cut her off. "You must be jesting. My father is the only family I have."

She put up a hand as I was about to rise from my chair. "Hear me out. You may leave when I'm finished telling you what you need to know."

I sank back into my chair. Fine. I'd see what other kind of insanity the witch could concoct.

She pinned me with her eyes and went on. "My name is Maud Lequerc. Otta, your mother, was my daughter. Cedric is my son. He's not your father. He is your uncle."

"How can this be?" The chair scraped across the floor as I pushed it away from the table.

"I will explain." She said, annoyed with my interruptions. "Your mother was in love with King Lelund. He had taken her as his mistress against Queen Vivienne's wishes. They kept it a secret from the jealous queen for as long as they could, but eventually she found out. King Lelund had to send Otta away to appease his wife, but he still visited her often. The king told your mother he loved only her, but being a king complicated their relationship. When your mother became pregnant with you, almost nineteen springs ago, King Lelund stopped coming to see your mother."

Maud closed her eyes and sighed deeply before continuing. "I knew your mother was heartbroken. I tried to console her when she came to see me, but she stole poison from my home in the kingdom and used it on herself after she gave birth to you."

I don't know when my jaw had dropped. "But—but that's not at all what my father told me about my mother. He said she was a whore who'd died giving birth to me. This tale of yours can't be true."

"Otta's maid found her dead on the floor with you crying in her bedchamber. She brought you to me. I knew I didn't have it in me to raise another child. So I took you to Cedric and asked him to raise his sister's baby. Queen Viv realized King Lelund had been in love with your mother when he fell into a depressed state after her death. She killed him in her rage and was executed for it. My son and I were the only ones who knew the truth of Queen Viv's rage—until now."

I ran my hands down my face. "No. This can't be true. Queen Vivienne lost her mind. She wasn't jealous of some love affair. King Lelund was a *good* king. My father loved him."

"He was a good king. He just wasn't a good husband."

I stood up so quickly my chair crashed to the floor. "Why are you telling me this? And why now?"

She placed her hands on the table and bowed her head, wisps of silver hair falling around her worn face. "You deserve to know the truth. You have royal blood in your veins *and* magic. You must be careful which path you choose to follow."

"This—this is too much." I raised both my hands and backed toward the door. "I need to speak with my father—my uncle... *whoever* he is!"

She got up off her chair too, but she didn't try to stop me. "I understand. You may leave if you like, but I'd prefer if you sat with me a while longer. Don't you wish to hear more about your mother?"

I closed my eyes and counted my breaths. When I had calmed my racing heart, I opened my eyes and set the chair back upright. I sat down. "What was she like?"

"Sweet—beautiful. Your mother had a good heart. So did your father." She got up and replaced my wine with water.

I took a long drink then asked, "Do you think she loved me?"

My grandmother's face softened as she placed her hand on mine. "I know she did. She was so broken when she had you though. But yes, she loved you."

Her words warmed my heart. I believed her. Why would she make her story up? My father was the one who'd deceived me. I pulled my hand away. "Why did you give me to my fa—to Cedric? You must have known he was a torturer."

She folded her hands in her lap and told me honestly, "I knew Cedric was a torturer, you're right. But I didn't think he'd subject you to his work. He was once a soldier you know? An honourable man. Not that there isn't honour in forcing answers from our enemies, but he's let it blacken his heart so much, he may as well be working for the Dark Lord."

I hissed at her opinion. Is that what she thought of me too? "We—he does his work in the name of Celestia. For the good of the kingdom."

"Yes, but love resides in him no longer. Only hate. I don't want you to end up like him."

I realized I agreed with her. I didn't wish to end up like him either. I gave her a slight smile and said, "I should go. Thank you for telling me the truth… about my mother."

She pushed herself to her feet, age slowing her down. "If you ever wish to visit, you're always welcome in my home."

I gave her knarled hand a light squeeze. "Thank you." I left her standing in the cottage as old as she, if not older.

I thought about everything my grandmother had told me on my return. I couldn't be an heir to the throne. I didn't *want* the throne. The illegitimate bastard of a dead king would never be accepted by the people of Terra anyways. Still, I'd had a right to know. By the time I reached the stables and handed my mount over to a stable boy, anger had crept back up on me.

I found my father inside his room, scratching words on a piece of parchment at his wide oak desk.

I stomped up beside him. "Hello, Father. Or should I say, Uncle?"

CHAPTER 14

M Y FATHER... MY uncle set down his feather pen and twisted
to stare at me. "Excuse me?"

"That's right," I challenged. "Your mother, Maud, told me everything."

"Did she?" He rose from his chair, slowly.

"My whole life is a lie, isn't it?"

But he didn't answer. He grabbed his cloak off a hook on the wall and strode for the front door.

"Where are you going? Tell me the truth." I followed him.

He slammed the door in my face, leaving me alone with no answers.

"Goddess dammit!" I slammed my fist into the wall, feeling pain tear across my knuckles. I ignored the wet sensation of blood beading on my skin as I wrenched the door open. My father was nowhere in sight. I headed for the palace. Perhaps he'd gone to speak with King Corbin—who was also my uncle. He could never know who my true father was. He'd view me as a threat even though I didn't want his throne.

Blaise stood on guard duty outside of the throne room. She blocked me from the giant double doors. "Seph, what's wrong?"

I ground my teeth and then tried to rein my temper in as I asked, "Is my father in there? Let me pass."

She stood firm. "No, I haven't seen him today." Her eyes flicked to my wounded hand. "Sepheus! Your hand! It's bleeding!"

I tucked my bleeding hand under my other arm. "It's fine."

"At least wrap it up so you don't get blood everywhere," she shot back. When I didn't move, she sighed and tore off a piece of the bottom of her surcoat. She held out her hand. "Here, let me see it."

I hesitated before letting her take my hand in hers. She studied the wound for a moment then clucked, wrapping the piece of material around it and tying it. "So are you going to tell me what's going on or not?"

"It's none of your business, Blaise."

Hurt flashed in her eyes. "Sorry for caring."

I took a deep breath. This wasn't how I'd wanted my peace offering with her to start. "No, I'm sorry. I—" I reached inside my cloak to pull out the pouch with the amulet in it, but it was gone. My brow creased with confusion. I must have lost it between the palace and Maud's cottage. "Never mind. I've misplaced something."

She snickered. "Were you about to offer me a gift?"

"Maybe I was. You'll never know now."

Her eyes grew rounder. "Why?" she asked, incredulously.

"It was nothing. Just some sort of symbol I thought you'd appreciate as a fellow warrior."

"Oh." She looked away and then smiled up at me. "Care to spar? I'm almost finished guard duty here."

I didn't want to spar. I wanted to find Cedric, but I didn't know where he'd gone. The hopeful expression on Blaise's face caused me to fold. It was sort of frustrating to care what another person thought of me, but kind of exhilarating at the same time.

Before long, we were in the training field striking and parring in leather armour. Blaise's weakness was also her strength. Her small size meant I could hit her with more force, but she was able to dodge my blows easier, and she was faster. It felt good to let out some of my anger. I welcomed the sweat pooling on my back.

We were interrupted by another soldier. "Sepheus, your father sent me to find you."

I whirled away from Blaise, letting my sword hang at my side. "Where is he?" I puffed out between breaths.

"In his torture chamber."

I didn't even spare Blaise a glance as I jogged to the chamber I'd basically been raised in.

I hadn't been inside the chamber since I'd helped question Leblond. It was as dark and horrible as ever, no sunlight able to penetrate the thick stone walls stained with blood. The rattle of chains told me my father wasn't alone. Shadows whispered to me, trying to pull me into the darkness I'd been born into. I ignored them and stepped beside Cedric, who faced the old witch chained on her back to a table.

Maud's lips curled up at the corners when my face appeared above her. "Good, he has brought you here."

"What did she tell you?" Cedric demanded.

I turned to the man I'd once called father. "She said my mother was in love with King Lelund and stole poison from her after she gave birth to me because King Lelund refused to see her anymore. She told me you are my mother's brother."

He laughed lowly, though there was no humour in it. "She got one important detail wrong." He took a thick blade from his belt and pressed it to her throat. "*She* was the one who gave your mother the poison. She thought Otta meant to use it on Queen Vivienne. With the queen dead, King Lelund may have recognized you as his son. It's *her* fault you're parents are dead."

I couldn't believe his words. My ears began to ring. He was admitting he wasn't my father... admitting I was King Lelund's bastard son. To hear them from the witch I'd just met was one thing, but to hear them from the man who'd raised me... My gaze fell back on Maud.

She inclined her forehead, causing more wrinkles under her hairline. "Now you know the truth." Her golden eyes shone unnaturally bright in the dark chamber.

I stepped back from the table. "No, this can't be—*I* can't be..."

"No one was supposed to know." Cedric pushed the blade harder against her frail, sagging throat. "I told you never to return," he hissed at Maud.

She smiled again and croaked, "My time is coming to an end."

"Then let us end it now." Cedric shoved the blade into her throat.

"No!" I tried to reach for the blade, but it was too late. Blood seeped from around the metallic blade and dripped onto the table beneath her. She'd given her life to tell me the truth... even if she'd twisted a small detail. She was *family*.

The colour drained from Maud's face as the life drained from her body. She took her last breath, a smile still on her face, and left this world with peace. She was happy to die now that her truth had been told.

"You didn't have to kill her," I hissed at my uncle. I'd do my damnedest not to be anything like him. I swore to myself then and there I'd reject the darkness festering inside my heart.

Cedric ripped his blade from Maud's throat and stuck it back in his belt without bothering to wipe it. I stood frozen... paralyzed. Until a rock scraped against the dirt floor, flinging everything back into motion.

I spun at the human-shaped silhouette the same time Cedric lunged for it.

I squinted in the torchlight, recognizing the face of the small woman. Blaise. Cedric had her throttled in an iron grip. She was choked, trying to speak, but she couldn't get enough air to get the words out.

Cedric was going to kill her—just like he'd killed Maud. No one could know the truth. But Blaise was my friend. Cedric had lied to me my entire life. I couldn't let him end her. She was the light in the darkness. I clung to that light like it was my last breath.

A green vine the size of a tree's root shot up out of the ground, throwing clumps of dirt through the air.

Cedric twisted to see what was happening, but he was too late. The end of the magical vine hit him with so much force it pierced straight through his chest and up toward the ceiling on the other side of him. His mouth tried to form a word but no sound came. Eyes still open, he slumped on the vine growing through his body.

Blaise's gasps were audible from behind Cedric's body. I ran to her and the enormous vine disintegrated, the body falling to the ground.

"Are you all right?" I tried to reach for her, but she shrank back and crouched on the ground.

"Pl—please! I won't tell a soul."

I realized she was afraid... afraid of me. "Blaise, he was going to kill you."

"Please let me go," she begged.

I'd never seen her this way, so frightened... so powerless. I moved out of her path. "You're free to go."

She scurried away like a mouse running from a cat.

I stayed inside the chamber for a long time after she'd left. I needed to pull myself together. The king would want to know what had happened to his torturer. I came up with the only plan my mind could put together.

First, I dragged Cedric's body away from any wood or other material that might catch fire. Then, I snatched the lit torch off the wall and used it to light Cedric's body aflame. I gagged and covered my face with the sleeve of my cloak at the smell of burning flesh. When Cedric was nothing more than a pile of ash on the dirt floor, I took Maud's body and threw it on top of the pile of corpses of criminals and vagrants all waiting to be buried in one big grave together. It was a bit of a shame she'd be buried with the lost and forgotten, but I couldn't risk someone recognizing her as Cedric's mother.

After the bodies were taken care of, I was granted an audience with King Corbin. The queen was busy with her ladies.

I fell to the floor before my king, eyes locked on the soft carpet. I couldn't make myself cry, so I let my shoulders drop as I breathed out with anguish, "My father... he's—he's *dead.*" I allowed myself to glance up at him.

The king was silent for a moment. He brushed a jewelled hand over his face before placing it on the back of my head. "I am so sorry. How did this come to be?"

"A witch," I explained. "He was torturing her when I arrived at the chamber to see what he'd fetched me for. He'd wanted assistance. I tried to help him, but she said a spell and the flame from the torch—it leaped onto the sleeve of his cloak and burned him alive." I squeezed my eyes shut and leaned forward so my head touched the floor. My life depended on the king believing my story. "I don't even get to give him a proper burial," my voice strained.

At last, I sat up on my knees and watched my king. He folded his hands together and blinked hard, staring straight ahead. He wouldn't let the tears in his eyes fall. He'd save those for solitude. "Where is the witch?"

"I—I killed her, Your Majesty. I apologize I did so without your approval, but I was so filled with hate. So angry at her for killing my father. I needed to end her life with my own hands."

King Corbin shook his head. "No need to apologize. I'm glad she's dead. It's been a long time since a witch has dared to use magic to harm another. I didn't believe they could even wield so much power. It's been watered down throughout the generations. Perhaps we need to find them all and snuff out their magic before they become more troublesome."

I didn't know if he wished to kill them or simply try to contain them. I needed to remain in control of this situation regardless. I clasped my hands before me and said, "Your Majesty, I beseech you. Let me help you in this quest. Let me choose a comrade to bring with me to find these witches."

"You don't wish to take your father's position?"

I winced. I most certainly did not. "No, Your Majesty. Apologies, but I'd like to remain as your knight. I feel there's more honour in this quest."

To my surprise, the king agreed. "All right, Sepheus. I shall find someone else to fill your father's place. You may have your honour. Do me proud."

I rose to my feet and bowed deeply. "I will, Your Majesty."

"You are dismissed. Go and get some rest. I will call for a death celebration to honour your father. I expect you to begin your hunt three sunrises after you say your goodbyes."

"Yes, Your Majesty. Thank you." I made to leave.

"Oh, and Sepheus," the king called. I paused and he said, "Your father meant a lot to me. I will miss him dearly."

I gave him one nod and left.

I needed to speak with Blaise. She could be the death of me. I had to convince her to keep my secret. If I could get her to agree, my life would remain safe.

Or you could kill her like you killed me, Claudia's voice said in my mind. "Shut up!" It wasn't an option. I was done with the darkness. "I'm sorry I killed you," I whispered to my ghost. "I know it was wrong. It was my fault you became a traitor. There. Are you happy?" I few passersby turned to stare at me. I clamped my mouth shut and kept walking until I reached my room in the soldiers' quarters. I didn't want to go back to the home I'd shared with my uncle.

I waited until after supper was served. I had no appetite after the day's events. When I was sure all of the soldiers had retired to their rooms, I knocked on the door to the one Elly and Blaise shared.

Elly answered and gave me a questioning look.

"I need to speak privately with Blaise" I said low enough only she could hear me.

She frowned and glanced over at her bed. "I'm tired. Can't you speak with her tomorrow?"

"Please, Elly."

She huffed. "Fine." She tossed on her cloak and turned to Blaise, who sat crossed-legged on the floor, polishing her sword. "I'll be back soon."

Blaise didn't answer, she stared straight at me as I entered their room and Elly closed the door behind her.

I sat down across from her and she went back to focusing on making her sword gleam. "What do you want?" she asked, scrubbing the cloth over the hilt harder.

"What you saw," I started. "I need you to promise me you'll keep it to yourself."

"I told you I won't tell anyone. What *are* you anyways?" She finally stopped polishing to glance back up at me. Her eyes searched my face for answers.

"The old woman you saw was a witch, so I guess that makes me a warlock," I confessed. I couldn't deny it. She'd seen my power.

She pinched her lips together then replied, "No, witches don't have that kind of power, Seph. No one's had that much power since the elementals walked the earth."

"Are you saying I'm an elemental?"

"No—I don't know. Maybe!" She flung the cloth down on the floor. "It doesn't make sense. Why would Celestia gift anyone with such power? The last time humans wielded elemental power they abused it and almost destroyed our world in the process."

I stared down at the space between us. "Maybe it's a mistake. Maybe I'm not supposed to have this power."

She scoffed. "Likely."

"Listen," I placed a hand on hers. "I didn't know I had this power in me. All I know is my father—Cedric—was about to kill you. My instinct told me to save you. I didn't want him to die." Most of it was true. I hadn't meant to kill him. I needed her to believe I hadn't been keeping the secret of my power to myself.

She studied my hand on hers. Finally, she relaxed a little. "Okay, but now what? What will you tell the king?"

"I've already spoken with him. I told him the witch killed my father and I took her life for doing so." I had to tell her the truth. Everyone would know of the story I'd spun to the king soon enough.

"You lied to the king?"

"I had to! If he knew the truth, I'd be executed. Cedric was a friend of the royal family. And if he believes my power to be a threat, he'll make sure I never breathe again. Blaise, I don't want to die. Please, tell me you'll keep this between us."

She tore her hand from underneath mine. "I said I will!" Then she asked between tight lips, "Is there anything else I should know?"

"Actually, yes. King Corbin wants me to find the witches for him. He wants to ensure none of them become a threat."

She tilted her head to the side and shook it back and forth. "No. This is wrong, Sepheus. You can't do this. Those witches are innocent. *You* are the one with great power. I won't help you harm those who've done nothing wrong."

"I need you. I asked the king if I could choose who I'd bring with me on this quest. I want you to come with me. We can find the witches with bad intentions. We'll only bring them to King Corbin. It was the only way I could keep him from eliminating anyone believed to have a speck of magic. If he gave this task to someone else…" Likely anyone he believed a witch would've been executed.

She glowered at me. I wasn't giving her a choice. The alternative was worse. "Fine. But it's just you and I. Leave Ger out of this."

I nodded and stood up. "We agree on that matter." I didn't want to be riddled with Ger's questions. I went to leave but paused to say, "I wish you didn't have to bare this. You should never have followed me."

I left before she had a chance to come up with some snide answer. It *was* her fault in a way. If she hadn't been there, I wouldn't have had to save her life.

CHAPTER 15

T HE WHOLE KINGDOM came out for Cedric's death ceremony. His ashes were buried next to where his own father lay, returned to the earth from which he came. Queen Nicola was one of the few who shed tears for him. He'd pushed most away in his later seasons in life, but he'd remained friendly with both the king and queen.

I felt relief as soil was placed over the remains of his body, a priestess speaking the rights of death. Never again would I be judged by the man who'd raised me. I wore a mask of grief until the death ceremony ended. Then, I excused myself. Ger tried to offer words of console, but I told him I wished to be alone.

Noctis De Celestia came and went. The king and queen travelled to Solis for the celebrations, along with a few other important members of court.

I didn't feel like celebrating the goddess that spring at the age of eighteen. I had nothing to thank her for. My life was a lie and my power a curse. Blaise wasn't in the mood for festivities either. Soon, we'd be scouring Terra and the surrounding area for witches.

Ger had heard about the witch who'd killed my uncle. Everyone had. The king himself made a statement about it at his death ceremony. Each time someone offered their condolences and well wishes in bringing down the witches, I noticed the judgment in Blaise's eyes. I hated it. I wanted to prove to her I could be better. I *would* prove it to her.

It took some convincing to get Ger to agree to let Blaise and I go on the witch hunt without him. I explained to him Constable Bouvant wouldn't want all of his most skilled guards away from the palace at once. He reluctantly agreed in the end. Sometimes it paid off appealing to a man's ego.

Two mornings after Noctis, we began our search. We started out in the kingdom, going from door to door. We searched houses for magical items such as potions, spell books and crystals. Usually, we found nothing incriminating.

The first house we'd found with magical evidence was near the slums. An older woman and her daughter lived alone in the cramped but cozy home. I held a potion up in front of her. "The king has banned magic in his territory. What do you have to say for yourself?" It was true, the king had given a speech and sent out messages to every home stating magic was no longer allowed in his kingdom except when used by one of his official healers.

The older woman shrank back and put her hands to her mouth. "I—I—that potion is harmless. It's used to make a woman fertile."

I dropped it on the floor and the glass vial shattered. Brown liquid seeped into the wooden floorboards. "If Celestia wants your daughter to have a child, she will."

The woman fell to her knees and her daughter, who looked close to my own age, rushed to her side. "Please, don't take my mother. She's harmless."

Blaise shot me a dark look then said to them both, "You aren't being taken anywhere, but you must not keep magical items any longer. It's for your own safety. Do you understand?"

The mother peered up at her with bleary eyes and nodded. "Yes, thank you. Thank you for sparing us."

Blaise led the way out. "I hate this," she shot over her shoulder as we went on to the next shack.

"If we scare anyone with magical knowledge and abilities enough to stop using those skills, they'll be safe," I explained, quickening my pace to catch up with her.

"I know," she said, "but some potions are harmless."

"Anything can be harmful in the wrong hands."

She couldn't deny it, so she kept her silence as we continued on.

House after house we searched. Most welcomed us and stood back as we scoured their homes. They knew we'd find no evidence of magic. Others reluctantly let us in and crouched in a corner until we left. Some people were simply intimidated by having two guards show up at their door. Those who tried to refuse us, they were usually the guilty ones. Anytime we found items which could've been used for magic, we destroyed them and gave the owners a warning. We didn't find many witches in Terra, and none seemed harmful.

After we'd finished endless days of searching the capital, we moved on to the surrounding areas. One day, we searched a small village south of the wall and were told by almost everyone who lived there to check a certain house with a large garden not far from the village. No one ever visited the place because everyone was afraid of the mysterious woman who dwelled there. She never went out during the day, and anyone who stepped foot inside her house had disappeared. No one could say for sure or not if she was a witch, but when the baron sent someone in to question her, he'd come back different. He told the village she was nothing but an innocent woman who wanted to be left alone. I suspected she'd used some type of spell on him, but the commoners were in no position to question their overlord.

As we neared her garden, I noticed the abundance of fruits, vegetables and herbs growing. I'd never seen plants so lush and bountiful. Maybe she was a skilled gardener and the rest of the village was only jealous.

The wood house appeared like any other normal house. Except the glass covered windows were small and high enough up no one could peer inside.

I knocked hard and loud on the wood door. Blaise waited behind me. No one answered. I listened carefully for movement inside... nothing. I tried the door handle. It was locked, of course. I turned to Blaise and shrugged when the door creaked open a crack.

I spun around, but found no one there. "Madam? Is anyone in there?" No answer, but a hint of a strange smell drifted out. "We just want to ask you something, Madam." I pulled the door open slowly. It groaned like it hadn't been opened in decades.

"Maybe we should leave this place alone. It appears as though no one dwells here," Blaise suggested, holding tightly onto her sword.

I smirked. "Are you frightened? I can go in alone."

"Don't be stupid. I don't think anyone's here, is all. We're wasting our time."

I continued through the door. "Let's just be sure. Something feels wrong."

The floor whined with each step we took. I worried one of us would step on a rotted board and fall through, but it held firm. It was dark; so dark inside the stuffy space. I could barely see my hand when I held it in front of my face. I felt my way around and came to the entrance of another room.

A candle burned lowly on a small round table. I could barely make out the shape of a bed beside it. I'd found the bedroom. I picked up the candle and riffled through the drawers along one of the walls. I found nothing but clothing and cosmetics used to powder faces and colour lips. I didn't know where Blaise had ended up, but she wasn't in the room with me. I picked up the candle and took it from the room to search the rest of the house.

I came to a hearth in the main room. It was strange for a house in this part of Sarantoa to have one. It never got cold enough to need a fire. The only places usually containing them were owned by wealthy people.

A scream startled me into almost dropping the candle. It sounded like Blaise.

I fumbled around until I found a set of stairs leading up. Her scream had come from up there. I unsheathed my sword and rushed up the steps. The smell grew worse the higher I climbed. Light beamed from a room down the hall on the top floor. I strode toward it and raised my sword.

I froze at the sight inside.

Dozens of candles flickered from shelves lining the walls. A strange symbol with letters I'd never seen in each corner was painted on the center of the floor. In the middle of the symbol stood a gorgeous woman with painted, red lips and long, silky hair. Her skin was unusually pale.

She smiled seductively at me. "Guests, what an honour it is to have you both in my home."

I tried to look away but found I couldn't peel my eyes from her. Her perfect body called to me. Her eyes were full of hunger. It was like she was breath itself, and without her, I would die. Something was wrong, but I couldn't figure out what.

"Sepheus!" Blaise's voice tore me from the spell, and I looked away from the beautiful woman.

Terror replaced lust as I noticed the bodies lining the wall Blaise faced. The corpses were husks, completely drained of blood by the slits on their wrists.

"I needed to go hunt for more blood. How lucky am I it came right to me this time?" The woman laughed, a low, thick sound.

"Blood magic." I faced her again, biting out the accusing words. I'd heard stories of witches who used blood to strengthen their magic. Until now, I'd only believed them to be fables told to frighten young children. These witches were said to use spells to make them appear younger and to strengthen their magic.

The witch laughed again before she shot toward Blaise.

Blaise raised her sword, but the witch knocked it from her hand before she could strike her with an unnatural speed.

"I've caught you now, pretty little girl," the witch cooed, running a long, sharp talon down her throat. A line of blood appeared where the witch's nail had traced. She made a show of sucking on her fingernail and then bared her teeth at me. I had to get us out of there before she feasted on us both.

"Let her go." I dove at her with my own sword.

The witch reached out her hand and grabbed the blade of my sword. Though her hand bled, she gave no sign she'd felt the pain. She stared at me with eyes full of wickedness. She believed she had us both in her web. I glanced down. My feet were on the edges of the symbol painted on the floor. I didn't understand its purpose, but I didn't want to find out.

Something moved in my peripheral vision. I turned my head and sent a silent prayer to Celestia.

The bloodless cadavers had come to life.

I yanked my sword free of her grasp. Blood dripped to the floor, but the witch laughed again as she licked the cut on Blaise's neck, smearing crimson on the side of her face.

A moan from one of the pale corpses tore my attention away from them. Empty eye sockets stared back at me. I swiped my blade out as it grabbed for me. Skin tore like paper, but the lifeless body didn't even notice. A common weapon wasn't going to work on these abominations.

Another corpse shuffled closer to join its partner. At least they moved slowly.

Blaise tried to yell something, but her words were muffled by the witch's hand on her face. I needed to kill her. She commanded the cadavers.

I called to my power. It came so easily, that spark deep within my spirit, like green lightning. I didn't need blood to strengthen my magic. It was right there at my fingertips.

Vines broke through the wooden floor, ripping boards apart behind her as decaying fingers with inhuman strength wrapped around my ankle.

I ignored the bruising grip and poured all of my focus into my power. My green ropes twisted around the witch's body. Her eyes widened with shock as the vines wrapped her up like a spider with a fly caught in its web.

She let Blaise fall to the floor and uttered more words I didn't understand. The vines began shrinking away at the spell. The ones still touching her turned brown and died as though she were poison.

The hand on my ankle loosened and I kicked backward connecting with the cadaver's face, sending it flying to the floor. It didn't get back up. The others didn't move either while the witch concentrated solely on my vines.

"Are you all right?" I asked Blaise as she dragged herself closer to me.

"Yes," she managed. "Kill her."

The witch was ripping my dying vines off her body when I sent another wave of power out.

More vines burst through the floor. This time, I didn't give her a chance to respond. A wire thin vine whipped around her throat so fast she didn't have time to scream before her head slid off her body and fell to the floor. It rolled out of the symbol before the rest of her body crumpled at the center.

The witch's cloudy eyes—eyes clear and golden moments ago—stared up at me. Her perfect skin had wrinkled and thinned, showing off the bones beneath.

"Let's get out of here." Blaise tore my attention away from the decapitated monster.

Disgusted I'd almost fallen into the witches trap; I swallowed the sore taste in my throat and nodded.

I helped Blaise down the stairs and out of the house.

Blaise twisted out of my grip, putting her hand to her wound. The cut wasn't deep. She'd heal without a scar. "When I agreed to this witch hunt, I didn't believe we'd actually find evil witches."

"I know. Me neither, but now we have news for King Corbin."

"Let's head back to the village. I've had enough for today." She strode for the spot we'd left our horses without a backward glance.

"I have too." I said to myself.

We arrived back at the inn we'd stopped at that morning. We'd asked the owner for any information they could offer us when we'd secured our room for the night.

A tavern took up most of the main floor, and the owner chatted with some of the locals when we sat down for supper. He spotted us and came over to the table we'd chosen, in a corner of the tavern.

"Any luck?" he asked placing both hands on the table. "You're alive so I assume she wasn't there."

"She was," I told him. "She won't be a problem anymore."

Twin bushy silver brows rose. "You mean you…" he made a slicing motion with his hand.

"It was self defense. She tried to kill us," Blaise snapped at him.

He backed up a little. "Ho-ho, no need to convince me. I'm happy the woman's dead. The village will feel safer for it. In fact, your dinner is on the house." He turned and whistled. The crowded tavern went quiet. "Listen up folks! These two great soldiers have rid us of the mysterious woman in that old house! Turns out she was an evil witch. You and your children are safe now!"

Everyone cheered and raised their mugs of ale. I sank a bit lower in my chair. Blaise smiled brightly and kicked me in the shin. "Be proud. We did a good thing."

I forced my lips into a smile.

The owner had a serving wench bring us warm plates of juicy chicken and fluffy, buttered potatoes along with two mugs of frothy, cold ale. We graciously accepted the meal. I even allowed myself to drink the ale for once. At least ale didn't go straight to your head like wine did.

A few people worked up the courage to come congratulate us. Some even had a few questions, which we answered truthfully... mostly.

When both our plates were empty, I suggested we turn in for the night. We wanted to start back home at dawn. I let Blaise take the single bed while I took the pallet on the floor.

"We did right by this village," Blaise commented. She'd changed into a tunic long enough it reached her knees. I'd waited outside the door while she got out of her uniform. "I take pride in these types of tasks. Helping rid the world of monsters, it's why I joined the army."

I hit my straw-filled pillow, trying to rid as many lumps from it as I could. "I thought you wanted vengeance for your parents' deaths."

Blaise pulled back the thin blanket and sat on the bed. "Yes, but people like that witch are the reason they're dead. I hope to save others from similar fates."

I laid my head down on the pillow and rolled to face her. "I wish my reasons were as good as yours."

She bit her lip. "I believe there's good in you, Seph. You've save my life—twice. Thank you for that."

"If I didn't know any better, I'd say I must like you." I allowed myself to smile up at her.

She lay down and pulled the blankets over her body, but not before I caught a glimpse of her perfect thighs and hips. "Shut up," she replied. But when she closed her eyes, her mouth curved up pleasantly.

I found it difficult to fall asleep sharing a room with such an attractive woman. I closed my own eyes and tried to block out her perfect image, but I couldn't stop picturing the rest of her body beneath that thin, white tunic. It was no wonder I felt so exhausted when dawn broke.

CHAPTER 16

B LAISE AND I stood before the king and queen of Terra. Other's waited nearby impatiently for their chance to speak with their rulers. Sunlight from outside the large windows brightened the throne room, the curtains fluttering gently in the soft breeze. Queen Nicola's cat rubbed against her leg and she reached a hand down to stroke its fluffy, white fur.

"What news do you bring us?" King Corbin asked, scratching his silver streaked beard.

"We found a witch who was using blood magic to strengthen her power and youth, Your Majesty. She tried to capture us so she could bleed us both dry. We managed to kill her." I explained for both of us.

"A blood witch?" Queen Nicola gasped, her hand pausing on top of her cat's head. "I believed them only legends."

"I saw what she was doing with my own eyes," Blaise confirmed. "She had corpses in her home. They'd all been drained of blood. And she was unnaturally strong."

"Thank goodness you found and stopped her," the queen exclaimed as her cat bunted her hand for attention.

"Indeed," the king added. "Likely there are more evil witches out there. Tell me, which areas have you searched?"

"We only have the eastern villages left," I answered.

"Good. Be sure you don't miss a single home. And next time you find a witch like her, bring me their head."

"Of course, Your Majesty." I bowed and Blaise gave them both a deep curtsy.

Queen Nicola leaned toward her husband and whispered in his ear. "Ah yes. And keep a look out for a young lady with bright red hair," he told us.

"Your Majesty?" I questioned, wondering why he'd care if we saw anyone from Solis.

The king adjusted his crown. "Queen Adelaide's cousin has gone missing. She sent men here in search of her. We've questioned every lady with red hair in this kingdom, but none of them are Zephyra Caldura."

I placed my hand over my heart, a promise to my king. "We will watch for her."

"Very good." He waved us off and beckoned to the next person seeking an audience with him.

Once we were away from the throne room, Blaise sighed, "I suppose the blood witch only proved King Corbin right about the witches. Still, I don't believe most of them are harmful."

"You might be right, but he is our king, and he fears the danger of magic."

She gave me a sideways glance. "And what would he do to you if he knew…"

"He'll never find out," I assured her. Still, I couldn't help the dread creeping up my spine. He'd burn me alive if he knew of the magic dwelling inside of me. I shrugged off the thought and suggested we find Ger. We hadn't yet seen him since we'd arrived home.

Before long, we were on the road leading away from Terra again. Autumn had crept up and turned some of the leaves fiery orange and ruby red. The flowers had mostly died for the season, already in slumber until spring. Birds still chirped high above in the trees that remained leafy and green throughout the winter season. Birds from other parts of Sarantoa migrated to Terra during the coldest season to get away from freezing climates and left in the spring. There was never a lack of birdsong in our kingdom.

The village, Birkshire, was a day's ride away from the palace. We visited a busy tavern first. It was usually the best place to gain information. After asking around, we learned there was a man the villagers believed might be a warlock. They said he kept to himself since he'd arrived in Birkshire a few springs ago. We decided we'd check out his house in the morning.

There was no inn in the small eastern village, but a kind middle-aged woman offered to let us stay the night in the home she shared with her family. They had two children, whom they'd let sleep with them for the night.

"It's small, but you two may share Ethan and Leopold's room," the mother, with her chestnut hair pulled back into a neat bun, offered.

"You are most generous," Blaise said, smiling at the little boy who handed her one of his wooden toy horses.

"We don't get many visitors around here, as you may have guessed," the mother told us both. "There's not much reason to come to a farming village unless you have family here."

"Well, we thank you for taking us in for the night," Blaise handed the toy back to the boy, who turned and ran back to his brother. She had a way with people. If only they saw her fiery, warrior side. A memory of her shooting an enemy through the chest heated my blood.

The home was small but well kept. Though the furniture was worn, I couldn't spot a speck of dust on it. The scent of smoked meat set my stomach begging to be fed. We enjoyed the tender bison, along with fresh baked bread, with the family once the woman's husband had returned from working in the field. The hay Terra fed its horses mostly came from Birkshire.

We turned in early for the night. "We could share the bed," Blaise suggested. "There's plenty of space for two."

It was true there was enough space for two, but I'd never slept next to a woman. Copulated with them? Yes, many, but there was something more intimate about sharing slumber with another. Unconsciousness meant vulnerability.

"Sleep on the floor then," Blaise said, mistaking my hesitation for refusal.

"No, I'll share the bed. As long as you promise not to bite."

She clanked her teeth together and laughed, but she slid over.

I let her have the blanket. It wasn't cold anyways. I blew out the candle and lay on my back. I closed my eyes. The darkness only enhanced my other senses. Her soft breaths were like a sighing wind. I could faintly smell the scent of her floral soap. And her body... the warmth drifted over my skin, a welcoming sensation begging me to move closer.

I told myself to think of other things... count to ten.

Maybe sleeping on the floor would've been easier.

Temptation ate me from the inside out. I lifted my hand, so carefully. My fingers touched her shoulder. I felt her stiffen as my fingers stilled on her satin-smooth skin.

And then she relaxed, taking my hand in hers. She brought it to her face... to her lips, and so gently that I barely felt it, she kissed the back of my hand.

I rolled to face her. Her back was still to me. I trailed my other hand against her neck. She shivered, but I felt her smile against the hand she still held to her mouth. Warmth spread through me like the sun breaking through the clouds on a cold, rainy day. *What am I doing?* I'd never felt anything but lust for another. But this wasn't lust. This was something else. I cared how Blaise felt, what she thought of me.

As she took my hand and wrapped my arm tightly around herself, something inside of me grew. The darkness seeded deep inside of my heart shrank a little to let some of that light in.

I fell asleep wrapped around the woman who'd walked into my life and changed absolutely everything.

Blaise wasn't in the bed when I awoke to the sounds of children laughing and dishware clattering. I found her in the kitchen helping our hostess, Alice, prepare eggs and ham to break our fast.

Her cheeks turned pink as she turned her face away, concentrating on the ham she held over the flame on a meat fork.

"Good morning, Sir Sepheus," Alice said as her two boys chased each other through the kitchen. "Food's almost ready. I figured you'd want to eat before you set out."

"Yes, thank you," I replied. Blaise still hadn't acknowledged me. Shame, I realized. She was ashamed of the intimate moment we'd shared.

"That looks well and cooked," the woman said to Blaise, taking the ham from her. "Come on, boys. Food is ready," she hollered to her sons.

My comrade inclined her head at me and took a seat at the dining table.

I sat across from her and the two boys sat beside me. I didn't spare them a glance. Children made me feel awkward. "Your husband isn't joining us?" I asked Alice, who'd taken her seat beside Blaise.

"Varis gets up early to work the fields," she explained. "He eats his oats while the children are still asleep."

"He's missing out," I said after my first bite of fluffy eggs.

The woman shrugged her slender shoulders. "He gets to break his fast with us once every seven sunrises. He makes many sacrifices for his family. We appreciate him."

Blaise scraped the last of her food into her mouth and then said, "Your cooking is delicious. We can't thank you enough." She still kept her eyes adverted from my gaze. She hadn't spared me a glance the entire meal. A bit of that light she'd put inside my heart ebbed away. She'd been lonely last night. I was only a temporary comfort. She'd never want more from me. I didn't blame her.

The boys had made a mess of their faces. Alice fetched a cloth to clean them up with. "It was a pleasure to have company. Good luck with your task." We'd asked her about the man others believed to be strange, but she didn't know anything. Her family kept to themselves, usually too busy with their farm to venture to the heart of their village.

Blaise replied with a smile and we said our goodbyes.

We walked in silence on the way to the man's house.

I couldn't take it any longer. I stopped and touched her arm. She looked down at my hand. I removed it. "Listen, about last night…"

"It was… I didn't…" She searched for the right words.

"I know. It's all right. I can't stand this awkwardness. Let's just focus on our task."

Her rigid shoulders loosened. "Yes, Sir Sepheus."

I couldn't help but smile. I preferred her teasing to the invisible wall that'd wedged its way between us.

We continued on to the man's house and knocked on the door. At least there was no garden outside full of bountiful plants; a good sign.

"May we come in, sir? We have a couple of questions for you," Blaise asked, standing before the very tall man with a slouched back. He was skinny and his long black hair needed a wash and a comb. I held my breath as the odour of sour milk and rotten vegetables wafted at me.

The man's dark eyes darted back and forth between us. When we didn't move, he opened the door. "Yes, all right. I don't see why not." His voice was soft for a man of his size.

I cringed as I took in the disgusting state of his home. Food growing green fuzz littered the floor, a meal for the flies swarming around the hot, smelly room. I scanned the area. I didn't spot anything that could've been used for magic, though it was hard to tell with the mess.

"We need to search your rooms," I stated, still trying to hold my breath.

The man's gaze darkened. "What for? What's the meaning of this? I've done nothing wrong."

Blaise raised her brows and uttered, "The state of this place is wrong."

The man shot her an angry look but, before he could argue, I said, "Some of the villagers believe you're a warlock. We've come to see if they're right."

The man jumped back as though he'd been struck, and then he put his head in his hand. "Oh, no," he mumbled. "I'm no such thing. You may search all you want. You'll find no evidence of magic here."

I eyed him before moving on to his bedroom. It was almost as disastrous as the rest of the house. Clothes laid on the floor, unwashed and stinking of body odour. I gagged and riffled through his drawers, only to find more clothes and letters. I stared at one of the letters.

Blaise stopped beside me. "What does it say?"

I stared at the words scrawled across the page. It would take me too long to decipher the words without her realizing I couldn't read well. "Nothing."

"Let's see." She grabbed for the letter. I tried to pull it out of her reach. She ripped the letter out of my hand. Her eyes scanned the page. She dropped the letter back into the drawer. "It's a love letter." She turned to me. "You can't read." A statement, not a question.

My face heated. "I told you it was nothing. You're so infuriating sometimes."

She laughed. "It's nothing to be ashamed of, Seph."

"There's nothing here." I stalked out of the bedroom. At least we were back to normal.

The man sat, his head hanging low. "I know I'm not ordinary, but I'm no warlock," he blubbered. "My wife died before I came to Birkshire. I cannot escape the sadness she left me with."

He was nothing but a sad, old widow. "I believe you," I said, handing him the love letter. "Clean yourself up. Maybe people won't be so leery of you. Or don't. I don't care."

I left the disgusting house and sucked in the fresh air outside. Blaise was close behind.

We spent the remainder of the day visiting the homes of other Birkshire locals, just in case someone else was using magic. We left empty handed.

In the next village we only found a lonely little lady with a spell book that had belonged to her dead mother. I took the spell book from her reluctant hands and burned it outside.

We found nothing in the last village east of Terra. Relief filled me as we turned home, our quest finished at last. Though it had been my idea, it was not something I'd wanted to do. I could only hope King Corbin would be satisfied the witches would no longer be a problem for him. Not that they were a problem to begin with, save for the one blood witch we'd killed. My lie had condemned all magic users.

We ran into more of a natural sort of danger on our way home.

We'd stopped to eat around midday and let our horses drink from a narrow trickling creek. I bit into a chunk of hard bread when Blaise suddenly shrieked. Her water skin hit the ground and rolled toward me.

"Ow! Ow! Ow! Ow!" She rubbed her ankle, hopping on one foot. "You slimy bastard!" she yelled at the grass. A bright orange snake with a white diamond pattern slithered away through the tall grass.

I helped her to a rock large enough for her to sit on. "You've been bitten by a corandor. Let me see." I held out my hand, and she lifted her ankle for me.

"It hurts." She winced and sucked air in between her teeth as I touched the flesh beginning to swell around the two red marks.

"This is bad." She gave me a look of panic, but there was no sense lying to her. "They're not lethal, but we'll have to camp here for the night. The side effects of a corandor's venom aren't pleasant." One lesson my father had taught me was which animals were dangerous and what could happen if you came across one. A corandor's venom caused full body pain and delusions.

"I'd prefer *not* to stay where there could be more snakes." She glared at me.

I set her ankle down. "I'll set up our tent. We'll be fine." We had brought a small deerskin tent with us in case of emergencies. This was the first time we'd had to use it.

As soon as the tent was up and Blaise rested inside, I took one of my tunics and soaked it in the cool creek water. "Here, put this on your ankle," I said, pushing through the flaps of the tent.

She sat up to accept it. She pressed the tunic against her apple-sized ankle. "I can feel it spreading. My leg hurts."

I sat down beside her and offered her some water. "I'm sorry I don't have anything stronger."

"Curse you and your sobriety," she shot, but she accepted the water.

I smiled. "You'll live to scold me another day."

She passed the water skin back.

I'd lost count of how many I'd seen suffer in pain. I'd never felt sympathy for the suspects my father and I had tortured. But I'd never cared about those people. And watching Blaise, I suffered with her as she screamed through the night.

"It feels as if I'm dying." She clawed at my chest, pulling herself up to stare into my face. "You lied to me! The venom is lethal!"

"I didn't lie," I said calmly. "You'll get through this."

"Arrrgh!" She wrenched away and cried into the blanket I'd set out for her.

It was hard to see her squirm and writher like a worm being burned by a reflection in the sun.

When the world had darkened, she finally stilled, the pain subsiding. Her shoulders shook with what I mistook as sobbing. But when she lifted her head I saw she was laughing. "I'm alive. And everything is wonderful!" Her hair stood up in places, wild like her personality. She held the blanket to her cheek. "How did you come by such exquisite material?"

"It's wool, Blaise." The delusions had kicked in.

Her eyes widened, and she put the blanket over her head. "Why must you always lie to me?"

"I'm not lying."

She threw the blanket off and scrambled for the flap of the tent.

"Where are you going?" I followed her outside. "You should stay off your ankle."

She wasn't listening though. She turned her face up to the sky and opened her arms. "The stars are singing! Can't you hear them?"

"No, I can't. Blaise, get off your ankle—Blaise..."

"Shhh. You're not my mother." A tear dropped down her cheek as she realized what she'd just said. "I miss my mother."

"I know. I'm sorry." I put my arm around her to help take the pressure off her ankle.

"You've been so kind to me." She swallowed. "I thought you were cruel... thought you hated me when I first came to Terra. But you, your—" A daring look crept across her face. She touched my cheek. "So beautiful."

My eyes locked with hers. *It's only the venom coursing through her veins,* I told myself. But as she stretched her neck and reached out for me, I did nothing to stop her. I leaned down and our lips touched. So soft, so delicate. I had wanted this, so much, for so long.

And then the voice inside my mind interrupted the moment I'd been longing for since that night at Queen Nicola's ball. *She's too good for you.* The voice was my own. I couldn't even blame it on Claudia's ghost. She hadn't haunted me since I'd told her I was sorry.

I pulled back and let her go.

She almost lost her balance. I stiffened as I steadied her body against mine. "I'll help you get inside. You should sleep so we can go home at first light."

"Yes, Your Highness," she mocked.

I stilled. Had she meant it, or was it only a jest? She knew about my magic, but had she heard who my real father was? We'd never discussed the night I'd killed my father. I didn't know how long she'd been in the torture chamber.

I decided to believe it was a jest.

I helped her into the tent and pulled the blanket over her.

Soon, her soft snores filled the small space, joining with the song of the crickets outside. My shoulders sagged with relief. Her delusions could've gone worse. She could have seen visions that only existed in her nightmares, and it would have sent her in a downward spiral. I thanked Celestia she'd had the most pleasant experience we could've hoped for. Her ankle would hurt for a few days, but the worst was over.

I packed up our belongings, including the tent I'd dismantled, and helped Blaise onto her horse. I wasn't sure if she'd remembered the night before... our kiss. She was quiet and awkward like she'd been after our night together in Birkshire, so if I had to guess, I'd say she did.

We rode back to Terra, silence hanging between us most of the way. When the wall around the kingdom came into view, Blaise started, "Look, about what happened last night—"

"Forget about it. Nothing happened."

Her gaze met the ground. Was that disappointment shadowing her features? She wiped the expression off her face and stared ahead. "Right, nothing happened."

I rode forward and we entered through the gates of Terra. Contentment filled me. We were home, permanently this time.

"Good," King Corbin said when we'd recounted our time in the east to him and the queen, who sat idly by his side. "Should anyone see or hear of anyone using magic, they are to report directly to Constable Bouvant. I've already informed the court."

I bowed my head in acknowledgement. I'd have to be very careful no one found out about my power. It was bad enough Blaise knew.

"Now, go rest. Tomorrow we will feast." The king slung his arm over his wife's shoulders. She leaned into him, smiling down at us.

Blaise and I took our leave, going separate ways. Her to probably bathe and see a healer about a balm to alleviate the pain still throbbing in her ankle, and I to The Watering Hole to fill my aching stomach.

"My goddess." Ger set his mug of ale down as I entered the tavern.

"Have you spent the whole time I was away slacking off?" I teased as he got up to embrace me. I thumped him on the back. "I missed you too."

"So, the witches are dead?"

"The evil ones are. The rest were warned not to use magic," I said, waving to a serving wench.

"Cook's made chicken soup. Would ye' like a bowl?" the wench I hadn't seen before asked in her unrefined tongue.

"Very much so," I gave her a charming smile as I placed two coins in her rough palm.

The luscious little tart winked at me before sauntering away.

"She new?" I asked Ger.

"She showed up here shortly after you started your witch hunt. Too pretty to be a serving wench if you ask me. She seems to like you. I'm sure you could use a tumble in the bedchamber." He nudged me.

I chuckled, shaking my head at him. "Drink your ale, you brute."

"Much obliged." He guzzled back the golden liquid, and I laughed again. It was nice to be home.

The wench brought out my meal, bending low to place it in front of me. "Let me know if there's anything else you need, sir." She squeezed my shoulder and batted her lashes.

Ger tilted his head. "Go, I'm almost finished here anyways."

A memory of Blaise flashed in my mind, her lips on mine. *You're beautiful.*

I flashed a smile at the wench blessed with a voluptuous figure. "Thank you, but I find myself tired after my travels. You have a good night."

She removed her hand. "Perhaps another time." Her hips swayed as she walked away.

My friend gawked at me. "When did you become such a gentleman?"

"Since now, apparently."

He shook his head at me and snickered. "It's good to have you back."

"It's good to be back," I answered through a mouthful of food.

Ger left me to finish my meal alone, probably to seek out the wench looking for a little *fun.*

I quickly devoured the roasted pork and seasoned potatoes and washed it down with a cup of water. I needed to find Blaise. I didn't want things to go back to the way they were before. I was tired of empty, meaningless nights spent tumbling with women who meant nothing to me. *She* was my light, *she* was my salvation. And I had to tell her so.

Chapter 17

I BANGED ON Blaise's door with my fist.

The door opened. "Seph? What is it?" she asked. Worry lines were etched between her brows.

"Blaise, I—"

A moan sounded from across the room.

"I can't speak right now," she said. "Elly's not well."

I peered over her shoulder into the room to where her roommate was indeed lying in bed. "What's wrong with her? Where's the healer?"

"She was wounded taking down one of the two men who attacked the Temple while we were gone. I sent the healer to get some sleep. She was here all day."

The words I'd come to say vanished from my mind. "Why didn't King Corbin inform us of this? Were they Redeemers?" Anger rose. I'd thought we were done dealing with those vermin.

She shook her head. "They may have once followed Leblond. They were acting in the name of Vesirus though. They—they killed a priestess."

I hissed through my teeth and made a fist. "I can't believe we were kept in the dark."

"They've already been dealt with. King Corbin probably didn't want to ruin our welcome back. I'm sure the constable would've informed us when we saw him."

Perhaps she was right. It wasn't the king's job to keep us informed.

I loosened my fist. "Care to take a walk with me?"

Elly moaned again and Blaise looked over her shoulder before setting her gaze back on me. "I can't. She needs me here."

"You're not her healer."

She narrowed her eyes. "She's my friend."

I pressed my lips together and then said, "A serving wench offered to tumble with me tonight."

"Then go tumble with her."

I winced inwardly. Wrong choice of words judging by the heat now in her eyes. "That's... it's not what I meant." Why was this so hard?

Blaise raised her chin, defiant... waiting. Her luscious lips curved downward.

I reached forward and slid a finger across those lips. In the blink of an eye my own lips replaced that finger.

The kiss was intense... ravenous, as though it would satisfy both our hungers.

It ended as quickly as it had begun.

"I have to go," Blaise breathed. And then I was standing on the wrong side of the closed door.

I left frustrated and alone. I did not slumber well that night.

The Guard, along with some of the most favoured courtiers, dined with the king and queen the night after we'd returned home.

Elly did not attend. The wound on her forearm wasn't healing properly according to Blaise. Infection had set in. The healer worked hard to fight it, but she would likely loose part of her arm.

"I've been given a new task," Blaise revealed as she sat beside me, picking at her piece of apple pie.

"Have you?" I set my fork down and turned to face her. "What task?"

"I'm to collect taxes from the outlying villages. With Reynard."

I breathed deeply and counted to ten before replying, "We only arrived home yesterday. Constable Bouvant would send you out so soon? When do you leave?"

"Tomorrow."

I slid my chair back and stood up. I strode to where Constable

Bouvant sat close to the rulers. He chuckled at something Ger had said from across the table. I tapped the constable on his shoulder. "A word, sir."

He eyed me before wiping his hands and excusing himself. Once we'd exited the hall so we could speak in private, he crossed his arms. "What's so important you can't wait until we're on duty?"

"You're sending Blaise to collect taxes *tomorrow*. Her friend will likely lose her arm, and we only just returned home."

The constable flicked his eyes over me, and I saw the man who'd once been Terra's best soldier. "The king trusts her with his coin, and she agreed to go. Not that I owe you an explanation."

I was taller than him, but he made me feel small. Still, I didn't back down. "Send me in her stead."

The constable breathed through his nose and closed his eyes, releasing me from his wrath. "You're needed here, in case more vermin show up in the name of Vesirus. I trust your comrade told you about that." He opened his eyes again, they'd warmed a little. "And you are to help with training some of the new soldiers. You're a knight. You don't get to do the menial tasks."

"She deserves better than this." I still fumed.

Constable Bouvant ground his teeth and moved closer to me, that steel creeping back into his gaze. "Stand down, Sir Sepheus." He moved past me and muttered, "Maybe you need some time apart."

I was too furious to return to the hall. The feast was nearly over anyways. King Corbin would forgive me. I'd rather be rude by parting this way than saying something I regretted in front of the rulers.

So I went to the room Elly rested in.

The healer answered my knock, her mouth set in a thin line. "She's resting."

"I can watch her until Blaise returns."

The healer looked me up and down. "But you are a man."

I put my hand on the door to open it wider. "I am a knight and her comrade. It offends me to think you believe I'd cause her any harm."

I held her stare, a battle of wills.

She backed down. "Fine. I've left some tea. Don't give her too much at once." She picked up her pack of supplies and said, as she moved to pass me, "I'll return tomorrow to remove her arm."

I paled. "It can't be saved?"

"It's either her arm or her life."

My tongue suddenly wouldn't work.

"Good evening, sir," she huffed and marched off.

A pallet sat on the floor along one wall. Elly lay in the bed across from it covered in white cotton sheets. I took a seat beside her.

She cracked her eyes open a bit. "Sepheus, what are you doing here?" she asked, sleep making her voice rough.

"I'm taking care of a friend." I picked up the cloths from the bedside table and pressed it to her forehead.

She managed a soft laugh. "What's the real reason?"

I sat back. "I'm waiting for Blaise, but I am concerned about you. How's your arm?"

She lifted her bandaged forearm. Red streaks crept from beneath the cloth wrapped around the wound. I noted the sheen of sweat on her face. Fever had taken hold. She lowered her injured arm and accepted the tea I handed her with her uninjured one. "I'm going to lose it thanks to the filthy bastards," she scowled.

"You'll do fine with one arm."

"It's my sword arm." She sipped the cup of tea, to hide the tears threatening to fall.

I took the cup back from her and set it down. "So we'll train you to use your other arm."

"Thank you for trying to make me feel better. If only you could bring back that poor priestess too." She swallowed and then continued, her voice stronger. "I wish those two sacks of scum were still alive so I could kill them again."

"You killed them both?" I didn't hide my surprise.

"I had help, but yes."

I patted her hand, the one she'd be keeping. "I'm sorry the priestess was lost. You did good nonetheless."

"I know." She squeezed her eyes shut. "These are dark times. People are acting in the name of the Dark Lord... *the Dark Lord,* Sepheus."

"Anyone who worships Vesirus is a fool. We will annihilate each and every one of them. Most of the people of this realm are devoted to Celestia," I said more to myself than her. "I doubt many would turn to the Dark Lord."

"I hope you're right."

Before I could answer, Blaise entered the room. She froze when she saw me beside Elly. "You left the feast early," she said to me, smiling at Elly as she picked up her arm to inspect it. She sighed and set it back down softly.

"I was angry," I explained.

Elly's eyelids fluttered shut and her breathing deepened. Effects of the tea.

"What are you doing here?" Blaise asked, pulling out her sack from beside her pallet. She'd have to repack it. Even though she'd probably just *unpacked* it from her last quest.

"Why did you agree to go on a menial errand with Reynard so soon? Aren't you happy to be home?"

She busied herself with stuffing a pair of breeches and a tunic into the sack. "Of course I'm happy to be home, but King Corbin trusts me with this, with carrying his coin. I'm not going to refuse."

"I should go with you." I walked over to stand over her.

"No, stay. Ensure nothing like this," she waved her hand at a slumbering Elly, "happens again."

I sighed, crouching down to take her hands in mine. "Be careful. There's a chance you could end up collecting from one of the Dark Lord's devotees."

She squeezed my hands. "I'll be fine. I'll be back before you realize I'm gone."

I brushed a strand of hair off her cheek. "I doubt that." I didn't want to let her go. I needed her to keep the darkness at bay. But we had our orders, and we couldn't ignore them.

Her amber eyes sparkled as she pressed her lips to the back of my hand. "When I return, let's go for that walk."

I could only nod as Elly stirred in the bed.

Blaise glanced at her sack. "I should finish packing and get some sleep. Will you watch out for her while I'm away?"

"Of course. She's part of The Guard. She'll be back to her own duties by the time you return."

Relief softened her features and she let go of my hands. "Thank you."

Hope, she'd given me hope. Maybe she wasn't ashamed to be with me. Something inside my chest, my once cold heart, warmed.

As I wandered back to my own room, I couldn't help but smile.

CHAPTER 18

I TURNED NINETEEN at some point over the winter.

Elly's arm had been chopped off at the elbow and cauterized. She tried to hide her self-pity, but it simmered beneath the surface anyways.

I paid her visits while she healed and, once she was well enough, I began training her to fight with her left arm. She often stormed off the training field, frustrated. But she always returned the next morning, more determined.

When I wasn't training with Elly, I trained young soldiers alongside Ger. We hadn't discovered any other worshippers of Vesirus. Perhaps the two who'd raided the Temple and killed the priestess had been the only ones foolish enough to turn to the Dark Lord. I believed that to be the case until spring, when everything changed.

Blaise and Reynard returned with sacks of coin a few days before King Corbin and the queen were to set off for Noctis De Celestia in Aquila.

They had arrived in the middle of the night while I was asleep in my room. I heard the news in the morning and intended to ask her for that walk later that night. After she'd had time to settle in.

I planned to tell her how much she meant to me. How she'd been a speck of light against the darkness inside my heart.

But on the day I planned to reveal my heart to that fierce, beautiful woman, my world turned upside down.

Elly didn't need me for training anymore. I was confident she could kill with her left hand now. And Ger and I had given our trainees the day to rest after getting beaten up and knocked down the three previous afternoons. Constable Bouvant had us guarding the gate instead.

I had busied myself with polishing my sword while Ger leaned against the wall half asleep when two riders came cantering up.

Ger was instantly alert and had his hand on the hilt of his sword. I dropped the polishing rag and pointed my sword forward as they halted their horses.

Both riders were covered in filth. Dirt caked the face of the male with ebony hair. His tunic and breeches were faded and torn, so was the female's riding dress. The woman's hair had come loose from its braid, and strands stuck to her sweat-coated face. I took in the bright red shade of her hair and wondered... *could she be the lost royal from Solis?*

The woman swung off her horse and clasped the front of my uniform so fast I didn't have time to react. Her emerald eyes flashed bright and wild as she said in a hoarse voice, "Take me to your king."

The black haired male had dismounted. He and Ger had both unsheathed their blades.

"Please," the woman begged. "I need to warn your king. I'm trying to save this kingdom!"

I cocked my head at her. She could be a mad woman—or she could be Queen Adelaide's cousin. Maybe she was both. I eyed Ger and the man she'd come with. Both waited, ready to strike at the first sign of threat. I rested my gaze back on the freckled woman. "Might you be Zephyra Caldura?"

She lifted her chin a little. "What does it matter if I am? We're all doomed anyway unless you take me to King Corbin."

She hadn't denied it. If she was the missing royal, King Corbin would wish to speak with her. I turned my gaze to the ebony-haired man. "If your friend gives up his sword, we'll take you to see the king."

She released my uniform and nodded to her friend. "Give it to him, Percifal. We'll get it back after we see the king."

Percifal flipped his sword over and handed it hilt forward to Ger. My friend kept his unsheathed but lowered it.

We escorted them to the throne room.

King Corbin took one look at the pair and bellowed to the courtiers, "Leave us!"

The lords and ladies lucky enough to live at court scattered and disappeared through the exits and out into the corridor. Before long, only the four of us stood before the rulers. We all bowed respectfully.

I was about to explain the interruption when the woman met the king's eyes and said, "I am Zephyra Caldura, and I have come to warn you of an evil meant to destroy your kingdom and the rest of Sarantoa."

Queen Nicola froze beside her husband, but he simply tapped his short, pudgy fingers on his knee a few times before stating, "You're the lost royal from Solis. Your kingdom's been looking for you."

"Did you not hear the rest of what I said? Your kingdom's in danger." Her eyes bore into his, unblinking... unfaltering. She was used to dealing with royalty.

"Speak to the king in such a manner again and I'll throw you in the dungeons regardless of your status," I warned, but King Corbin held his hand up to silence me.

Percifal shot me a glare from the other side of Zephyra.

"Tell us then, what is this evil you speak of?" King Corbin pressed.

"You must not travel to Aquila for Noctis De Celestia. King Zaeden has joined forces with Vesirus. He's marching toward Terra with an army as we speak." Still as a statue, she waited for him to answer.

Everyone except Percifal had lost their tongues. The queen appeared absolutely horrified. She was buying the story. Ger likely felt the way I did. The warning was absurd. The Dark Lord of Mnyama wouldn't bother with a mortal king. Yes, he had followers who'd committed hideous acts in his name, but Vesirus himself...

As if King Corbin had read my mind, he asked, "Why would the Dark Lord help King Zaeden? I've heard King Zaeden wanted to go to war with the rest of the realm after we refused to back him on his foolish conquest against the island, Gwon, but I never imagined he actually had the balls to come after the other three kingdoms."

"In exchange for aiding him in conquering all of Sarantoa, King Zaeden is working with Vesirus to bring the dark world here. I don't believe he could've accomplished this without the aid of a mortal." Zephyra looked to Percifal. "We still don't know all of the details... like why he's chosen to attack here first."

When King Corbin looked like he was about to dismiss Zephyra's warning, Percifal interjected, "Your Majesty, if I may?" King Corbin nodded. "I understand this all sounds like madness, but Zephyra's telling the truth. I've witnessed it myself. Phyra, show him," he urged the Solis royal.

Zephyra stepped back from the rulers and held out her hand, palm facing the domed ceiling. Her eyes focused on the space above her palm. Flames instantly appeared upon it. They danced along her fingertips like courtiers at a ball. She dropped her hand to her side and the fire disappeared as if it'd never been there. Her skin remained untouched, not one sign of a burn mark as she showed it to us. She had *magic*. And not just the simple kind. Magic like mine. More powerful than any witch.

I saw the fear glowing in King Corbin's brown eyes.

I moved to apprehend Zephyra, but Queen Nicola spoke before I had my sword out from its sheath. "An elemental." Zephyra bowed her head to the queen. "No one in this world has had such power for centuries. Why would Celestia gift us with it now?" The queen twisted a piece of chestnut hair around one of her tiny manicured fingers.

An elemental, is that what I was?

"I believe you've just answered your own question, Your Majesty," Zephyra replied. "Celestia knew her brother... Vesirus would try and take us from her. She knew he would need to be stopped." She pled to King Corbin again. "Why would I make this up? If I meant you harm, surely I would have attacked you already."

King Corbin looked at his queen. She whispered something into his ear. He took a deep breath before answering. "While I don't believe the goddess or her brother would bother with our world, my wife makes a good point. We don't wish to take the chance. We'll stay in Terra for Noctis De Celestia and will set up our defenses." His face fell flat as he leaned forward and said, "If you try to harm anyone in my kingdom, I will have you executed, and your head will be sent to Queen Adelaide."

"Thank you, Your Majesties." Zephyra curtsied gracefully.

"Find someone to assist them," Queen Nicola ordered me and Ger, wrinkling her small nose. "They're both in need of baths and clean attire."

We bowed again and took our leave of the rulers. Of course the courtiers waited right outside the doors with listening ears. Soon the whole kingdom would know about the elemental who'd come to warn us all. Gossip was the one thing that could be counted on at court. If

Vesirus still had worshippers in Terra, they'd be rejoicing.

I had been so sure King Corbin was going to lock Zephyra up for her power. If my power was like hers, maybe he'd let me live as well. Regardless, I couldn't imagine sharing my ability with him. He trusted me, and that meant me not keeping secrets from him. If this enemy was truly coming, I decided I'd fight it with a sword.

On my way to find Constable Bouvant, I spotted Blaise. She wasn't alone. She walked along the pathway with Reynard, both of them laughing as she leaned in and said something in his ear. My stomach dropped.

Noticing me watching, Blaise stopped laughing. "Sepheus, I've been looking for you."

"I've been busy," I said through my teeth. "It looks like you have been too." I set my sight on Reynard. Of course they'd grown close. They'd spent the whole damn winter together. She'd be happier with him anyways.

Blaise put some distance between Reynard and herself as she said to him. "Go on ahead. I'll see you later."

I started to back off too, but she grabbed my wrist. "What's wrong with you?"

"Vesirus is coming," I spat.

She froze, her hand tightening around my wrist. "Are you jesting?"

"I wish I was. The lost Solis royal showed up at our gates. Turns out she has *elemental* magic. Apparently King Zaeden is working with Vesirus. He and his army are marching for us now."

"But—that's—you—"

I cut her off before she could articulate her thoughts. "I need to find Constable Bouvant. We need to prepare our defenses."

She finally released my wrist. "Listen, Reynard and I, we're not—"

"It doesn't matter. We'll all be dead soon if we don't find a way to stop Vesirus." I left before she could get another word out.

She deserved to be happy. Reynard, as much as we butted heads, was a good man. I could let her go, release her from my darkness. It would have been the hardest thing I'd ever done, but for her, I would do it.

I swallowed the hurt creeping up from my chest. I didn't have time to wallow in self-pity. King Corbin may not have believed the Solis royal, but I did.

King Corbin waited in the courtyard for his subjects to gather. Queen Nicola, dressed in gold and orange like the setting sun casting its rays across the world, scanned the faces of those already there from one side of her husband. Zephyra stood to his other side, wearing a pale yellow gown of silk and chiffon… a gift from Terra. The fire elemental and Percifal, who I learned was her lover, were given anything they needed during their stay at the kingdom of earth.

The unforgiving ball of sun beat down on us from high above in the cloudless sky. All had been invited to hear what their ruler had to say this high noon. The wealthy, the poor, the soldiers, the children. All who were able had come.

So when the courtyard outside the palace was full of people of every shape and size who hailed from Terra and its surrounding villages, King Corbin began his speech.

"People of Terra!" he started and all conversations ended. "King Zaeden is marching toward Terra as I speak."

Audible gasps swept throughout the crowd, and a few ladies waved their silk fans at their faces.

King Corbin continued, "Fear not, my loyal subjects! Our goddess, Celestia, has sent help. She has not abandoned us, her children, to die." He beckoned Zephyra to step up closer to him. "This woman is a fire elemental from Solis. She has agreed to help us fight this battle. With her power and the might of our army, we will annihilate King Zaeden and his army of dogs!"

The crowds murmured their agreement. Some whispered to their neighbour. Though King Corbin was assuring his subjects all would be well, I felt unease in the air, saw the fear on their faces. I glanced at Zephyra. She had gone pale making her freckles stand out starker. Percifal stood behind her and placed a hand on her elbow, a steady hand of reassurance.

"We have increased our guard at all entrances to Terra, and our soldiers are preparing for war. Should any of you see any sign of King Zaeden's army, you are to alert the nearest guard," King Corbin, the two women and Percifal stepped off the platform. A priestess took their place.

Her long brown hair hung loose down her white robed shoulders like ribbons of silk. "Today we pray to Celestia for her guidance and protection…"

I didn't hear the rest of her words. My eyes fixated on Zephyra. She was frightened. I felt the same fear pounding in my heart. I had to find out more about her power. I had to get her alone.

When the priestess had finished the prayer, and the crowd began to leave the stone courtyard, I started after Zephyra and Percifal. But someone snagged my arm. I peered over my shoulder. Blaise stared up at me with big amber eyes. I hadn't spoken to her since I'd found her and Reynard swooning over each other.

"You—" she started.

"Not here." I glanced in the direction of the palace orchards… my favourite place as a child.

I led Blaise to the blooming trees that would soon be ripe with cherries, or apples, or peaches. White and pink flowers emitted sweet aromas, promises of juicy fruit in the hotter season. White balls of fluff from the poplar trees lining the outside of the orchard floated through the air as we wound our way through the fruit trees and along the lush grass until we were out of earshot.

I stopped walking and faced Blaise. "I know what you're going to say, and no, I don't think it's a good idea."

She stared up at me and set her jaw. She said it anyway, "You have power like the fire elemental. You should help her."

"I will not break King Corbin's trust. If he knew I was keeping this secret… I can't believe Aquila's king is working with the Dark Lord. I knew he'd been determined to go to war since his greed had gotten his wife killed, but this… it's madness."

I'd heard the story from Cedric. King Zaeden had stolen gold from the island of Gwon. The island's ruler retaliated by killing his wife, Queen Thea. Ruthless, but it was King Zaeden's own problem. He was throwing a tantrum because none of the other kingdoms would join forces with him.

Blaise let out a breath and shook her head. "I don't think you have this power by coincidence, Seph. This Zephyra knows more than you do. Perhaps you should confide in her about your earth magic."

"Earth magic? You think I'm the earth elemental?"

She batted a piece of floating fluff away from her face. It landed in her hair instead. "It makes sense, doesn't it? You're able to grow and control vines with your magic. Have you been able to do anything else?"

I studied the cherry tree behind her. I remembered the day I'd coaxed the cherry tree to produce fruit even though it was the wrong season. I looked back at Blaise. "Nothing that doesn't have anything to do with some type of plant." She was right. She had to be. But why? Why had I been given earth magic?

And then I remembered my bloodline. My *true* bloodline... Dirva. Dirva had been the daughter of Terra's first king. It was because of her power the kingdom never froze. *Maybe I should speak to the fire elemental.* Still, I wasn't about to let my king find out this piece of information. And I damn well wasn't letting Blaise get in the middle of it. "It doesn't matter." I began to stride past her. "I'll use my sword in this battle, nothing more."

"You're being a coward."

I closed the distance between us. Fury clouded my judgement. "I'm sure Reynard will protect you."

"I don't need protection," she snarled back. "And he's just my friend. Which is more than I can say about you." She was small, but she was mighty as she clenched her fists and threw the words in my face.

We didn't utter a word for a few breaths.

She reached up and gripped the sides of my face to pull me down to her height. She kissed me with the heat of a thousand fires. I could barely react, so shocked by the impact. Our fingers interlaced and then she tore away and stormed off through the orchard, leaving me feeling raw and utterly confused.

I'd find her later. We both needed time to cool off, but Reynard... they were only friends she'd said. Could jealousy have made me so blind? So thick-headed?

I headed back to the palace to try to find Zephyra, but when I found her, she was with Percifal. *Damn,* I thought. I wanted to speak to her alone. I didn't know or trust the man she'd come to Terra with, but they were always together.

I trailed them for a while down a corridor but was cut off by Ger. "There you are. I'd begun to wonder if you'd decided to tumble with one of the ladies," he teased with that wide, yellow-toothed grin of his.

"Hmm," I replied, watching Zephyra and Percifal disappear around a corner, only half-listening to what he'd said.

Ger turned his face to where I'd been looking and chuckled. "I'm afraid that one's already got someone to tumble with."

Giving up hope of speaking with the fire elemental for the day, I turned my full attention on Ger. "What do you want?"

"Cheerful today, aren't we?"

I waited with a raised brow.

Ger continued, "Constable Bouvant wants us all performing drills until sundown."

I gestured with my arm. "Lead the way."

Constable Bouvant had us busy from sunrise to sunset on the days leading up to Noctis De Celestia, preparing for battle. When we weren't doing drills, we were taking our turn at scouting the perimeter outside of the wall in case King Zaeden or anyone else who meant us harm showed up early. I was unable to find time to slip away to try to speak with Zephyra. Maybe it was for the best. If I told her about my power she'd probably demand I use it to help her battle.

I studied the blade of my sword as I sharpened it the evening before Noctis. It was a more reliable weapon. I was *good* with a sword. I had no idea how much power I had in me. The sword was the right choice. It had to be. We wouldn't truly be fighting Vesirus. We'd be fighting a deranged king acting in his name. I told myself that over and over. If the Dark Lord had gifted King Zaeden with some dark magic... well, I'd think about that when the time came.

I couldn't think about what Blaise's kiss in the orchard had meant. I needed to focus on the upcoming battle. For her, I needed to focus for her. So she could live in the light and not be forced to suffer in darkness.

I heard a commotion outside my door. I opened it to see what was going on. A small group of soldiers had gathered just down the corridor from my room. Blaise was with them.

She noticed me watching and strode toward me. She placed a hand on my doorframe. "Two people from Aquila showed up outside the gates today," she informed me. "A man and a woman."

I didn't move. "Were they taken to the dungeon?" Aquila had deemed itself our enemy. Its subjects were a threat to Terra. It only made sense to keep them locked up. The only reason the man from Aquila wasn't currently rotting in a cell was because he'd come with

Zephyra, who seemed to be on our side.

"They were, but they've been released. They're friends of the fire elemental and her lover."

I pressed my lips between my teeth, and then said, "I don't trust this… any of it. Why would Aquila's own people come to aid us?"

Blaise stepped closer, challenging me. "Maybe some of Aquila's people don't want to work with King Zaeden and the Dark Lord of Mnyama." She bit her lip and then whispered, "Some say the woman is a water elemental."

I didn't miss the pointed look she gave me. I slowly pushed the door shut while I said, "Good luck tomorrow, Blaise."

CHAPTER 19

B EFORE THE SUN showed its face on the day of Noctis, the army
was dressed and ready for battle. We gathered outside the
entrance to the soldiers' quarters.

King Corbin walked back and forth across the line of soldiers,
dressed in glinting armour of his own. "Today we fight against
darkness," he shouted so we could all hear. "You honour Celestia and
your kingdom today! Many of you won't see tomorrow, but your
sacrifice will *not* be forgotten. You will be given a place by Celestia's
side. It is those of us who survive who will feel the loss."

A few nodded, some raised their swords above their heads. All who
were there were prepared to fight. We knew not all of us would make
it. And I knew if I died that day, I'd die a hero, my heart no longer
darkened by the shadows of my past.

King Corbin's armour clanked as he continued to pace. "Today, we
fight for our wives and our children. Today, we fight for our honour.
We fight for our kingdom." I cheered along with my comrades, my
brothers and sisters. "We may not be thanking Celestia by celebrating
on this night, but we *are* thanking her by fighting in her name. We will
end King Zaeden's tyranny and show the Dark Lord that as followers
of Celestia we will *not* be defeated!"

We roared, brandishing our weapons. I'd fight for my king and my
kingdom… for my comrades, who were my family by bond. It could've
been me up there giving a speech to this army if King Lelund had
claimed me as his son. I shivered at the thought of having so many eyes

watching me. I wasn't born to be a king, and I never would be one. Everyone who knew the truth was dead… except me and perhaps Blaise. And I was sure she'd agreed I'd make an awful ruler.

As I headed for the wall surrounding Terra with the rest of the army, King Corbin stopped me. "Queen Nicola is pregnant," he said lowly to me. "Ger and Reynard are guarding her chambers. If it looks like we're going to lose the battle, ensure they get out of here safely."

I stilled at his proclamation. An heir to his throne, he and his supporters had been waiting for this blessing. If they had a son, the throne wouldn't be passed to one of his distant cousins. Terra's throne always went to a male, unless there were no males to take it. If that happened, it would go to a female until a male within the royal bloodline was born. I met my king's softened gaze and nodded. "Yes, Your Majesty. I will do everything to protect the queen and your unborn child." I meant it. Everything Cedric had taught me, everything I'd ever accomplished, had been for the good of the kingdom.

King Corbin smiled slightly. "Thank you. Now, let's go obliterate our enemies."

We took up our positions outside the wall, in amongst the thick forest surrounding the kingdom. Birds and insects went on chattering as though we weren't about to break out in war. I knew Blaise was up in a tree somewhere with the other archers, bow and arrow ready to pierce the hearts of our enemies. I could shoot an arrow well enough, but I lacked the skill of hitting my target every time. We all had our strengths. A sword was mine.

Somewhere near the back of our army, the fire elemental and her friends were positioned to take on anyone who made it through our defenses. They had been told to be careful with their powers. King Corbin wouldn't have them destroying his kingdom with their elemental power. They were lucky Queen Nicola believed their magic came from Celestia. If she hadn't spoken up in their favour, I was sure they'd all be dead by now.

All day, we waited for King Zaeden to arrive. Squires brought around skins full of fresh water a few times. Armour clanked as soldiers shifted from foot to foot, growing restless. The calm before the storm.

At last, when the sun had set through the trees and the big, round moon woke from her slumber to light the night, we heard Aquila's army approaching.

I readied my sword, its blade shining in the silvery moonlight. When I saw the first of Aquila's soldiers, my heart stopped. They moved through the trees like mindless corpses. Their eyes glowed bright green-blue. Something wasn't right. They moved unnaturally, like they were being controlled by some unseen force. My breath caught in my throat as I realized... *Vesirus.* I had never feared my enemies, and I wasn't about to start.

I bellowed a cry of rage against the king who believed he could take my kingdom, my home. I charged with my comrades and met my enemies with a crash of steel. I hacked, chopped, ducked and parried. Limbs flew through the air and hot blood sprayed my face. I impaled a soldier through the gut, but he kept coming at me with those unseeing eyes. I wrenched my sword from his body, leaving a gaping wound in his belly, and swung it at his neck. He fell to the side like a tree toppled by lightning from the impact.

I finished the job in time to swing out of the way of the axe about to implant itself in my chest.

I stabbed my blade through the soldier's foot, but he didn't seem to feel a thing as he swung again and caught the top of my shoulder. I grunted, clenching my teeth against the pain, and bashed him in the face with the hilt of my sword. Stunned, he hit the trunk of a tree, giving me an opening to stab him in the heart. He stared at me for what felt like eons, unblinking, before falling to the ground.

The dirt turned thick and muddy with the blood of both friend and foe. The air reeked of death, and screams from both armies echoed off the trees.

A spark of orange lit up the corner of my vision. Zephyra had set a woman on fire. The burning woman fell to her knees, but no sound came from her mouth as she burned alive. These soldiers of Aquila didn't feel anything.

An arrow fletched with green and red feathers punctured the throat of the soldier charging at me, and I wondered if it'd been from Blaise's quiver. A sick whistling came from her throat as she tried to breathe. She fell only after her face turned purple. At least these soldiers did go down. It just had to be a killing blow.

I fought and fought, my body weakening with each kill.

The wall grew closer as I was continually knocked backward, and the enemy advanced.

A thick fog the colour of the soldiers' eerie eyes seeped through the trees and along the mossy ground from where I'd spotted King Zaeden. He was weaving some type of magical spell. It was the only explanation for such a strange fog. If only I could get nearer to him. But he seemed untouchable, as if that fog gave him some type of power.

I cut off the head of a large brute with no hair, watching it roll when a whip of water cut through a group of soldiers and sent them flying.

Sprays of water erupted from the ground and added length to the liquid whip as it snapped again.

Clouds blocked out the glowing moon, and rain poured down in sheets upon the carnage.

Some of the archers had jumped from their trees to fight with swords… others had fallen and fought to keep standing. Where was Blaise? I hadn't seen her once since the battle broke out. It was a relief to know Ger was safe, guarding the queen.

An enemy soldier with a long, black braid and a face painted in blood knocked my sword from my grip.

I reached for the twin daggers I'd strapped to each vambrace. I sliced and cut at the male soldier who'd gouged my leg with his blade.

As I stabbed one of my daggers through his glowing eye, I saw Blaise fighting for her life with a blade, her face coated in dirt and blood. She could only block the blows the soldier dealt her with an inhuman force.

I stumbled over to her defense but I wasn't fast enough.

The enemy disabled her.

Now weaponless and barely standing against exhaustion, Blaise was about to meet her end. And I wasn't going to make it in time.

I took a deep breath and released my power into the ground beneath the lumbering enemy's feet. A vine wrapped around his ankle. The soldier pitched forward, face first, onto the blood soaked soil.

Blaise regained her feet with a pain-filled howl. She stomped on the soldier's neck, crushing it and ending his life.

I released the breath I'd been holding onto as our eyes locked and a knowing smile crept over her lips. She was the reason I'd used my power. For her, I'd do anything. A realization that shook me.

That one smile… that one second…

I noticed the other soldier approaching too late as she reached down for her sword.

The soldier threw his dagger. It flew through the air, spinning hilt over blade.

I cried out, too late, as the blade implanted itself right under Blaise's collar bone. She pitched backward, her sword still lying on the ground.

I heard myself yelling her name as I scrambled to her. But I was too late. That one smile had cost her everything, had cost *us* everything.

The woman soldier who'd thrown the dagger had reached Blaise. She grabbed a handful of her golden brown hair and wrenched her head back to bare her neck.

Eyes glowing brilliant blue-green, the soldier pulled the dagger out from the chest of the woman who'd been my light in a world of darkness and used it to slit her throat.

I screamed her name as blood flowed like a crimson river from her throat and the fire left her eyes.

I lunged for the pair and impaled the enemy soldier in the gut with my sword. Blood erupted like a fountain as I put my foot on her chest and wrenched my blade free from her body.

I turned and slid on my knees in the mud. "No, Blaise, please," I begged as I held onto her limp body. Her eyes didn't see me. I'd been too late.

She was gone, gone before I'd been able to reach her… before I could even tell her how much she'd meant to me.

Enemy soldiers turned their attention on us. They lumbered toward where I kneeled, holding the woman who'd come into my life and changed everything. They'd taken her from me. This enemy who'd sworn themselves to Vesirus.

I roared as I slammed my fist into the ground.

A crack appeared where I'd struck the blood slick soil, spreading outward like fractured glass. The crack cut in front of the soldiers ambling toward us.

It grew and fractured until a sound like thunder shook the forest.

The ground split open. Enemies and friends alike plunged to their deaths into the large crevice that had opened. Those who were close paused to gape. Some took the advantage to land a killing blow.

I stared at the wreckage, still holding Blaise's body in my arms. Had my power done this?

Soldiers began making their way around the crevice. Others still fought behind me. The shock had begun to wear off. The fight would continue. Glowing gazes turned to me. I couldn't leave Blaise's body there to be trampled and forgotten, pecked at by the crows. I picked her up and spoke to her unhearing ears, "I'm so sorry, Blaise." I'd loved her. I'd never admitted it, to myself, or to her. I had been a coward and a piece of me went with her as I dropped her into the crevice my power had created to return her to the earth from which we'd all been born.

The thick, green fog had spread, swirling its way toward the wall, King Zaeden completely concealed behind it as though it were a blanket offering protection from the cold.

A bruised and bleeding soldier snarled at me, axe in hand. The wall was right behind us. Terra wouldn't win this battle. I had one purpose left to fulfill. Keep my queen safe.

I turned to sprint for the gates when a hand clamped down on my shoulder.

A woman with hair bright as fire clenched her pale fingers around the iron covering my shoulder. Even through the layers of blood and dirt coating her face, I knew who she was.

Fire erupted from her other hand and sent the soldier with the axe stumbling backward. His skin melted and turned to ash as Zephyra Caldura declared, "We've been searching for you."

CHAPTER 20

I OPENED MY mouth to reply to Zephyra, but Percifal, the man she'd come to Terra with, rode up on a dark bay horse. He held a woman with black hair that flowed to her waist against his body. Her eyes were shut, her body slack.

A line formed between Zephyra's brows as she rushed to the horse. "Is she…?"

"She's alive," Percifal assured her.

"Thaimis?" Zephyra questioned, but Percifal shook his head.

She turned back to me. "We must leave, *now*. Terra is lost."

I couldn't leave. Not until Queen Nicola was safe. I had to get to her. I stepped up to the fire elemental, a challenge. "You don't tell me what to do."

"Easy," Percifal warned.

I ignored him and appealed to Zephyra. "I will save my queen."

"You're the earth elemental. We need you to help us rid Sarantoa of the darkness King Zaeden has brought." Her bright emerald eyes searched my face. If she was looking for heroism, she'd find herself sorely disappointed.

Percifal dismounted, careful not to pull the dark-haired lady down with him. "Phyra, get Chel away from here. I'll help this man save his queen, and then we will find you."

Zephyra's lips parted. The battle continued growing closer to the wall. Terra's soldiers fought relentlessly, but our numbers had dwindled. The enemy pressed us back further and further. I needed to get to my queen.

"Head west through the forest," I said to her. "There are a number of abandoned farms. Hide. Once my queen is safe, we will look for you." I could try to convince them they didn't need me once I'd fulfilled my promise to King Corbin. I didn't even know if he was still alive. I'd spotted him fighting once during the battle, but I'd lost track of him. And with the fog so thick… He had to still be alive.

Zephyra climbed into the saddle behind the other woman, who groaned but didn't open her eyes as the fire elemental shifted her. "Celestia be with you," she said with a longing last look at her lover, and then she took off.

The fog edged closer to the wall, along with enemy soldiers. I bent down and took a uniform off a dead soldier, a black surcoat with a silver V embroidered on the chest. I tossed it to Percifal. "Put this on." I went to another fallen soldier from Aquila and did the same to disguise myself. Aquila was winning. We'd have a better chance of escaping alive dressed like them.

Percifal bent down and pulled a helmet off a dead soldier and placed it on his own head. He slid the visor down to cover his face. "Many in Aquila's army know me, especially King Zaeden," he explained, breathing through the vented metal.

I nodded. "Better keep that on then."

A horn blew, the signal for retreat on our side. Water pooled around my boots and dripped off my hair and into my eyes from the rain still pouring down hard.

I raced for the palace, Percifal right behind me. Some of Aquila's soldiers had already fought their way through the gate.

One of Terra's soldiers was about to try to stop me, but she paused when she recognized my face. Elly's eyes roamed over the V on my chest.

I raised both brows at her, as if to say '*let us pass.*'

She took the hint and turned her back on me. She stuck her blade through the back of a soldier who'd been fighting with one of our comrades. Having only one good arm didn't slow her down. She had her weapon ready in time to clash steal with the next enemy. As her trainer, I couldn't help but be impressed.

I didn't waste any time. I slipped inside the palace and dashed down the corridors with Percifal. He didn't get through unscathed. Blood weeped from a gash on one of his arms.

We reached Queen Nicola's chambers. Relief filled me when I found Ger and Reynard still guarding the closed door, weapons readied.

Shouts and clangs echoed down the corridors. Ger raised his sword, ready to strike. I raised both hands. "Ger, it's me. We need to get the queen out. *Now."*

His eyes widened as he recognized me. Reynard was still sizing up Percifal.

"He's with me," I told them. Reynard relaxed a little but still kept his blade pointed at Percifal.

Ger had Queen Nicola out the next moment, her face hidden beneath her cloak's deep hood.

When the queen saw me and Percifal she let out a yelp and tried to twist away.

"It's all right, Your Majesty," I assured her, making sure she saw my face. "Terra is lost, but I'm helping you escape."

"Sepheus?" I could hear the anguish in her voice. She was losing her kingdom... her home, and we had no idea if King Corbin was alive.

I nodded and the four of us ushered her to a set of stairs leading down to the dungeons. Courtiers screamed as King Zaeden's soldiers ripped them from their chambers. It was about to be a slaughter, and the queen couldn't be part of it.

We descended deep down into the bowels of the palace, our only light being the torch Reynard snatched from one of the walls. Just before we reached the door to the dungeon, I stopped and felt along the cool, stone wall with the palm of my hand. Where was it? Every piece of stone I touched was solid... until my fingertips drifted over the edge of one with a bit more space around the sides. I gripped the stone and pulled. The invisible door opened enough for me to get my fingers around the edge. I clenched my teeth and heaved as hard as I could, dragging the heavy door open enough for a person to slip through. Reynard went first with the torch, pulling the queen in after him.

Ger slid through next but stopped and turned when I hesitated to follow. "Come on, Seph."

I eyed Percifal. He shook his head and spoke before I had the chance. "If Seph doesn't come with me, there will be no kingdom for your queen to return to."

"King Corbin entrusted me to ensure the queen escapes safely." I lowered my voice to a whisper and turned my gaze back to Ger. "She may be carrying the heir of Terra."

"You've done as you promised," Percifal answered. "You've helped the queen escape. If Vesirus brings his dark world to Sarantoa, it will all be for naught. You *must* help the other elementals."

Ger's eyes darted back and forth between Percifal and me. "Seph, what's he talking about."

It killed me inside to let the queen go without me, but if there was a chance my power could send King Zaeden and the Dark Lord to the pits of Mnyama, I had to take it. I squeezed my eyes shut and then opened them. "I'm sorry, Ger. I don't have time to explain. Percifal's right. I have to go with him. Follow the tunnel. You'll exit behind Cheyanne Falls. Take the queen far away from Terra. Protect her with your life."

"Are you coming, or am I to take the queen and leave you behind?" Reynard's voice came from the other side of the door.

"I have family east of Birkshire. We'll wait there." Ger clasped my forearm. "And I'll die before I see the queen harmed."

"I'll see you soon, Brother." I clasped his arm in return, and then he disappeared into darkness. I slammed the door shut behind him.

We ascended the stairs, taking two at a time, to the ground floor. At the top, I hesitated, taking in the sight of dripping splatters of crimson covering the walls and stone tile floors of the palace. Guards and courtiers lay dead and wounded at our feet. Aquila's soldiers paid us no attention, mistaking us for one of their own.

Stepping over bodies, we exited the palace. The green fog had made its way to the courtyard. My stomach sank. It stopped at the Tree of Ends, pooling around its trunk. The bark was turning black and dripped with slime. Its roots moved like living tentacles, burrowing into the soil. The scent of rot caught in my throat, making me gag.

"The portal to the dark world," Percifal stated from beside me, staring at the Tree in horror. "This is the reason King Zaeden chose to attack here first."

My tongue failed me as I watched King Zaeden standing beneath the Tree. Rain soaked his black and silver uniform, and his sopping hair was impossibly dark against his gaunt, white face. His soldiers gathered around him and sank to their knees, bowing their heads.

Aquila's king spoke in a language I'd never heard... an ancient language not meant to fall from the tongues of mortals. A black shadow of nothingness rose from the ground and the mad king laughed, the sound reverberating through my bones. I could only stare as he absorbed the shadow into himself. At first, it seemed as though it'd disappeared, but then black veins spidered along his skin like a growing web. They appeared beneath his sleeves first, shooting over the skin on his hands. And then they crept up his neck and along his jawline until his face was covered in the inky lines. His eyes flashed pure silver before fading back to deep blue.

His soldiers rose and stood ready to hear their king. Their eyes glowed brighter as King Zaeden clenched his fist, as though he controlled them all with the palm of his hand. "Followers of Vesirus," his voice snaked around the army like a vicious serpent. "We've succeeded this day. Vesirus has given us power. But there is still much to be done. Celebrate tonight. You've earned it. Tomorrow, we begin setting our sights on the rest of Sarantoa. We will not stop until the realm belongs to us, and to our Dark Lord."

The soldiers roared, stomping their feet in unison. They were ready for more bloodshed.

"We will not stop until nothing but darkness covers the land!"

The cheers from the soldiers were deafening.

I looked at Percifal. "What's wrong with them?" No sane mortal would follow a worshipper of Vesirus... even if that worshipper was a king. How did he get a whole army to support him?

"They're possessed by dark spirits," Percifal explained, watching to see if anyone was listening. They weren't. The soldiers marched into the palace to join their comrades.

We followed them. I tore a cloak off a cooling corpse and threw the hood up to hide my face. We had to remain inconspicuous until we could escape.

The soldiers of Terra who hadn't gotten away were crammed into cells in the dungeon or killed. Courtiers were forced into the soldiers quarters while Aquila's possessed soldiers claimed the luxurious chambers for themselves. Lords and ladies found themselves forced to be personal slaves. If they refused to scrub their new master's stinking toes or perform other hideous acts, they ended up broken and bleeding.

The citizens of my home kingdom watched us with disgust and horror, believing us to be one of their enemies. We kept our heads down and didn't dare meet anyone's gazes. We didn't need our regular eyes giving away our identities. Orders had been given; no one from the kingdom of earth was permitted to leave.

On the way to the throne room, we concocted a plan. Percifal, helmet still on, veered off from the group to take over guard duty at the gate. I was to meet him there as soon as I could get away without drawing unwanted attention.

Surrounded by my enemies, I watched as King Zaeden sat on Terra's throne. Blaise's face flashed in my mind, catching me off guard. Blaise... she'd been the light in the dark, and she was gone. Gone like she'd never existed. We should've been celebrating this night of our goddess together. I imagined myself asking her to dance under the light of the moon. Would she have said yes? I'd never know. And as King Zaeden sat on that gold and wooden throne, it took everything in me not to march up to him and tear his heart out.

My anger was like a beacon to the coldness that had settled in my heart. I didn't have the power to defeat King Zaeden alone. Not with Vesirus' dark power running through him. No, I'd wait until I had the other elementals to back me up. If I'd learned anything from my time as a torturer, it was patience.

King Zaeden sat with his fingers in a steeple, a slight smile permanently carved on his lips as his soldiers destroyed each portrait of every ruler who'd ever reigned over the kingdom of earth.

The larder had been raided, and the palace cooks had been given the choice to prepare a meal for Aquila's army or be sent to the dungeon, a promised meal for the demons on their way to our world. All had chosen the former. Crumbs, chewed off chicken bones and wine stains littered the emerald carpet.

After the room had been torn apart, King Zaeden placed his chin in his hand. The smile had given way to a rather bored expression. He came to some sort of conclusion and sat up straight, clapping his hands together thrice. The room went silent.

King Zaeden pointed to a young soldier with curly black hair across from him. "You, bring us two courtiers."

The soldier gave him a blank stare.

"Now!" King Zaeden's eyes flashed silver as he shouted, causing the soldier to rush from the room to fulfill his task. He sat deeper in the throne and waited while his army went back to celebrating.

Someone clapped me on the back. I bit my tongue to keep from snapping at the lanky soldier grinning at me. "We did it!" he exclaimed. "We ruined the night of the weak and pitiful goddess of light."

The corners of my mouth tugged up in a viscous smile as I pictured his head being severed from his body. "All hail Vesirus," I responded flatly and moved away from him.

It was difficult pretending to be part of a group of people when you wanted nothing more than to brutally end each and every one of their lives.

"Wait. Your eyes…" he called after me.

I spun on him, knocking him back with my body. I wouldn't let this fool ruin my ruse. I narrowed my gaze at him from beneath my hood. I was about to answer when King Zaeden leaned forward, placing his hands between his knees, and said, "You're eyes do appear rather dim, soldier."

My shoulders tightened as I turned my face to the mad king. I shoved back my hood and bowed. "Your Majesty. I do not know why the others eyes glow, but I am a devoted follower of the Dark Lord. I have been my whole life."

"A true devotee?" The king's lapis eyes glittered.

"Do you question my faith, Your Majesty?"

He placed his finger over his mouth, deep in thought. Instead of answering, he said, "If what you say is true, you won't mind the events about to unfold."

The curly-haired soldier had returned with two courtiers. The lady I recognized right away… Bridgette, one of Queen Nicola's handmaidens. The other was a polished lord, whose name I couldn't remember. His usually combed brown hair was in disarray, and his grey tunic was torn in places. Everyone made space as they were brought before the king.

Skin covered in those ugly black veins, the king flashed his canines at the pair in a wicked smile, like a demon from some nightmare. "We find ourselves in need of entertainment." His voice carried throughout the room. "You two will fight until one of you no longer draws breath."

The soldiers shouted their approval, surrounding the courtiers so they had no way to escape. I forced a smile. I'd never hated myself more. *For my queen,* I told myself. I'd do this to save my kingdom's future.

"N—no," Bridgette whimpered, clasping her shaking hands together.

"I will not harm this woman." The lord clenched his fists, daring to defy the mad king.

King Zaeden inclined his head and sat back again, draping his hands over the arms of the wood and gold throne. "Refuse and we'll bring in some of your friends and make you watch while they die slow, painful deaths. Trust us. This choice will be much easier for you."

Bridgette began sobbing as the lord eyed her.

"Shall I give them weapons, Your Majesty?" the giant of a soldier, who I assumed to be Aquila's constable, asked. I'd seen him give the others orders. He only answered to the king.

"No," King Zaeden replied to the soldier whose armour couldn't hide his overly large muscles. "Let them fight with their bare hands."

Soldiers had begun passing coin around, placing bets on who would win.

The dishevelled lord put both hands up and appealed to Bridgette. "I'm sorry, but I have to keep my family safe."

Bridgette didn't wait for the lord to attack. With a high-pitched cry, she lunged at him and wrapped her hands around his neck.

Panic flashed across the lord's face, but he quickly recovered by bringing his knee up and into her stomach.

She let go of his neck and bent over, coughing, trying to suck air back into her lungs.

The lord grabbed her by the hair and slammed her face into the floor.

She struggled until she was able to get onto her back and scratched at his face. Mean, red lines formed where her nails had dug into his skin.

"*Bitch!*" he spat and back handed her across the face. It's amazing what one will do when the lives of their loved ones are in danger.

The woman spat out a gob of blood and tried to squirm out of his grasp, but he had her pinned down. He wasn't budging.

The soldiers cheered and shouted at the pair. It seemed most had betted on the lord. It appeared they were going to win. But then Bridgette got her hand into the top of her simple dress and pulled out a small, hidden blade.

Before the lord could blink, she jabbed the blade into the side of his neck with a howl.

The lord released her to place a hand where the blade still protruded. Blood soaked his hand and drizzled onto Bridgette's beige dress.

And then his eyes rolled into the back of his head and he fell forward onto her.

Two soldiers pulled the dead lord off the handmaiden and another helped her to stand. Her blood soaked chest rose and fell as he raised her arm above her head. "We have a winner!"

Bridgette didn't resist. I caught a glimpse of her gaze as the room cheered, and by the nothingness in it, I knew she was gone.

One of the soldiers who held her began to take her away, but King Zaeden held up a hand. "Wait." The soldier paused. "A gift for a true follower of Vesirus." He pointed at me. "Her life is yours."

Don't think. Just do it. Do it. Do it.

She turned her empty stare on me. She didn't beg me to spare her. She didn't look scared. It was like she wasn't even there… like she had already left her body and joined Celestia.

And I had no choice. So I ignored the image of Blaise's horrified face as it blinked into my mind.

I drew my sword and drove it through Bridgette's heart.

She blinked down at the blade, once, before collapsing to the carpeted floor.

Now… *now,* I hated myself even more.

CHAPTER 21

I T WAS NEARLY dawn by the time most of Aquila's soldiers traded celebrations for sleep. The rain had let up and the clouds parted, revealing the bright face of the full moon. Even in the lightening indigo sky, it shone like a beacon against darkness.

I led two horses to the gate. Percifal leaned against the wall, staring up at that moon. His pretend comrade, one of Aquila's soldiers, glanced at the horses. "Have somewhere else to be?" He stepped forward and faced me. The glow in his eyes had dimmed. Though, the green-blue colour still swirled through his irises like curling smoke.

"By the orders of the king." I grunted from beneath the hooded cloak.

"What orders?"

"None of your business." I pointed at Percifal. "You, come with me."

Percifal pushed off from the wall and shrugged, his helmet still on.

The soldier glanced at Percifal. "He's terrible company. Doesn't talk much."

"Good," was all I said as we mounted the horses and took off through the forest.

When the wall of Terra had disappeared from our sight, Percifal took off his helmet. "Did you have to give me a pony?" he asked, running a hand through his cropped onyx hair to fluff it up.

I smirked. "I admit your mount is short. I took the first two I could catch." While that was partially true, I had given him the pony on purpose too. If I changed my mind and decided I didn't want to join him and his little group, I could easily out run him.

Percifal grunted. "I should've gotten the horse."

I responded by edging my mount faster. He trailed me through the trees and out onto the small path I knew led to the farmland west of Terra.

The sun crept into the sky and warmed my face, flickering through the branches as though darkness hadn't just fallen on Sarantoa. Birds continued to serenade the morning with their songs, animals still poked their heads up from eating grass to watch us ride by. Celestia had not yet turned her back on her world. I decided that though my heart may have darkened, the rest of the world didn't deserve to. I would ensure my unborn cousin had a future in this realm. Blaise's death wouldn't be in vain.

I couldn't forget the look of utter nothingness in Bridgette's eyes right before I took her life. Her blood stained my hands. Along with Claudia's and Cedric's and every other person's life I'd ended. My hands were clean of Blaise's blood. But her death hurt the most. I hadn't let myself think much about it until now. There hadn't been time. I was so angry that she was gone. Angry at her for getting herself killed, angry at King Zaeden for starting this war… most of all, I was angry at myself. Angry for not being able to stop that woman soldier from slitting her throat.

I nudged my horse into a gallop, shoving those useless emotions down. The time would come. King Zaeden and his army of dark spirits would regret their decision to steal my kingdom.

The forest thinned and the land flattened as we rode west. We pushed our horses through meadows of knee-high grass. By late afternoon, we crossed through fields of corn and hay.

The first abandoned farm we came upon had been empty. The house had collapsed, but the old barn would still make for a decent shelter. I held onto our mounts while Percifal checked the faded wooden barn to see if the women were inside. He came out shaking his head. "No one's been here."

We refilled our water skins from a small creek and continued on through the fields of green. I kept silent and Percifal didn't press for conversation. We reached the second farm as the evening sun said its goodbyes. The house was still intact, and I wondered if perhaps someone still dwelled there. We hobbled our mounts and let them munch on fresh grass while we inspected the little house with a peaked roof. Dust covered every piece of furniture, every drape. The floor was coated with dirt... untouched. No sign of a farmer or an elemental woman.

"No one's been here," I said, stepping back outside.

"Let's check the stable." Percifal didn't bother waiting for me.

I followed him. I still didn't understand why he was with the elementals. If he had magic of his own, he had yet to show it. I didn't really care why he was helping them, to be honest. He didn't ask questions, so neither did I.

The stable was large enough to hold about a dozen horses. Dust floated in the beams of sunlight peeking in through the spaces in the boards of the walls and ceiling. I swore I heard a whisper as we passed by the stalls, but each stall we passed was empty.

Percifal came out from the room used to store grain and tack as I peered over the last stall. The fire elemental sat beside the lady she'd rode off with... the elemental who'd formed water into a whip. She lay curled beside Zephyra, her face covered in streaks of dry, dirty tears.

"Phyra?" Percifal came up behind me and pushed the stall door open.

"Percifal!" She threw her arms around his neck, bits of old straw clinging to her fire red hair.

The water elemental moaned and put her hand over her face before rolling over to face the stall wall. Her obsidian hair was tangled like the cobwebs hanging from the ceiling. She and Zephyra both still wore the leather armour they'd donned for battle.

Percifal released Zephyra and tilted his head at the water elemental. "Is she all right?"

Zephyra bit her bottom lip before answering, "No, not really." She crouched back down beside the water elemental. "Chel, Percifal's brought the earth elemental here."

"I can see that," the water elemental—Chel—mumbled, still facing the wall.

Zephyra winced at me. "Sorry. She hasn't been herself since Thaimis died. Chelela is the water elemental and Percifal's sister. And who are you?" She cocked her head.

"My name is Sepheus." I didn't bother giving her my last name—Dirva, a royal last name which still didn't feel right. "I know what it's like to lose someone."

"Do you really?" Chel mocked in a hoarse voice, sitting up enough to pin me with a cold, sapphire stare. "Do you know what it feels like to have the person you loved more than *anything* ripped from your life?"

I narrowed my own eyes at her. She had no idea.

She mistook my silence for denial. "That's what I thought. Leave me alone." She plopped back into the dusty, old straw.

Zephyra grabbed Percifal and I both by an arm and led us out of the stable. "She needs time."

"We don't *have* time," Percifal argued. I couldn't agree more. I had lost the only person I'd ever loved, but I wasn't wallowing in self-pity. No, I would take my pain out on my enemies.

"She's not in her right mind right now." Zephyra swung her arms out.

I waited silently while the two bickered.

"I understand she's grieving, but while we sit here waiting, King Zaeden's planning his next move. I saw it, Phyra." He took her by the shoulders. "I saw the portal open and Vesirus bestow King Zaeden with more power."

Zephyra opened and closed her mouth once before saying, "It's true, then? There is a gate to Mnyama in Terra?"

"Yes, it was under some tree in the courtyard."

"The Tree of Ends," I muttered beneath my breath.

Both turned to look at me.

"It's the tree where we hang criminals once King Corbin gives the order for execution."

Zephyra looked to the sky and shook her head. "You used the tree to send dark spirits to Vesirus. It's no wonder it's a gate to the Dark Lord's world!"

"No one knew such a thing was possible," I challenged.

The fire elemental threw her hands up in the air. "Did you not believe in our gods?"

"No…"

Her emerald eyes sizzled as she gave me a pointed look.

"Yes? I'm not sure."

"They're *real*." She put a hand to her forehead and sighed. "I've been visited by Celestia."

"Have you?" I asked incredulously.

"Yes, I have. She's come to me in my dreams."

"In your dreams?" I smirked. Who did she take me for?

"Watch yourself," Percifal warned.

But we all stopped as Chel walked between us with two packed sacks. "Are you people going to stand here and bicker all day, or are we going to go make King Zaeden wish he were never born."

Zephyra raised a red eyebrow at Percifal. He shrugged and followed his sister without another word.

It seemed our conversation had ended. It didn't matter what I once thought about our goddess and her brother, Vesirus. I knew at least one of them existed. I'd seen all the proof I'd needed. And if Vesirus was real, Celestia likely was too. So I said to the woman staring after her friend and lover, "We all want the same thing. So how about you stop questioning me and focus on figuring out how to kill King Zaeden and send Vesirus back to Mnyama."

She sized me up, not backing down, but in the end she relented. "I find you rude, but you're right. Let us focus on the task at hand." She jogged after the others. I followed her. When she caught up with Chel, she touched her elbow. "Are you sure you're ready?"

The dark-haired woman kept walking. She either didn't notice, or didn't care that her appearance was out of sorts. "I have no choice. I heard your conversation. There's no time. A gate has been opened."

Zephyra's expression turned sympathetic. "I'm sorry. I wish we didn't need your help."

"I would help even if you didn't need me. I will exact my vengeance on King Zaeden for the deaths of Thaimis and my father, and I will enjoy every moment of it. Perhaps I'll join them by Celestia's side once the realm is safe."

"You shouldn't say such things," Zephyra replied.

"There's a high chance we could all die in battle." Chel approached the horse they'd ridden to the farm together, who currently chomped on a mouthful of grass in the pasture. The two were still hobbled by the house.

Zephyra gave up on trying to console her friend. She was right of course. We could all be giving our lives up to save Sarantoa. It was the cost every soldier was willing to pay. Was Zephyra a soldier though? Was Chel? I guessed we'd all find out soon enough.

"Zephyra and I will ride together," Percifal offered. Of course he did. This way, he wasn't stuck with the pony.

When it came time to mount the horses, Chel looked at me with eyes as blue as the sea, put her hand on her hip, and stated, "I'm *not* taking the pony."

Oh, we were going to get along very well, her and I.

I caught Percifal's smile as I climbed into the pinto's saddle. My legs were awkwardly too long for the short mare. I sighed through my nose and clucked to get her moving. Payback was a bitch.

"We need to obtain supplies before heading north to Ventosa," Chel advised from beside Zephyra and Percifal.

I, of course, took up the rear.

"Ventosa?" Zephyra exclaimed. "We're going to Solis. King Zaeden will most likely attack my cousin next."

"We *need* the air elemental. I'll bet you all the jewels in the world they reside in the kingdom of air. We won't have enough power to defeat the mad king without them," Chel argued.

Percifal and I kept our mouths shut during the exchange.

Zephyra gripped her thigh with her hands as she twisted toward Chel from in front of Percifal. "Queen Adelaide will come to our aid. I can't go off to Ventosa without warning her first."

Chel brushed an invisible piece of dirt from her arm as she said, "Surely Solis knows what King Zaeden is doing by now."

"Terra didn't."

"Word will have spread since the attack. If you want to help your cousin, Ventosa is your best chance."

Zephyra didn't answer for a few moments, but when she did, fire crackled in her voice. "*You* can go to Ventosa. *I* am going to help my queen."

"We're not splitting up," Percifal broke in. "King Zaeden is more likely to invade Solis first and Queen Adelaide will need *our* aid. We'll go to the kingdom of fire first. Then, we'll make the journey to the frigid kingdom up north."

"Fine," Chel ground out and fell back behind them to ride by me.

Percifal pulled a compass out of one of the sacks tied to their mount and turned his and Zephyra's horse. "This way."

We trod through the field of weeds and grass at a steady pace.

"Seems the princess got her way," I commented when the others were far enough ahead.

Chel urged her horse into a trot until she was at the front, leading the way without a glance back. I guessed she didn't wish to converse. Fine with me.

We stopped at a market in the first village we passed to obtain supplies for the rest of our journey to Solis.

I hadn't brought any coin, but Percifal had enough to share. I accepted the plain dark green tunic he bought me after we discarded the uniforms we'd taken from King Zaeden's fallen soldiers. We stocked up on dried meat and bread. We didn't need to worry about water. Chel could call it up from the earth whenever we needed. Both Chel and Zephyra hadn't said a word to each other since their argument. I could see the hurt in Zephyra's eyes, but Chel pretended not to notice, though a storm brewed beneath the surface. She tried not to care if the other elemental was upset. I could tell Percifal felt awkward as he tip-toed around both women. I, on the other hand, welcomed the peaceful silence.

With sacks so full they were almost bursting, we mounted our horses again and left the village.

"If we shared a horse, we could use the pony to pack our stuff," I suggested to Chel on our way out.

She scoffed, "No, thank you."

"Unbelievable."

We rode as fast as the horses could handle through the grassy plains between Terra and Solis. Stretching green meadows and endless blue sky was our only view for days.

We only stopped when we were too tired to go on. We slept with blankets on the grass underneath a limitless world of radiant stars.

I pulled my blanket tighter around my body and shivered. It was too dangerous to build a fire out on the open fields where the wind blew strong. It would've been too easy for it to spread, to burn out of control. So we made due with the wool blankets we'd purchased. Luckily, summer was almost upon us, and Solis was the second warmest kingdom in Sarantoa.

Percifal and Zephyra had the advantage of sleeping together, their bodies warming each other. When I'd looked at Chel, she simply sniffed and stomped off to find a place to set her blankets down. A place I heard soft sobs coming from as I closed my eyes, trying to sleep.

The water elemental put on a strong face most of the time, but when no one watched, she let herself fall apart over and over again. I knew what it was to be broken. Her pain was a mirror. Looking at her was like staring at my own reflection.

I tried to shut Blaise out from my memory during the day, but I'd dreamed of her every night since her death. I dreamed of our kiss the night she'd been bitten by the corandor, I dreamed of her asking me to dance, and each time I refused her. I woke up hating myself more and more each morning, cursing every sunrise. If only I'd told her how perfect I'd thought she was… how beautiful. If only I'd told her how much I… I didn't let myself finish the thought.

The landscape changed the further we rode. Plains turned to rolling hills. Hills turned to mountains. Grass became sparse, a thing of the past. And when we reached the dusty, red sandstone cliffs surrounding the kingdom of fire twenty some sunrises later, Zephyra's back had stiffened, her chin tilted higher.

She was a royal, and she was home.

Chapter 22

As soon as Zephyra showed her face, we were admitted into the palace. The guards immediately recognized her. They knew Queen Adelaide had been searching for her since the day she'd left. Two guards escorted us to the Solis queen, fearing punishment if there were to be any delay in reuniting the cousins.

With our horses taken from us to be cared for, we rushed down corridors lined with red drapes and tapestries of Celestia and her first elementals. We were ushered through an ornate, golden door. I stepped inside after the others. I marveled at the impressive stone throne with a red velvet seat and celestial suns etched upon its surface. A pair of gold dragons made up the arms of the mighty throne. Slender, pale hands rested on each of their polished, triangular heads.

Percifal, Chel and I all bowed before the young queen dressed in a red and ivory gown. A golden crown rested upon her twisted, sunny blond curls.

Queen Adelaide let out a choked, very unqueenly, sound before rushing from her throne to embrace Zephyra tightly. "Zephy! It's really you!"

"I've missed you too, Addy," Zephyra managed to get out, returning the embrace.

When Queen Adelaide released her, Zephyra passed her hand down the sore state of her dress. "Apologies, we weren't given time to clean ourselves up before visiting you."

Queen Adelaide waved her off. "I don't care how filthy you are. I'm just happy you're here."

"Is Peyton… Are you…" Zephyra began.

"He is king. We married shortly after my coronation," she said, beaming.

"How wonderful! I'm so happy for you." Zephyra smiled at her cousin before her expression turned somber. "I wish I could've been here for you."

The queen's smile faded, but she quickly replaced it with a new one. "You are here now, that's all that matters."

"I'm afraid I come bearing dire information." The fire elemental folded her hands in front of her.

Queen Adelaide waited for her to continue.

"I know this is going to sound insane, but King Zaeden has found a way to join forces with Vesirus. He's trying to conquer all of Sarantoa. And if he succeeds, Vesirus will bring his dark world here." Zephyra paused to study her cousin, who remained unwavering, and then added, "You don't believe me, do you?"

The queen looked away before she huffed. "I believe you. I'm already aware of King Zaeden's plans. I was told when I visited Aquila for Noctis De Celestia. Someone slipped a note into my dessert. I don't know who or how. And no, I didn't believe it at first, but I knew something wasn't right when we were told King Zaeden was having his mother host Noctis this spring because he'd fallen ill. And not only was King Zaeden absent, King Corbin didn't attend either.

"The note stated King Zaeden had gone to attempt to conquer Terra. I left before dawn. I told the queen of Ventosa she should leave if she knew what was good for her kingdom. I don't know if she received a note or not. We didn't have time to speak more, and I was worried about being overheard."

"We plan to travel there next," Percifal said, stepping up beside Zephyra. "We came here first to warn you, and to ask for your aid in this war."

Queen Adelaide inclined her head at him. "You have no need to ask. Anything you need is yours. We must all come together if we are to win this war."

Zephyra beamed at her cousin. "I knew you'd help us."

"Always," the queen answered. "Some of Terra's subjects have already arrived here in seek of refuge. We've accepted their soldiers into our own army and have given everyone else a place to stay. But enough of this for now," she said, running her hands down the length of her scarlet skirts. "We can catch up over dinner. You've all come a long way. I'll have some of the maids assist you and meet you in my private dining chamber for third meal."

"That sounds lovely," Zephyra replied.

Once we all had a chance to bathe and were given fresh attire, we were taken to Queen Adelaide's chambers, where we were formally introduced. Queen Adelaide was ecstatic to learn Percifal and Zephyra were lovers, as was King Peyton. The king with short flaxen hair and kind eyes questioned the pair about where and how they'd met as we devoured our meal of roasted venison, buttered potatoes and glazed vegetables.

Chel beckoned the servant to bring her more wine off the small cart parked in the corner of the burgundy carpeted chamber. She'd downed the first goblet of red wine as if it were water and, when he poured the second, she took such a big sip that I thought she'd finish it too and ask for a third. I believe the only reason she held back was due to the royals' presence. Caught up in conversation, no one appeared to notice, except for me. Her pale cheeks already flushed pink from the wine.

She nudged me and pointed at my still full goblet. "Aren't you going to drink that?"

I swallowed the last bit of my food and answered, "No. I don't drink wine."

"Pah!" She tossed her dark, glossy hair over her shoulder. "That's preposterous."

"You drink it," I slid the crystal goblet closer to her.

"I want you to drink it." She crossed her arms in front of her chest. She wore an elaborate silk peach gown with a bodice that pushed up her perfect bosom.

Zephyra cleared her throat, clearly upset by the interruption.

Chel remained with her arms crossed and a dark eyebrow cocked at me. Everyone had stopped talking to watch us.

I sighed and snatched the goblet off the table. I took a long sip and set the goblet down. "Happy?"

Chel feigned a smile and then went back to her own wine. By the time I'd finished mine, she was on her third. Some people liked to drown their sorrows. She was one of them.

We had finished our supper and were enjoying fruit tarts when Queen Adelaide grabbed a hold of Zephyra's hand from across the table. "I have some exciting news to tell you."

Zephyra swallowed her tart and asked. "What is it?"

"You're an aunt. We had twins!"

Zephyra bounced up off her seat. "Truly?"

"Yes," Queen Adelaide said with a bright smile. "Two girls. They are with their nurse."

Zephyra sat back down. "My—my vision! It was true. I knew it. Oh! Did you receive my letter? Did you find the man named Algor?" She peered down at her hands, clasping her yellow skirts. Percifal put a comforting hand on her back. "He—he was horrible."

"Did he hurt you?" Lightning sparked in the queen's eyes. "I knew something bad happened."

"He did, but—but Percifal helped me… Percifal and Celestia." She gave her cousin a small smile.

Queen Adelaide pursed her lips and replied, "We found him burned to death. We also found the dungeons you spoke of in your letter and the remains of four women. Our guards arrested his staff. They're living out the rest of their lives in the dungeon here."

"He burned to death?" Zephyra's eyes widened almost as big as the plates now being cleared away from the table.

Chel had the male servant refill her goblet, as well as mine.

"Yes, it was the strangest thing," Queen Adelaide said. "Only he burned, and no one could explain why."

"Because of me," Zephyra confessed.

King Peyton gasped. "You set a man on fire?"

"Well… yes. I didn't mean to, but he was about to hurt me. You see, I—I'm a fire elemental."

The queen and king exchanged a look as though they could read each other's minds.

Chel set her goblet down and grinned at the royals. "And I am a water elemental."

When I didn't say anything, Chel kicked me under the table.

"Ah! I'm the earth elemental," I confessed. I scowled at Chel, who had turned her attention back to her wine.

"Well, this is unexpected. But good, this is very good for Sarantoa," the queen mused.

"Indeed," King Peyton added, rubbing the scruff on his chin. "We may have a fighting chance against King Zaeden with the three of you."

"You believe us? Just like that?" Chel looked skeptically at our hosts.

The golden queen set her regal gaze on the water elemental and said plainly, "My cousin wouldn't lie to me."

Chel simply shrugged as the queen dismissed her to turn back to Zephyra and Percifal. "What about air?" She tucked a piece of blond hair behind her ear.

"We believe she'sss-in Ventosa," Chel slurred and shot Zephyra a glare. "Where we *need* to go."

Percifal shut Chel out and appealed to Queen Adelaide. "We plan to find her once we leave here. We need a few things from you, if you will, before we make the journey north."

"What do you need?" The queen spread her hands.

"Warm clothes, tents, food, coin and good horses," he replied.

"Done."

"What about you?" Zephyra asked the queen. "What if King Zaeden attacks Solis while we are off searching for the air elemental. We should stay and help you fight."

I finally spoke up, the wine already going to my head. It was an effort not to slur like Chel. I focused on the words, refusing to appear like a bumbling fool. "The three of us couldn't stop him in Terra. Surely we can't do so here."

"What's one more elemental going to do?" Zephyra argued. "If three can't stop him, how will four?"

I narrowed my eyes at her. "You're the one who receives visions from our dear goddess. You tell me."

Chel smirked into her goblet. "I agree with him."

"Enough!" Queen Adelaide sliced the air with her hand. She was a queen through and through. Authority rang clear in her voice. "Celestia created the four elementals for a reason. We would not be here without all four. I will give you what you need for your journey to Ventosa. In the meantime, I am preparing my army for battle. We don't even know if King Zaeden will come here first."

"Yes, Your Majesty," everyone except King Peyton mumbled simultaneously, put in our places.

"Good. We are finished here. You must all be tired. We will meet again tomorrow to go over our plans with my constable."

"One more question." Zephyra's eyes searched her cousin's face. "My parents…"

The queen grimaced. "I'm sorry. Your father left with his mistress after you ran away. Your mother… I gave your mother an estate on the outskirts of the kingdom. It keeps her out of my way."

Zephyra's lips pulled up pleasantly. "I'm glad my father found someone who makes him happy." She didn't have anything to say about her mother. I guessed their relationship wasn't a good one. I could relate to that.

I was surprised Chel could walk mostly straight when we left the queen's chambers for our own for the rest of the night. I, myself, had a difficult time not stumbling, and I'd drunk only half as much as she.

Zephyra knew her way around the palace, having grown up within its walls. She and Percifal found their own way to their bedchamber. A maid led Chel and I down a corridor to a separate wing. Her frizzy, orange hair bounced with each clipped step. She stopped at a closed door and motioned us to wait outside while she bustled into the guest chamber and lit half a dozen candles. Motes of dust still hung in the air as she returned to us, offering the room to Chel for the evening.

She was about to take me to my own temporary sanctuary when Chel grabbed my wrist. "Stay with me," she said, peering through thick lashes. I was about to refuse, but she pouted and added, "Oh, come on. I'm simply not ready for slumber. Don't flatter yourself."

I moved to leave. Her face fell and she softened her tone. "Please. I don't wish to be alone with my thoughts."

I considered her, the haunted look in those sea blue eyes. Maybe I wanted a challenge. Or maybe I wanted to forget my own ghosts for a while. I couldn't explain why I chose to go with her. Perhaps it was the wine.

The maid shrugged, keeping her thoughts to herself, and said, "There's another chamber across the corridor if you please." She strode away, leaving the two of us alone.

I stepped onto the fluffy peach coloured carpet inside the guest chamber. The bed sat in the center, covered in ivory blankets. A small unlit hearth faced the foot of the large bed. No fire burned within. Nearly summer; the nights at Solis were warm.

Chel bounced onto the bed, landing on her stomach. Her grin appeared from behind her curtain of cobalt-black hair.

I took a seat on the lounger placed at the end of the bed.

"Tell me how you discovered your power," she urged, brushing her hair off her face.

"I had a dream about it. When I woke up, I had power," I replied flatly.

"That's it? Seems so simple… too easy."

I leaned over to take my boots off. *May as well get comfortable.* When I didn't answer, she revealed, "I was only a child when I discovered my power. I fell into the sea… discovered I could breathe underwater. I spent many seasons searching for answers. I didn't find them until I met a sorceress. She taught me how to control my power. Do you know how to control yours, Sepheus?"

"Of course," I lied. Mostly, I knew what to expect when I called upon my magic. The split in the ground though, that had been unexpected.

She rolled over onto her side to lie closer to me. So close she could play with one of the gold buttons on the crimson doublet I'd been given to wear to dinner. "Not a man of many words, are you? Here I thought it'd be less boring with you in my chamber."

I bent my chin to peer down at her. She was bold, but that could've been the wine. "You're drunk."

She stopped fiddling with the button to stare up at me with those big, sapphire eyes. "I once fell in love with a mermaid, you know?"

I raised my brows. "A mermaid…"

"Yes, she wanted to keep me there under the big, beautiful blue sea, but I couldn't stay. I had to come back to Sarantoa to help Phyra save the world. If only I'd have stayed at sea, maybe I wouldn't have ended up killing the man I loved even more than the mermaid I deserted. So yes, I'm drunk. Actually, more wine would be *fantastic* right about now." She scanned the chamber as though she expected a decanter to be waiting for her.

"I didn't know mermaids were real," I said, ignoring the rest of her rant. I certainly wasn't fetching more wine.

"As real as you and I." She turned her attention back to me. "And I wonder, if you have as much control over your power as you say you do, why did you create the crack which killed some of your own comrades?"

The question caught me off guard, and I stuttered, "I—I... that was different. My power always produced itself in vines before. I didn't know it could do that."

"Maybe you could use a sorceress too. Or perhaps you lost the one person you cared most about." She sat up so close to me I could smell the perfumed soap she'd been washed with. I glanced at her full, pink lips. She leaned in closer, as if to press them against my own. She was intoxicating... dangerous.

I pulled back within a heartbeat, my head spinning from the wine, from her closeness. "I'm not here to replace your dead lover." The bitterness in my voice surprised me.

She stared at me for a moment before lying back down and turning her back to me. If she thought she could make me feel bad, she was mistaken. I owed her nothing. I let myself out, carrying my boots with me, and entered the bedchamber across from hers.

Sleep eluded me for most of the night, visions of Blaise plaguing me. Maybe I should've let myself be lured beneath the sheets by the water elemental. Instead, we were both condemned to spend the night with our memories.

CHAPTER 23

A FTER COPIOUS AMOUNTS of water, my head still pounded from the wine the next morning. Chel didn't seem to be suffering at all when we met with the queen and the leader of her army, Constable Creighton, to discuss strategies against King Zaeden and his possessed soldiers.

"Perhaps we can lure them away from Terra—away from the innocents so Zephyra can extinguish them all with her fire," the young constable, with coppery hair and a freckled nose, suggested. Queen Adelaide had already filled him in on all of the details about who we were and what King Zaeden was doing.

"Perhaps Zephyra can also use her fire to melt some of the ice around Seph's heart," Chel drawled from the other side of the round table.

Everyone glanced at me. Another might have turned red, but I wasn't so easily embarrassed. I brushed her words off like lint on a tunic and replied to the Solis constable. "We have agreed to go to Ventosa to find the air elemental first."

"That's preposterous," Constable Creighton exclaimed. "By the time you find them, King Zaeden might already succeed in crushing all of Sarantoa."

"We are not strong enough to beat him without the fourth elemental," Chel argued, placing her hand on the map unfolded on the center of the table. "And how exactly are we supposed to *lure* him out?"

"Maybe not lure him out, but we could meet him on his way here, catch him off guard." The constable held Chel's gaze. His own soldiers would have yielded, but she wasn't backing down.

"We tried that tactic in Terra. It didn't work," I said. As stubborn as Chel was, I agreed with her on this.

"Why didn't it work?" Queen Adelaide had been quiet up until this point. Her eyes were still on the map before us, as if the answer laid between the lines of ink.

"Well," Zephyra bit her lip. "We were told to hold back our powers as we were still close to Terra. A fire could've burned down the whole kingdom." She turned her face to me then. "Perhaps if you could split the earth again we could trap King Zaeden's army and I could then burn them."

"I don't even know if I could split the earth again. I've only done it once, and it wasn't on purpose."

Zephyra looked down at her hands, which were folded neatly in her maroon skirts. "Perhaps you could hone that part of your magic. It may be our best chance."

"What say you, Your Majesty?" Constable Creighton appealed to his queen.

She opened her mouth to answer, but then a guard in red and yellow Solis livery burst through the doors. "Apologies, Your Majesty," he said as he bowed, clearly out of breath. "More soldiers have arrived from Terra. You'll wish to hear what they have to say."

Queen Adelaide stood taller and lifted her chin. "Bring them to me."

We waited while the guard fetched the refugees, our discussion forgotten for the moment. He soon returned to the small octagon shaped room with two men and one woman. All three wore Terra's uniform. They each bowed deeply before the queen. She was not their queen, but she was still a royal and still an ally of their own king.

"Rise," Queen Adelaide ordered, regal to the bone. Born and raised to be a queen.

One of the men, the one with shoulder length brown hair and a scar bisecting his upper lip, spoke. "Your Majesty, we managed to escape from Terra and we seek a place among your own army."

"Granted," Queen Adelaide affirmed.

"Thank you, Your Majesty," the man with the scar breathed. I recognized his face, but I couldn't remember his name. "I would also warn you to be prepared. The things we've seen… the land around Terra… it's *dying*. And the—the creatures… they're not of this world." The man was clearly shaken.

The queen stiffened. "Creatures? What creatures?"

"They were—they were like hairless hounds with sharp claws, and they stood on two legs. Others were the size of my fist, but had wings and sharp pincers made for ripping flesh from bone. We—we saw them devour a large man within moments."

"Impossible," she replied, turning away from the soldier. She walked slowly around the table, tapping her knuckles on its surface, deep in thought. When she'd come to a full circle, she stopped. "I do not want to give King Zaeden the chance to bring Vesirus and his dark world here. I will send a soldier out to learn of his location. If he's still in Terra, we will wait until he marches again. Once he's on the move, we will attack, giving us the element of surprise. Having magic on our side also gives us an advantage. Elementals, are you with us? It's your decision. If you wish to go to Ventosa to find the air elemental, I won't stop you. But if you choose to fight with us, we could end this sooner."

I knew Zephyra's decision by the look of pride on her face. And the storm raging in Chel's gaze told me hers. I was the deciding vote as Percifal had no say. I set my eyes on the queen and said, "We'll fight with you. There's no sense in searching for a person we may never find when we could end this war now."

Queen Adelaide smiled, her eyes sparkling with hope. "Good. First, I need someone willing to find King Zaeden. I need a champion."

Percifal stepped forward. "I would be honoured."

Zephyra put a hand on his arm. Her brow creased with concern. "Percifal, are you sure? King Zaeden knows you."

He covered her hand with his own. "Yes, this is my chance for redemption. I could've stopped this before it began. Let me help end it. Besides…" He winked. "I've mastered the art of disguise."

Zephyra let out a nervous laugh and explained to the room, "He was posing as a vagrant when I met him. I'd never have guessed he was once a constable."

Constable Creighton gave him a measuring look, which Percifal answered with a wink.

"It's settled then. You will leave at dawn. As soon as you find out where King Zaeden is bound for, you will return here."

"My pleasure, Your Majesty."

Chel hadn't said a word, but I sensed the silent rage rolling off her in waves. She'd forgive us when King Zaeden was dead.

Queen Adelaide dismissed us, and servants came to take care of the refugees.

Zephyra and Percifal went their own way, needing time alone before Percifal left for his mission. Constable Creighton went to inform his soldiers of the plan and to prepare them for the battle ahead, leaving me and Chel alone together. Wonderful.

"I hope you know what you're doing," she fumed, marching past me.

"I don't, but this makes more sense than going on some search for a person who may or may not be able to help us."

She stopped and twisted to face me, fists clenched. "We found *you*, didn't we?"

I crossed my arms. "Maybe you got lucky."

"If you call losing the battle in Terra luck, maybe you deserve to die."

I couldn't help myself. I let out a bitter laugh. Didn't she know who she was talking to? "Of course I deserve to die. The sooner you learn that, the better off you'll be." I'd had enough. Screw not knowing my way around the Solis palace. I'd rather get lost than deal with the emotions that woman evoked in me. I left her in the corridor.

I found my way outside and ended up in the gardens. Courtiers strolled down the cobblestone pathways through the endless vibrant flowers. Ladies dressed in gowns as bright as the petals battered their lashes at me from behind silk fans. Lords gave me sideway stares, unsure what to think of the man whose face they'd never seen in their kingdom. I ignored them all as I found a bench to sit on and gazed into the fountain of bubbling water. How could a place be so beautiful when the world outside was turning to ash? I wished for King Zaeden's death. I wanted my own king to be back on Terra's throne so his child, my cousin, could one day rule. They were the only family I had. It was a secret they'd never know, but it mattered to me. I'd been raised to protect my king. And I would die to save his heir.

~ 179 ~

Percifal was gone by the time I woke the next morning. I ran into the woman who'd come with Terra's soldiers the previous day. I stopped her. "Have you heard word of King Corbin? Is he—alive?"

She squared her muscled shoulders. "All I know is he escaped during the battle. I do not know to where, but I believe he is still alive."

A knot loosened inside my stomach as I nodded. "Thank you." I stepped out of the way to let her pass. I hoped Percifal would return soon so we could get this over with.

Chel found me after I'd broken my fast. I had no idea where Zephyra had gotten to. She probably wanted to be alone after seeing Percifal off.

The water elemental wore a tight dress so dark the blue shade could've been mistaken for black. "Listen. I'm sorry about what I—"

"Don't worry about it." I cut her off. I didn't feel like talking about it.

She studied me before beckoning. "Come with me." But she didn't wait to see if I'd follow.

Curious, I trailed her out of the palace to a spot behind the royal stables.

She stopped and pointed at the ground. "Crack it."

"Pardon me?"

"Split the ground like you did in Terra," she clarified.

It was worth a shot. The ability to send my enemies falling to their deaths would be useful. I rolled my shoulders and crouched, splaying my fingers on the ground and waited... nothing.

I raised my gaze to Chel. She waited with a hand on her hip. "You do know how to use your power, don't you?"

"Of course I do." I focused my attention back on the ground and reached inside to where that spark of power slept. A moment later, a thick vine twisted up from the soil, sending chunks of dirt flying.

Chel tried not to laugh but it sputtered out anyways.

I straightened and glared at her. "I'm so glad you find humour in my failure, my lady."

She stopped laughing. "Try again."

I did, and the same thing happened. Over and over, vine after vine rose from the ground and then disintegrated.

"Think back to the moment you cracked the earth," Chel said over my groan of frustration. *"Remember* what happened."

I didn't want to remember. Blaise… her face, the empty look in her eyes as she bled out. I couldn't stop the images flashing through my mind. And as I felt the anguish—the loss—I reached for my power, sparkling and green.

The ground beneath my hand shook. A crack appeared, growing longer and longer, wider and wider, until the soil had split from where we stood to the base of a weeping willow where it stopped.

Chel smiled, staring down at the split soil. "We will practise again tomorrow." She left me, gaping at what I'd just done.

Every day for the next thirty sunrises, we met to practise using our powers. Chel sometimes used her own magic to fill the cracks with water, creating tiny streams around the stables. I'd admired the way her power came so naturally to her. She was quite attractive when she wasn't focused solely on her sorrows. Slowly, I gained more control over my magic, though I still felt more confident in my vines.

Zephyra worried more with each day that passed by without Percifal's return. She'd told us he'd shaved all the hair off his scalp and planned to grow his beard out so he would have a smaller chance of being recognized. If all went well, King Zaeden would never see him anyways.

Needing a distraction, Zephyra came with me one day to watch. Chel hadn't yet risen from bed. She told us to go on without her when I'd asked through her door. I guessed the wine she'd indulged in the previous night must have kept her down. She'd drunk more than usual after third meal. I'd left her and Zephyra alone in the fire elemental's private dining chamber once I'd finished my roasted hen and potatoes.

"Chel can be difficult at times, but she's a good tutor," Zephyra mused as we entered the meadows peppered with daisies. I'd destroyed enough of the ground behind the stables I'd had to find a new location to practise on. The master of horses scolded Chel and I for making the area dangerous to ride around and had to order his workers to fill the cracks in.

"I know," I replied, flexing my fingers. I no longer needed to touch the ground to use my powers.

"She taught me how to control my power too."

"I suppose being trained by a sorceress gives you the knowledge required to teach others." I reached inside myself to a place where only wreckage lay. I could feel the difference now between the two parts of my power. One was growth, the other… destruction.

Without too much effort, the ground right in front of us split with an earth shattering crack.

"Do you think Percifal is all right?" Zephyra asked as though I hadn't just ripped open the earth.

"I don't know. Probably."

"He should be back by now. I'm worried he's been caught." Her eyelids lowered as she stared at the ground.

"Listen, I'm not going to lie to you. There's a high chance he's already dead. There's a high chance we'll all be dead soon. This is what we decided though… what you agreed to. So if you're looking for someone to cry to, you've come to the wrong person." I adjusted my tunic and strode off back to the palace before she could reply. Sometimes the truth hurt. I was tired of waiting for Percifal to return too, but unless we wanted to seek out the air elemental, there was nothing else we could do. Worrying wouldn't do any good. Worrying wouldn't win the war.

I found myself reprimanded for my honesty with Zephyra later that night during third meal. We ate in the main dining hall, a modest room beside the great hall, which was reserved for larger, more important events such as Noctis De Celestia. Giant suns created with painted tiles stared up from beneath each round table. Numerous torches burned brightly along the stone walls, illuminating the whole area with warm, golden light.

Ready to dig into the rack of pork ribs a servant had placed on the table in front of me, Chel sat down beside me and said, "I don't know what you said to Zephyra, but she's been very upset since she came back from practising with you this afternoon."

I tore a rib off and shrugged. "You're one to talk."

Chel gladly accepted the wine offered to her by another servant as I refused it. "I admit, I haven't been the most pleasant to be around lately, but I've been hurting. I've said some things I regret."

"Maybe I've been hurting too."

She clasped her goblet of wine in one hand with her head tilted in thought before asking, "What's the one thing you want the most?"

I swallowed the juicy, smoked meat and replied, "To see my king and queen returned to their thrones. What do you want, Lady Water?

Or should I say, Lady Wine?"

She made a rude face and took a big sip from her goblet. "I want King Zaeden dead, and I won't stop until the deed is done."

"Then our goals are the same."

"Yes."

"I'm surprised you're not worried about Percifal too. He is your brother." I directed the conversation back to her.

"What makes you think I'm not?"

I saw it then, the dark circles beneath her eyes... the colour missing from her cheeks. She worried as much as Zephyra on the inside. I hoped he lived... for her sake. The realization hit me like a bolt of lightning. I wasn't supposed to care about these people. I only worked with them to fulfill my own needs. But there it was, that seed of morality.

Chel's gaze drifted to where Zephyra sat with Queen Adelaide. The fire elemental studied her food, but she'd barely touched it... barely noticed the conversations going on around her. Queen Adelaide was grinning at something King Peyton had said to their table. Her grin disappeared when the door to the dining hall flew open. Everyone turned to stare.

The crystal goblet in Chel's hand shattered in her grip when she saw the middle-aged blond woman enter with a silver-eyed king dressed in black.

Our enemy had found us.

CHAPTER 24

Z EPHYRA'S CHAIR CRASHED to the floor as she leaped up. "Mother?"

The blond woman with eyes the same emerald shade as her daughter's gave her a cold, cruel smile. "Zephyra. I'd heard rumours you'd returned. How lovely to see you."

Zephyra ignored her words. "Mother, what are you doing? King Zaeden is a *tyrant!*"

King Zaeden had used some type of cosmetic powder to cover up the black veins on his skin. He wore a gold and silver crown encrusted with obsidian jewels. He no longer appeared gaunt. No, an unnatural strength emanated from him, and a terrifying power flashed within his gaze. The unnatural silver had replaced the dark blue of his irises permanently.

"King Zaeden," the woman dripping with an ageless sort of beauty started, "has agreed to make me his queen, which is more than anyone else has ever offered me." She raised her chin to look down her nose at her daughter.

"You will pay the price for this treason, Mirrabel," Queen Adelaide said to Zephyra's mother, moving to stand by the fire elemental's side.

Zephyra's bottom lip trembled, but her eyes filled with a hatred I'd have thought her incapable of bearing. "You're stupid. He's using you."

"Where's your army, Zaeden? You think you can take my kingdom alone?" Queen Adelaide questioned, her voice booming through the hall.

King Zaeden presented her with a sly smile. "Why take the time to bring a full army when I could come alone and walk right into your glorious palace?"

Before Queen Adelaide had the chance to answer, the goblets began to rattle on their tables. In a flash of blurred motion and colours, Chel leaped from her seat, twisting toward King Zaeden and Mirrabel. All the wine and water rose from the goblets and flew toward the king in a giant red torpedo. The spinning liquid, about to smash into King Zaeden, met an invisible barrier. It splashed to the floor, staining the stone a deep burgundy as it pooled around his feet.

King Zaeden's laugh, laced with cruelty, was enough to make me want to jump out of my skin. "Chelela," he began. "We wondered where you'd gotten to. It appears Thaimis didn't make it out of the battle. Tell us, where's your traitorous brother?"

"I. Will. Kill. You!" she screamed, but it was Zephyra who shot a burning ball of blinding, white-blue flames at the mad king and her mother. The fire hit the invisible barrier and instantly burned out.

"So you're a Solis royal," he cocked his head at Zephyra. "If we'd have known this when you showed up at our palace, we would have held onto you."

"Leave this kingdom at once." Queen Adelaide strode up to him, hands clenched at the sides of her elegant, ruby red skirts.

"Or?" he challenged.

Queen Adelaide bared her teeth at him and ordered, "Seize him!"

But before any of the guards who'd surrounded the mad king and Mirrabel could move, King Zaeden yelled, *"Caperus!"* I'd never heard the word and knew it must have been a spell when a thick, white fog rose from the floor and shot straight into Queen Adelaide. Her eyes glowed a green-blue before dimming. *"Caperus."* King Zaeden shot again and directed the next plume of fog at Constable Creighton.

Another guard who was about to strike King Zaeden paused when Queen Adelaide held her hand up. "Halt!" The guard froze in his tracks, sword still raised. And then the queen stretched out her arm and pointed a finger at Zephyra, Chelela and me. "Kill them."

The confused guards glanced at each other, not sure what to do. It was treason to refuse their queen's command, but they knew she wasn't herself.

King Zaeden didn't waste a moment. He used their hesitation to work his spell on half the hall, including King Peyton. Mirrabel smiled like a little girl who'd just been gifted a pony.

I grabbed onto Chel's elbow and shouted, *"Run!"*

If King Zaeden recognized me from Terra, he didn't show it.

Swearing, Chel grabbed hold of Zephyra's hand and we bolted for the door. Zephyra knew her way around best. She led us around corner after corner. We didn't stop to look back, but I heard the guards trailing us. A bell of alarm tolled, echoing throughout the corridors. We weren't going to make it to the palace entrance.

Zephyra came to a sudden halt and pushed me and Chel into an empty chamber. She slammed the door shut and bolted it. Her chest rose and fell as she breathed deeply. "We need another way out." Her eyes moved to the window.

"No," Chel gasped. "It's too far down. Unless…" She looked pointedly at me. "Unless your vines are strong enough to hold a person."

"They're strong enough," I confirmed, rushing to the window. No glass rested in its frame, but the iron bars… those would prove a problem. It wouldn't be long before the guards discovered our hiding place.

"I can take care of the bars," Zephyra said, rubbing her palms together as she stepped up to the window. She closed her eyes and placed her hands on the bars. The iron turned red beneath her skin. The heat spread so every piece of iron on the window changed colour. Red, then orange, then white. The bars turned so bright, I had to look away. When the light dimmed, I saw the bars had melted into nothing but a bubbling puddle of black iron.

The guards tried to open the door. Realizing we'd locked it, they began pounding their fists on the thick wood. I moved to the window and peered outside. I could barely make out the moonlit ground far below. Holding my breath, I reached for my power. An instant later, a thick, twisting vine shot up and hooked itself over the windowsill.

The wood door started to crack against the hard pounding. I looked at the two elementals and said, "I'll go first."

Zephyra nodded. "Hurry!"

I loosened a breath and climbed out the window. The vine held strong. I slid down, as quickly as I could without falling. My arms and legs ached by the time I reached the ground. At least I could try to help the other two if they began to fall.

Zephyra's feet appeared out the window. She slid down the vine fast... too fast. I'd never be able to catch her at that speed. I used my power to call another vine up. The second vine wrapped around her ankle as she lost her grip on the first. She dangled in the air from the vine as it slowly lowered her. Face red, she reached the ground safely. Though, her hair and gown were out of sorts, and she appeared like she was about to retch. She adjusted her skirts and cleared her throat. "Thank you."

Chel was already half way down the first vine. On my command, it unhooked and lowered Chel to the ground with us. Her arms shook from the exertion of climbing half-ways down.

The bell still tolled. Sheer chaos had erupted inside the palace by the sounds of the screaming and crashing. A guard leaned out the window of the chamber we'd climbed from. He had no way down now that the vine was gone. "Outside, now!" he shouted to the other guards.

We had escaped from one of the side wings of the palace so we sprinted for the trees. Solis had no wall around it like Terra, but guards did patrol the perimeter. We were stopped by two who were on duty. Staring down at us from their horses, they drew their swords.

"Where do you think you're going?" A weathered guard who I'd have guessed to be in his late forties, asked.

"Let us pass," Chel ordered, her fingers flexed, ready to use her power.

"We cannot let you pass if you're an enemy of Solis," the younger guard put in.

The thunderous footsteps of the guards from inside the palace caught my attention as they charged outside and stampeded for us.

Zephyra stepped up to the two guards. "I am Zephyra Caldura of Solis, cousin of Queen Adelaide. Now, step aside."

The guards smirked at each other. The older one turned his face back to her. "We only take orders from Queen Adelaide or Constable Creighton."

"Please," Zephyra begged. "Your comrades and queen are being controlled by dark spirits."

The younger guard pressed his lips together, considering her statement.

We didn't have time for this. I felt for my power. A vine shot up and wrapped itself around the horse's ankle that the older guard rode. The black horse reared back, causing the guard to drop his sword so he could grab the saddle. But it was too late. The guards from the palace had reached us.

Glowing eyes promising brutal death advanced. My heart stopped. We were done for.

Chel threw up a spray of water, and the other horse bolted with the younger guard still on its back.

Zephyra stared, unblinking, at the guards who'd once protected her home. As the one closest to us readied to swing his blade, hot, hungry flames burst between us and the group of possessed men and women. Numb to pain, those who'd caught fire still came at us, flesh burning into ashes. It was enough. Zephyra's power had given us the chance we'd needed.

The three of us ran through the trees, burning guards chasing us until they breathed no more. That they felt no pain as the bright golden fire ate them alive was a small mercy. Or perhaps they did deep inside where a small part of the real them still dwelled, untouched by the dark spirit who'd invaded their mind and body.

We sprinted, dodging branches, not sparing one glance backward. We didn't stop until we could run no more.

Gasping for breath, Zephyra bent down and retched between her knees. She put her arms over her head, her body shaking with sobs.

Chel crouched down beside her, rubbing her back.

The fire elemental gathered herself enough to spit. She wiped her eyes. "Those people were good… were *my* people."

"You did what you had to," Chel stated. "War claims many victims."

"I hate it."

"I know." Chel helped her back up. "Believe me. I know."

Her slight nod was the only indication she understood her friend thought of the former lover she'd killed herself. "We need to find Percifal," Zephyra said, changing the subject.

"He could be anywhere," I argued.

"We have to *try.*" The fire elemental was nearly in tears again.

"We will head toward Terra and see if we can find him before we go on to Ventosa." Chel brushed a lock of dark hair off her sweaty forehead.

"This is my fault." Zephyra choked back a sob. "If we'd left for Ventosa like you wanted, we'd all be together. I'll never forgive myself if he's dead."

Chel narrowed her eyes at me as she answered her. "It's not your fault. Let's go find my brother."

"Fine," I said to them both. "But first we need horses."

"There's a village on the way," Zephyra offered as she began walking. "We'll find horses there."

We followed her through the trees. The summer night was warm and dry, the forest thinner than the one surrounding Terra. Not as many predators to worry about either. We navigated our way north until we cleared the cluster of aromatic pine trees. I ignored the sharp pain in the bottom of my feet as I stepped over the hard, rocky terrain.

We came to a village darkened by night. Only a few torches still burned in the quiet streets. Most had gone home for the night to sleep before arising for work the next morning. Only a few drunks straggled behind at the old taverns that kept their doors open for people such as them, addicted to the thrall of wine and spirits. We came up to the side of one such tavern where two horses tied to a rail waited for their owners. Zephyra marched up to the white one and began untying its rope.

"What are you doing?" Chel demanded.

"Taking these horses. We need them more than their drunken owners do. Are you going to help me?"

When Chel didn't move, I stepped up to untie the bay standing next to the horse Zephyra led away from the rail. "One of us will have to ride together," I commented, finishing loosening the knot in the rope.

Chel glanced at Zephyra's puffy skirts. "I don't think there's enough room in the saddle for both our gowns."

Zephyra put her foot in the stirrup and answered, "You ride with him. It's not proper for me to ride with another man."

Chel rolled her eyes. "Fine." She shoved her dark hair out of her way and then said to me, "Let me on first."

I held the horse still while she pulled herself into the saddle, and then I settled in behind her. I'd never ridden with a second rider. I awkwardly adjusted myself, but no matter my position, her body rested right against mine. I tried to ignore the way her warmth seeped into my body and heated my blood. It was difficult. I was a male with a beating heart after all.

One of the drunks stumbled out of the tavern in time to see us take off. "Come back, you thieves!" he hollered, but it was useless. He was a disappearing dot in the street.

We rode through the night, galloping only as much as we dared without putting the horses in danger. When the sky transformed into a paler shade of violet, we stopped at a small stream to let ourselves, and the horses, drink.

"So that was your mother," Chel remarked when Zephyra came up beside her to cup her hands full of water and drink.

"Yes," Zephyra replied, drying her hands off on the skirts of her gown.

"No wonder you ran away from Solis."

Zephyra stood and smoothed wisps of her fiery hair back. "I should have let her be executed all those springs ago when she planned to kill Addy."

Chel pressed her lips together, questions rolling across her face. But she simply said, "She's your mother."

"Zephyra's right," I chimed in from where I let the two horses graze. "She should've turned her mother in if she knew she was a traitor." It was a poor excuse for her to leave her kingdom. One's own problems had a way of catching up with them. It seemed it was her turn to face them now.

Zephyra's shoulders slouched. "She—she let King Zaeden in, and now Adelaide's in danger. Do you think he'll hurt her?"

Chel scowled at me as she walked over to Zephyra to put her hand on her back. "No, he needs her. She's under his control. I don't think he'll hurt your cousin while the dark spirit resides inside her."

Zephyra sniffed but nodded her head.

I wasn't so sure about her reassurance, but my honesty wasn't welcome so I kept my opinions to myself. "Come on. We've tarried long enough."

I tangled with Chel's mass of skirts each time we mounted. "If it were up to me," she bit out, "I'd be wearing trousers. Unfortunately, it's improper attire for a lady to wear at court."

"Perhaps we can trade some of these jewels Queen Adelaide gave us at the next village for coin and supplies," Zephyra offered.

"Yes, a splendid idea. What other use is there for such baubles? I once enjoyed my gowns and jewels, but I've realized their unimportance as of late."

"I still like my gowns." Zephyra absentmindedly smoothed her own skirts.

I silently wished I had my sword. We weren't permitted to bear arms when dining with Queen Adelaide so I'd left my sword in the guest chamber. Thankfully, I'd hidden a dagger in my boot. I knew Chel and Zephyra had hidden blades as well. We were never fully unarmed. Our best weapons, though, were our powers.

We led our horses through the market of the next village we came upon, bartering jewels for coin and goods. We'd need coin to obtain furs closer to Ventosa. The kingdom of air was high up in the Acuties Mountains where snow never fully melted. Anything to keep us warm would be valuable. The villages in the southern parts of Sarantoa didn't sell such items unless it was autumn or winter.

We bought saddlebags and packed them full until they nearly burst at the seams. The jewels we sold were worth a lot. The merchant's eyes had sparkled when we'd shown them to him. It was his lucky day.

We paid a farmer a small sum to let us have an afternoon nap in his barn. He frowned at the request, but accepted the payment. We had enough coin to get us to Ventosa, but we had to be smart with it.

We travelled through the grassy plains for days. Used to the heat, I basked in the summer sun shining down on us. Chel, however, hated it. She'd grown up in the cold, damp coastal weather of Aquila. I felt the stickiness of the sweat coating her bare arms as I steered our horse across the fields. She often complained the sun was going to be the death of her. I poured water down her back at one point so she'd stop complaining, almost getting us thrown off the horse. Zephyra tried not to giggle but failed. At least someone was having a good time.

Animal life disappeared the closer we ventured to Terra. An eerie silence fell like a blanket as we entered the forest surrounding the kingdom of earth. Not one bird… not even one insect could be seen or heard. Even more sinister, the usually leafy green trees had turned brown and wilted. It didn't make sense, until I recalled the words of the soldier who'd escaped from Terra to seek refuge in Solis. He'd said the forest around Terra had begun to die. I pushed down my panic as I realized the rest of what he'd told us was probably true. I didn't want to know what now lurked in these woods.

We came to a point where the horses would go no further. The bay mare Chel and I rode, tossed her head in the air and pawed at the ground when we tried to make her move forward. Zephyra's mount reared, clearly freaked out.

We dismounted and I said to both of them, "One of us has to stay here with the horses. The other two will go in further to see if we can find Percifal. I know you don't want to hear this, Zephyra, but it's a long shot. These woods cover a vast amount of space, and we don't even know if he's alive or what could be waiting for us in there."

She sighed. "I understand. If we don't find him soon, we'll go to Ventosa."

I handed Chel the horse's reins. "We'll make haste. If we don't return soon, leave without us. Here." I reached into my pocket and pulled out my compass. "Take this."

Chel frowned at the compass. "Who put you in charge?"

I stretched my arm out further. "I know these woods better than the two of you, and are you really going to make Zephyra wait here while we seek out her lover?"

"He's my brother." Her gaze flicked to Zephyra's sullen face. She snatched the compass from my hand. "Fine, but make haste."

"Yes, Lady Water."

Thunder and lightning filled her eyes as she gave me an annoyed look, but I turned away and marched past Zephyra. "Let's go."

Dead leaves crunched under out feet as we cautiously stepped into the dying forest. The smell of decay was so bad I almost gagged. The sky was as grey as smoke, not a shred of blue in sight. A crack echoed as Zephyra stepped on a fallen branch, causing her to start. She felt the same sense of impending doom as I did. We'd entered a world void of life. If this was only a taste of the dark world of Mnyama, what was coming to the rest of Sarantoa… nothing would survive.

An inhumane screech had us both halting to stare in the direction of the sound. The hush that followed was more unnerving.

"I should never have let him go," Zephyra breathed out on a whisper.

I didn't have any words of comfort to offer her, so I didn't say anything.

The air had turned cold and dry upon my skin, as though not a drop of water were to be found in the entire forest.

No matter how much distance we put between us and where we'd left Chel, we found no sign of Percifal—or anyone else for that matter.

About to suggest we turn back or risk becoming lost, a dark shape flashed through the trees. And then another not far behind it. I froze and grabbed Zephyra by the arm. She'd seen it too. Her face transformed into a mask of horror as the shapes loomed closer to us. They were not human.

We both turned and bolted, darting between trees and trying not to stumble on rocks. Celestia help us if one of us fell.

Faster. We needed to run faster.

The creatures gained on us. I could hear them snarling at our backs. We had to fight or they'd tear us apart from behind.

I stopped and spun, the warmth of my power rising. A vine smashed through the hard ground between us and the creatures. The vine caught the closest creature, with slick, black skin and a long snout, around its waist. It screeched at me, saliva dripping off its hooked, yellow fangs. Eyes the colour of fire watched me, promising nothing but a brutal, painful demise.

Its partner still chased Zephyra. She screamed from somewhere behind me. I tightened the vines grip on the creature… *demon* suited the thing better, but I could feel the vine dying. It was as if *I* was dying from the center of my core. My insides churned, my blood turning to sludge within my veins. The vine had begun to wilt where it touched the demon. I had to let go before my own power killed me from the inside out.

The vine disintegrated into dust as I released my hold on my power and snatched my dagger from my boot.

A flash of orange light to my left followed by an ear-piercing shriek told me Zephyra had thrown a ball of fire at her pursuer.

As the demon before me lunged forward, teeth bared and claws out, I jabbed my blade into its face.

It stumbled back, clawing where the dagger stuck out just below its eye. Dark green blood oozed from the wound around the blade.

It noticed me watching and gave up on the blade, snarling at me again. The demon narrowed its orange eyes and prepared to jump, but a swirl of sparking flames spiraled around it, engulfing its smooth, hairless body. The sounds erupting from it as the black skin melted from its bones had me and Zephyra both covering our ears.

Then everything but the crackling flames fell silent.

I'd have been that thing's meal if it weren't for Zephyra's fire. I faced her and huffed, "Thank you."

Her body trembled as she replied, "Let's get out of here."

"I'm sorry for..." I stopped, clamping my mouth shut. A misty, white shape drifted through the trees behind her and my stomach sank. Not again.

To my utter shock, the misty shaped formed into a shining white horse. No, I realized as I squinted to get a closer look, not a horse. A unicorn, so white it casted light through the dark woods, tossed its mane.

I pointed. My jaw dropped, unable to believe my own eyes.

Zephyra followed my finger to the where the unicorn watched us. Her eyes went huge as she breathed, "Antarus." She slowly tip-toed closer to the mystical being.

I'd heard the legends of Celestia's unicorn, Antarus. It was said she'd sent it to our world to help one of her first elementals. I worried this was a trap though. We didn't know if Antarus was real. I tried to tell Zephyra as much but she was already half-way to the magnificent beast. I jogged after her to catch up.

Almost to the unicorn, she reached out to touch its nose, but it shifted away.

"Zephyra," I reached for her wrist. "We don't know if it's Antarus. This could be a trap."

She didn't seem to hear me as she slowly stepped closer to the shimmering white unicorn, cooing gently to it. Completely enthralled, she reached out a hand again to touch it.

But then it vanished.

Sorrow and confusion crossed Zephyra's face right before a pair of hands reached out and pulled her into a cavern opening that had been hidden by dead branches and rocks.

CHAPTER 25

I COULDN'T WASTE time returning to Chel for help. Whoever, or whatever, lived inside the cavern could have killed Zephyra by then. I had no choice but to enter the dark cavern of packed earth and stone that the unicorn had led us to. Zephyra's muffled cries came from further down the narrow cavern as I jumped down through the hole. The fall wasn't far. I could only imagine what held onto her. The hands I'd caught a glimpse of appeared to be human, but it could've been an illusion. Surely a demon as horrendous as the ones who'd previously attacked us had taken her.

I thanked the goddess when torchlight revealed the faces of two human women trying to calm Zephyra down. Once my eyes adjusted to the dimness of the cavern, I realized I recognized them. They were the witches I'd ordered to stop using magic, the older mother and her full grown daughter who'd strove to become with child. They'd escaped the kingdom alive.

"*You!*" the older woman with webs of wrinkles spreading out from the corners of each eye accused. "You forbade us from using magic. How are we to defend ourselves against such darkness?"

I held both hands up in surrender as the women waited for my answer. "I come in peace. I didn't know such darkness threatened our kingdom when I warned you to stop. I was only following our king's orders."

"We're worse off because of you," the daughter spat. Her tangled mousy brown hair reminded me of a bird's nest. "You destroyed potions that could've helped us against these demons."

"Again," I reiterated. "I'm sorry."

"No use for apologies," the older woman said with a note of defeat. "Help us with this man if you wish to do something right. We found him injured nearly a fortnight ago, but his healing's been slow."

Zephyra had been quiet up until that point. She broke her silence by saying, "Take us to him."

The witches wasted no time. They led us farther into the cavern, toward the sound of trickling water. I didn't believe it possible until I saw it, but there it was, a slow but steady stream of water running beneath the dying forest. And off to its side, in a bed of cushiony moss, lay the wounded man. The man's head had been shaved, his dark hair only beginning to grow back. A dark beard covered half of his face, and I wouldn't have recognized Percifal lying there in tattered clothing, which had been ripped away from his wounds, if not for Zephyra's stifled cry. *"Percifal!"* She dropped to her knees beside him and inspected the wounds that had been covered with a thick, colourless salve.

"You know this man?" the older witch questioned.

"Yes." Tears gleamed in her emerald eyes as Zephyra looked up at her. "He's the love of my life, and we've been searching for him. Oh, thank Celestia! I knew it was Antarus. She sent him here to guide us."

I couldn't quite believe it. Yet, neither could I deny it. We *had* seen a horse with a gold horn. And it'd led us to this cavern. Maybe Celestia was aiding us.

Zephyra wiped Percifal's forehead with a piece of material one of the witches had dipped in the cool stream. "Percifal, can you hear me? It's Phyra."

At first he didn't stir, but then a moan escaped his throat. His eyes opened a crack. "Zephyra?"

"Yes, it's me. I've found you." She pushed him back down as he tried to sit up. "No, stay down. You're weak."

"I—I don't know how you found me, but thank goddess you're here."

Zephyra glanced up at me then. "I had a little help. But tell me, what happened? How did you end up like this? Did you see King Zaeden?"

Percifal winced as he adjusted himself on the bed of moss. "I spotted King Zaeden leaving Terra. He didn't see me. I followed him, but then these… I don't know what they were—demons I suppose—they attacked me. I thought I was dead." He glanced down at a red gash in his ribs, now cleaned and covered in salve. It would leave a nasty scar. There were more, shallower, wounds on his arms and legs. "I was nearly dead when the witches found me," he finished.

"I'm surprised the demons didn't eat you," I commented. Zephyra shot me a disapproving look. "What? The ones we fought seemed like they wanted to have us for dinner." I tilted my chin down to stare at Percifal. "What did the demons look like?"

"They were nothing of this world, more like shadows with claws like knives. Once they're upon you, there's nothing solid to fight. I found myself engulfed in a black fog, slashed at from every direction. I went down, and the demons slipped away. I passed out and woke to these witches dragging me down here. If not for them, I *would* be dead."

Zephyra rose, dusting the dirt from her hands, and walked right up to the older witch and threw her arms around her. "Thank you," she said into the witch's greying hair.

Taken aback at first, the older witch stiffened, but she patted Zephyra's back lightly. "We couldn't leave him out there to die."

"We need to get him out of this forest," I said to them, and then to Percifal, "Think you can walk?"

Pain was written on his face, but he nodded anyway. "With help, yes."

It took the four of us to get him off the ground. Once he was on his feet, Zephyra and I were able to hold him up enough that he could walk—slowly.

"Take this with you." The older witch held out a jar filled with the salve she'd dressed his wounds with. "It'll help hasten the healing and alleviate the pain."

Zephyra accepted the jar. "What about you?"

"We've got enough jarred food to last us a few more fortnights," the older witch answered. She set her gaze on her daughter. "There are others trapped like us. If we can find them, we may have a chance at out-smarting those demons."

Her daughter's jaw tightened as she looked away.

"You could come with us," Zephyra offered, adjusting Percifal's arm over her shoulders. I wished she'd get on with it.

"No," the older woman shook her head. "But thank you for the offer."

"She wants to wait for other witches," her daughter put in, throwing her arms up. "It's foolish if you ask me, but I can't make her change her mind."

"Mind your tongue," her mother reprimanded. "I won't abandon my sisters."

"At least tell us your names so we may remember you when this is all over," Zephyra said.

I scoffed, but she ignored me. Percifal was already having a tough time staying up right, and we still had a ways to go.

"It's Lucile, and my daughter is Emeline."

Zephyra gave the old witch a nod. "I'm Zephyra. Percifal and I thank you both. May Celestia be with you."

"And you," Lucile replied, a genuine smile stretching out her thinning lips.

Finally, we started down the cavern back toward the entrance. If we ran into anymore demons, I doubted we would've all made it out of that forest. For the first time since I could remember, I sent a silent prayer to Celestia. She did send Antarus to help us, so maybe she'd listen to my plea.

"Where's my sister?" Percifal managed to get out, dragging his feet as the opening of the cavern came into view.

"We had to leave her with the horses," Zephyra explained, wiping sweat from her brow. "They refused to come further in these woods."

I used a vine to carry the three of us up out of the cavern. Dragging Percifal up would've been nearly impossible without harming him and possibly us.

"Ah, mine did too," Percifal huffed when we once again stood on solid ground. "He threw me from his back when I tried to push him. "Took off and left me on my own."

I raised an eyebrow. "Can't say I blame him."

"Me neither," Percifal admitted.

We didn't speak the rest of the way, saving the rest of our strength to get Percifal out of those woods. I'd strapped his sword to my back. His other supplies the horse had taken off with. The leather scabbard bit into my back with Percifal's weight on it.

In its unnatural state, I didn't recognize the forest I'd once known so well. I worried we'd become lost, but the smoky sky eventually gave way to a deep shade of blue, and the wilting trees thinned. Celestia must have heard my prayer because we didn't run into anymore demons wishing to eat us for dinner.

We came across the tracks we'd left in the dirt and followed them out of the woods.

We saw the two horses first, and then Chel. She sat against a tree, her cobalt hair ruffled, and her gown dirty and torn. A dark storm brewed in her eyes, but she took one look at her brother and all the anger drained from her face. She jumped up and rushed to him. "You're alive," she choked out, pushing me aside so she could inspect him herself. She froze when she saw the wound on his ribs. "We need to get him to an inn so he can heal."

"What happened to you?" Percifal rasped, indicating his sister's dishevelled state.

"I'm fine," she assured him. "I ran into some sort of flying creature not from this world. My water was slow to come through the dying earth. It got me with its claws before I could drown it, is all."

"You shouldn't have been left alone," Percifal made sure Zephyra and I both heard him loud and clear.

"I'm *fine*," Chel repeated.

I untied Zephyra's horse, not bothering to argue with Percifal, and said to the other two, "Help me get him up."

The women brought him up beside the horse, and Zephyra helped him lift his leg and placed his foot in the stirrup. Percifal grabbed a hold of the saddle and pulled himself, letting out a cry of pain while the rest of us helped push him on. Zephyra swung up behind him.

Chel scrunched up her face as I climbed up behind her in our own saddle. "You reek of decay."

The smell of the rotting forest stuck to our hair and clothes, but without a bath and change of attire, there was nothing we could do. "Then hold your breath," I said, taking up the reins to move the horse forward behind Zephyra and Percifal.

She shifted away from my chest as much as she could without falling off.

Once we were well away from the forest surrounding Terra, Chel asked, "How did you find him?" I knew she meant Percifal.

A puff of air escaped from between my lips. "Don't laugh... a unicorn led us to the cavern he'd been taken to by two witches. They saved him."

"A unicorn…" Chel began.

Having heard our conversation, Zephyra twisted in her saddle, careful not to wake a dozing Percifal. "Antarus. Celestia sent him to us." She was convinced we'd seen Celestia's warrior unicorn.

Chel stayed quiet for a moment, contemplative. "Either you're both trying to fool me, or you truly did see Antarus," she replied.

"If mermaids and demons are real, is it really so shocking unicorns are too?" Zephyra pointed out, turning her head back to steer her horse.

"I suppose not," Chel admitted.

"You said your water was slow to come to you?" I asked Chel.

"Yes, the land is drying up, making the water hard to call… a disadvantage of my power." When I didn't say anything else, she peered over her shoulder at me. "Why?"

I didn't meet her eyes. "Because my vine didn't live long once it touched the demon I'd fought. Actually, if it weren't for Zephyra, I could be dead right now. Seems her power is the most reliable against Mnyama's demons."

"You're welcome," Zephyra said over her shoulder.

"It was spectacular, the way you shaped your flames," I admired.

"Is that a compliment?" Chel asked, utterly shocked.

"I suppose it is."

Zephyra spoke up, adjusting herself in the saddle, her skirts draped like a blanket over the horse. "I've never done that with my flames before. I acted on instinct. Even I was surprised by the way they formed around the demon."

"You're gaining more control," Chel said to her. "The more we use our powers, the more control over them we'll all have."

"Fire seems to be the only useful power in the dark world," I pointed out again.

"That's because fire is *part* of the dark world," Chel said. "I doubt it will be effective on its own against Vesirus himself. We'll need all four to beat him back to Mnyama."

"I hope you're right. I hope we can send him back to his forsaken world," I replied, steering our horse between two boulders.

We came to a small village with a lake. In the distance behind, the northern mountains stood proud. Those mountains were the beginning of our trek up to the cold peeks of never-ending winter, to the kingdom of air. We couldn't make the journey north until Percifal had healed well enough.

We found a cozy inn just off the lake with a cramped tavern on the bottom floor.

"Two rooms for seven sunrises please," Zephyra told the innkeeper, handing him the right amount of coin. "We may need to stay longer," she added. "We'll give you more coin if needed."

The short, chubby man, whose cheeks were red and shiny, set down the book he'd been reading and accepted her coin. "Uh-huh."

"Two rooms?" Chel questioned her as we followed the innkeeper upstairs.

"Yes," Zephyra confirmed, helping Percifal along. "One for me and Percifal, one for the two of you. We can't afford to be wasting our coin just so you can both have your own room."

Chel grumbled something inaudible, and I reminded her, "You didn't mind when you were drunk in Solis."

She gave me a rude gesture.

"It's late," the innkeeper said as he scratched behind his ear, reminding me of a cat. "I'll get the maid to bring you some food."

"Thank you, good sir," Zephyra smiled at him and disappeared with Percifal into the room he'd unlocked for them.

The innkeeper moved on to a door further down the hall, with me and Chel in tow. He opened the door and let us inside. "Eve will be up with some stew soon."

We thanked the aloof little man. He waved us off, waddling back down the stairs to return to his book.

The room had seen better days, but it would do. An old mattress laid to the far side against a faded blue wall. A chunk had been broken off the corner of the table beside it, and the window was covered in a layer of dust.

The mattress beneath the yellowed blankets sank as Chel lowered herself down onto the edge and started unlacing her corset from the front. I turned the other way as she shrugged out of her worn gown. "Don't worry about me," she stated. "I haven't a shy bone in me. Gwon saw to that."

"Gwon?" I turned to frown at her. She still wore her undergarments, but the lines of her body showed beneath the thin fabric. "What in Mnyama were you doing there?"

She shrugged one shoulder and sat back further on the bed, curling her legs underneath her. "It's a long story. One I'd rather not get into right now."

Someone knocked on the door. I opened it and found a quaint, little maid holding a tray with two bowls of soup, two buns and a pitcher of water with two empty cups. I let her inside and thanked her once she'd set the tray down on the old worn table.

Keeping her eyes averted, she rushed back out the door and squeaked, "G'night."

I joined Chel on the bed, as there were no chairs, and placed the tray between us. I dipped a stale bun into the thin stew and bit into it... bland, but edible.

We ate our meal in silence and washed it down with cool water.

Chel placed the tray back on the table and went to her saddle bag. She fumbled around until she found what she'd been searching for. "There you are," she said, dangling the metallic flask between two fingers. She settled back down on the bed, pulled the lid off the flask and took a swig.

"Where'd you get that?" My eyes followed the flask in her hand as she held it out for me.

"It was in that drunkard's saddlebag we stole the horse from."

I grimaced.

"Don't worry, I washed it off," she assured me.

I sighed. "Why not? Just one sip." Her lips curled up playfully as I accepted the flask. I sipped slowly, cautiously swallowing. As soon as the liquid hit the back of my throat, I sputtered and coughed. "Strong stuff," I said when I was able to speak again.

"Whiskey usually is," she eyed me, taking the flask back and recapping it. "Why do you think you deserve to die?" she asked frankly, surprising me with the turn of conversation. At my blank stare, she clarified, "In Solis, you told me you deserve to die before you walked out of the bedchamber."

Ah, that. I leaned back on my arms on the mattress, taking a moment to think of the best way to answer her. "Because my heart is dark, and I've done terrible things to all sorts of people."

She tilted her head at me, causing her loose, dark curls to fall off her pale, bare shoulder. "I don't believe darkness is the only thing filling your heart, not really."

"No?"

She smiled. "No. Even the smallest of sparks can ignite in the dark."

Her words, the way she was looking at me… I felt that spark as the bond between us flickered and came to life. This time, I leaned forward and brushed my lips against hers. She responded by pressing her lips closer and returning the kiss. But this time it was she who pulled back. A tear fell off her cheek like a single rain drop.

"Not the reaction a man hopes for when he kisses a lady," I said as she brushed away the wetness left from the tear.

She looked away and shook her head. "I'm sorry. It's just that—that I've been so sad for so long. I never thought I'd feel this way again." Tears filled her sapphire eyes.

"What way?" I asked with curiosity. It was so strange to see her like this. So vulnerable.

"Alive," she breathed.

I raised a brow. "I make you feel alive?"

She laughed at that. "Shut up."

A little bit of the darkness lifted as she watched me with those glittering eyes. "What was he like?" I asked. "Thaimis, I mean."

She ran both hands through her hair and then shook her head. "He was an ass." Her lips lifted a little at the corners. "But he was so much more than that. He was a good man, and I loved him. I loved him and I *killed* him." She looked down, but not before I saw the shame written on her face… shame and regret.

I touched her hand and tried to understand. "I'm sure you had no other choice."

"I didn't mean to." Her voice cracked as she lifted her face back up to meet my eyes. "He was possessed by one of those dark spirits. If I didn't stop him, he would've—he would've killed me and then he would've moved on to more innocent people."

Nothing I could have said would've made her feel better, so I offered her the only thing I could think of, a secret of my own. "The only woman I've ever loved—maybe the only person—died never knowing how I felt about her."

Chel leaned back, thoughtful. "I'm sure she knew."

"No, she didn't… because I never told her. I believed she deserved better than me. I let my belief get in the way. And when King Zaeden brought his army of possessed soldiers to Terra, she died right before my eyes. She died, and I couldn't save her." I should've saved her. I realized then, finally admitted to myself, that I felt responsible for her death. It was foolish, but there it was. Maybe I had been right. I never deserved her love. I set my jaw and grabbed the flask off the mattress and took another drink.

"What was her name?"

"Blaise," I offered in a strained voice. I hadn't spoken her name since the battle in Terra. I hadn't even had the chance to tell Ger of her death. I hoped he was safe where he had gone with Queen Nicola. I didn't let myself consider the fact they could both be dead too.

Chel smirked. "I suppose we have something in common."

"That's not funny."

She tossed her locks over her shoulder and got up off the bed. "Come on. Let's not spend the night wallowing in our regrets. I'm tired of trying to drink the pain away. It's a vicious circle of misery, exhaustion and pounding headaches. Revenge will taste much sweeter."

"Where are you going?" I asked.

"You still smell of that wretched forest, and there's a lake just outside. I'm not sleeping in this bed with you until you've dunked yourself in fresh water."

"Someone may see you in your under-garments," I warned.

She waved her hand. "Pff. It's late. Everyone's inside their rooms."

I set the flask on the table and grinned. "As you wish, Lady Water."

It turned out everyone had retired for the night except for the innkeeper, who sat at his desk behind a pile of paperwork. He gaped at Chel as she strutted passed him and out the door. If she'd noticed his gawking stare, she didn't care.

We strolled through the grass and down a packed dirt path to the nearby lake. We had to watch our steps to avoid stumbling down the steep, rocky beach. The warm summer air was still that night, but when Chel walked into the water she yelped and giggled. I discovered the lake was indeed cold as I dove in further to catch up to her. My body quickly became used to the temperature.

I couldn't remember the last time I'd felt so refreshed. Glittering starlight reflected off the dark surface surrounding us. Chel beamed at me as she treaded water into the middle of the lake. I'd never seen anyone so delighted. This was her element. I couldn't imagine how she managed being so far from the ocean she'd been raised next to.

I stayed where my feet could touch the bottom of the lake. I wasn't a good swimmer and didn't want to embarrass myself.

"Oh, I've missed this," Chel exclaimed, spinning in a circle. She sunk deeper and dunked her head into the water. She didn't come back up right away. If I didn't know she could breathe underwater, I'd have panicked, believing her to be drowning.

A loon wailed from somewhere on the other side of the lake. An eerie, yet beautiful song. So peaceful there in that part of Sarantoa while darkness consumed the land in the south… changing into a place which resembled the dark world of Mnyama.

Chel broke the surface, water droplets flying from her slick, black hair like tiny, iridescent crystals. She brushed the water off her face and lifted her gaze to the stars.

My blood warmed as she studied me from the middle of the lake. I needed to keep Vesirus from taking Sarantoa from us all. Not only for my unborn cousin, the heir to my kingdom, but for Chel, and for the other elementals whom I'd begun to care about. They were the only ones who understood what it was like to be different… to have great power. I'd lost Blaise. I wouldn't lose them too.

When my fingers were wrinkled, Chel had finally had her fill of the lake and reluctantly agreed to go back inside. The innkeeper was gone from his desk when we'd returned.

I peeled off my sopping wet clothes, leaving only my undergarments on and crawled under the not so soft blanket. Chel was perfectly happy sleeping in her dampened undergarments with no blanket. Her lips curved into a soft smile as she drifted off to sleep.

CHAPTER 26

S OMETHING LANDED ON my legs, startling me awake.

"Get up, lazy ass." Chel stood at the edge of the bed, dressed in black trousers and a loose blue tunic cinched around the waist with a leather belt.

I sat up and picked up the clothing draped over my legs. I blinked at Chel. "You went shopping?"

"Yes, I figured we could use some new clothing and you were sleeping like an infant so I left you and went to a merchant's shop. I hope it fits," she added the last part playfully.

Once I'd donned the simple white tunic and brown trousers, we met Zephyra in the dining room to break our fast. She wore new clothing as well. Though, her new attire was a pale pink riding dress. Her royal self wouldn't be caught dead in trousers.

"How's Percifal?" Chel prodded as she nibbled on a puffy pastry.

"Rest has helped, but the wound on his ribs is still a bit sore."

"We mustn't waste time," Chel replied. "If he's not well enough to travel by tomorrow, we leave without him."

Zephyra shot her a dark stare. "We will not be leaving him behind. We *need* him."

Chel's dark brows drew down. "And Sarantoa needs *us*. He's my brother. I don't want him risking his life more than he has to."

"I don't either, but it's his decision."

"Fine. We'll ask him tomorrow," Chel relented, though the way she stabbed her slice of pork told me she wasn't happy about it.

I smiled cautiously. "Ladies, I'd love to stay and listen to you bicker, but I'd like to purchase a sword before we continue on."

"Merchant shops are that way," Chel pointed, not bothering to glance up from her food.

I welcomed the silence as I ambled along the pathway behind the inn, passing by a line of little wooden shops. I peered in each window. Jewelry sparkled from behind the polished glass of one shop. Another displayed the colourful works of a local weaver. Silver glinted, catching my eye from one of the windows near the end of the pathway. I entered and an eager merchant met me with a blade in his hand. A thick, white polishing cloth dangled from his other hand. "Welcome, warrior. This blade is waiting for a man like you to slay enemies with." The merchant held the long sword out for me to get a closer look.

The blade was indeed a fine piece of craftsmanship. I pressed my finger against the edge to test its sharpness. A line of blood appeared on my skin where the blade had touched. I studied the solid gold hilt with the unique twisted design. I would've loved to own a sword like that, but I couldn't be greedy and spend all our coin when we needed it for more practical items. So I politely declined. "Not this time, but do you have something simpler?"

The merchant's face dropped with disappointment, but he fetched another sword and brought it to me. "This one is sturdy and sharp. She'll do well by you."

I accepted the sword from the merchant and turned to take a practice swing. The blade was well weighted, and the leather wrapped, iron hilt felt comfortable in my palm. "How much?"

"Two golds, one silver."

I dropped the coins into the merchant's hand and left the shop with my new blade.

I returned to the inn to find Percifal downstairs sipping on a bowl of soup. I raised my forehead at him. "You're out of bed."

"I need to keep up my strength. It seems my sister will leave me behind if I'm not ready to leave tomorrow."

"*Will* you be ready to leave tomorrow?" I eyed him suspiciously.

"Is that concern you have for me, Seph?" Percifal jested. When I just stared at him he added, "I'm fine."

"Honestly, I'm glad it won't just be me and those two. Sometimes I worry they'll kill each other before Vesirus even gets his chance."

That got a laugh out of him, though he couldn't hide the wince at the pain in his ribs. He was a stubborn fool for wanting to stay on this journey. I couldn't have said I wouldn't have done the same if I were in his position. As soldiers, we couldn't stand by and watch while others went to war. We'd rather die than sit idly by while our friends fought.

Zephyra entered the dining room with Chel behind her. "You're back," the fire elemental commented. "Come and pray with us. There's a Temple not far from here."

I looked at Chel. Her face seemed to say, *'if I have to, so do you.'*

"What about him?" I gesture to Percifal, who focused on drinking his water.

"He has not been gifted by the goddess, and he needs as much rest as he can get before we leave tomorrow," Zephyra said.

"All right," I agreed. "If only to pass the time."

Zephyra scowled. "Do you even remember the last time you prayed?"

I thought for a moment before answering her. "No. Sometime when I was a child and my father had taken me to Terra's Temple."

Chel's brows rose as Zephyra said, "It is time you reunite with our goddess then. We need Celestia's guidance more than ever."

I held out my arm. "Lead the way."

"Not a devoted follower either, are you?" Chel whispered as we followed Zephyra out of the inn and down the pathway leading past the shops.

"No, I never believed the goddess cared much for a torturer's son."

"You're more than that now," Chel assured me.

Zephyra's braid bounced like a rope of fire with each of her bouncy steps. "She's right. If Celestia didn't care about you, she wouldn't have given you earth magic. No wonder the goddess has only chosen to visit me and not the two of you. You've both been ungrateful."

"I'm sorry, but I don't feel thankful Celestia chose me to fight her brother of darkness in this war," Chel shot.

"Well, she did," Zephyra countered.

I sighed loudly through my nose and asked, "Will you two ever get along?"

They both gave me a look that could turn stone to ash, so I shut my mouth and we walked the rest of the way in silence.

The Temple wasn't as magnificent as the one in Terra, but it had still been beautifully built. Its long diamond-shaped windows were filled with clear glass that was cut to send prisms along the inner walls when the sunlight hit from the right angle.

We stepped inside and were met by a priestess with long, white hair. Her pale skin crinkled as she smiled at us. I couldn't guess how many Noctis' she'd lived through, but she had aged with grace and still moved like water. "Good day, my friends," the priestess welcomed us in a soft voice, barely above a whisper.

"Good day, Priestess," Zephyra replied, bowing her head to the elderly woman. "We've come to pray. Do you have offerings available for us to give?" She held a gold coin out to the priestess.

The priestess accepted the coin and nodded. "I do, please wait here."

We did as told, removing our boots while we waited for her to return. Bare feet were custom when making an offering to the goddess. It allowed the devotee to be closer to her with nothing between skin and earth.

The graceful priestess returned with a cup of water and a cup of soil in one hand, a candle and incense clasped in the other. She handed the items to Zephyra and said gently, "Celestia is ready to hear your prayers."

We stepped into the main part of the Temple to where a statue of Celestia rested with both hands out as if waiting to welcome her followers in a loving embrace. Zephyra handed the cup of water to Chel and the cup of soil to me. She kept the candle and the incense and bowed her head, closing her eyes. "Celestia, hear me now. I am here to thank you for the gifts you've bestowed upon me and upon all of your children. I thank you for the fire that burns inside my veins, and for giving me the chance to fight in this war against darkness." She opened her eyes and the candle's wick flickered to life, the glowing flame burning bright and steady.

When no one said anything, she nudged Chel, who kneeled beside her. Chel closed her eyes and spoke to the goddess. "I kneel before you and offer my thanks for the gift you've given me, and for the gift of life given to your children. Please accept my offering and give us aid in this war." The water swirled up out of the cup and shot in a spiral to the statues feet, soaking the ground beneath the white marble.

I closed my eyes and tried not to feel awkward as I spoke to a statue. "Celestia, I thank you for the gift of earth magic, and for the life you've given us all. Please accept my offering." I opened my eyes and focused on the cup of soil in my hands. A tiny vine sprouted from the center of the cup, growing until it budded and bloomed into a white flower. I lay the cup before the statue, and then I sat back on my heels.

"As air is not yet with us," Zephyra started. "I would like to thank you on their behalf. Please accept this offering for the gift of air." An ember glowed on the tip of the incense she held, a stream of scented smoke floating from the stick and filling the Temple with the scent of sandalwood. "Please guide us with your light in this war against darkness," she whispered as she set down the incense into the holder at the statue's feet.

We rose and made our way back to the front of the Temple to fetch our boots.

"May Celestia be with you," the priestess offered as we left.

"May Celestia be with you," Zephyra replied, bowing her head.

It was true, I hadn't prayed to Celestia like that since I was a boy. It started by making excuses about having no time but, in the end, I didn't believe myself a worthy enough follower. Somehow, she still believed in me enough to give me her gift. Perhaps she regretted that decision, but Zephyra's devotion had been inspirational. I'd try to be worthy of the magic I'd been given.

As dawn lit the sky through the window with brilliant shades of liquid gold and fuchsia, Zephyra burst into the room Chel and I shared with a smile on her face. "Celestia came to me last night," she beamed.

Chel rubbed her tired eyes and yawned. "Did she?"

"Yes," Zephyra confirmed, ripping the blanket off Chel. I had already dressed in my new clothing and straightened from tying up my leather boots. "She said to find the air elemental. She said they are the *key* to stopping her brother."

"Isn't that what we're doing?" I put in from a corner of the room.

"Yes," Zephyra said, "but it means it isn't all for naught. We're on the right path."

"Did she happen to tell you where exactly this air elemental is?"

Chel asked, rolling to sit up and comb out her mass of dark hair with her fingers.

"No." Zephyra bit her lip. "But she has to be somewhere in Ventosa. It only makes sense."

"Of course she didn't," I muttered. "She can't even give us clear answers never mind come fight her brother herself."

Zephyra crossed her arms. "I'm sure she would if she could. Vesirus is only here because of King Zaeden."

"Let's go find us an air elemental then," Chel stated, reaching for her trousers.

Percifal was waiting for us at the front of the inn by the time we were ready to leave. The innkeeper sat at his desk playing a game of solitaire and sipping on a cup of tea.

"Do you know what's been happening in the rest of Sarantoa?" I decided to ask him. A lot of those smaller villages were a fair distance from any kingdom and didn't know much of what went on outside of their little community. All they worried about was paying taxes to the kingdom closest to their village.

The innkeeper peered up from his card game. "There's been word that King Zaeden of Aquila has conquered Terra. We belong to Ventosa though." He shrugged.

I cleared my throat before informing him, "King Zaeden has also conquered Solis and will be coming for Ventosa next."

The fair-haired man lifted his round shoulder. "It matters not to me which sovereign I pay tax to. They're all the same, all greedy for gold."

I felt Chel stiffen beside me as I tutted, "I doubt you'd feel the same if you knew King Zaeden is working with Vesirus to bring Mnyama here."

I watched as the innkeeper's eyes bulged and his hands shook. "You—you must be jesting!" he stuttered.

"I'm not. Tell your neighbours to prepare for war." I pushed the door open and left him speechless.

"I'll fetch our horses," Chel offered.

"That was mean," Zephyra said, coming up beside me.

I faced her. "If these people know what's coming… maybe they'll stand a chance if they're prepared to fight."

Zephyra brushed Percifal's comforting hand away. "Likely they'll run, and there will be nowhere to hide if King Zaeden and Vesirus win."

"So you'd rather lie and let these small villages die without even knowing what happened?"

"Yes—no—I don't know! You didn't have to be so cruel about it though. You've scared the poor man half to death."

I gave her a dark smile. "It's a cruel world, Princess."

"Don't call me that."

"Apologies… Princess." I couldn't help myself. She got worked up way too easily.

Percifal stepped forward, fists balled, to defend his lover.

I raised my hands in surrender just as Chel came back with the horses.

We tied our bags to the saddles and took off to the north.

"There's another village at the base of the Acuties. We can purchase furs and supplies before we make the trek up the mountains." Percifal told us. The Acuties… a vast mountain range the Kingdom of Ventosa nestled in. Snow covered their rocky peaks permanently, making them dangerous to travel through. I remembered hearing Queen Nicola once grumble about having to attend Noctis there. As I recalled, she hated the 'kingdom of ice and frozen hearts.'

A couple days rest had done Percifal well. He had more colour in his face, though he still hid how much pain he was in as we rode into the foothills at the base of the mountains.

My eyes widened as Chel rested her hand against my thigh. I smiled into her shiny hair and squeezed her softly with my arms. We'd spent the previous night sharing pleasant memories of our pasts. Mine few, hers many. My grief had turned from a sharp pain to a dull ache over our journey. The thought of giving my heart to another didn't seem so impossible now. I wondered if Chel felt the same as she let herself relax against me. The storm raging within the water elemental was turning into a warm, summer rain.

We stopped a few times to let the horses drink; besides that, we rode straight until darkness made it too difficult to see. We built a small fire and slept on the ground around it, covering ourselves with blankets. There was a kind of serenity to being out in the open all on our own. The night air stayed fairly warm at the bottom of the Acuties, the wind blocked out by the evergreen covered mountains. I rolled onto my back and watched the stars blink, wondering if my real mother and father looked down from somewhere among them with our goddess. I fell asleep wondering what my life would've been like if King Lelund would've claimed me as his son, only to wake up stiff the next morning from the long ride and the hard ground.

Each day went much the same the closer we grew to the trail that would lead us up the Acuties, until we reached the village Percifal had told us about five sunrises later. He knew the layout of Sarantoa well. He had been brought up to be King Zaeden's right hand. I trusted his navigational skills more than my own.

This village, much like the last, had merchants set up to sell their goods. Only, the items they sold were different. We purchased rooms for one night at the sole inn to allow ourselves a good night's rest before hiking up the Acuties. After seeing to our horses and dropping off our bags at the inn, we visited the merchant shops and purchased warmer clothing and more food. We still had coin, but it was beginning to run low. We'd have to spend it wisely to make it last.

"I wish we could've afforded our own room," I whispered in Chel's ear, glancing to the bed where Zephyra and Percifal slept entwined.

She smiled wickedly at me and reached for my hand. She slowly brought it up to her mouth and pressed her soft lips to my skin before saying, "Perhaps once we've saved the world we'll, have time for ourselves."

I hoped she was right. And I hoped Vesirus wouldn't snuff out that little spark of light that had kindled between us. For if that little spark died, I knew my heart would never escape the dark again.

We were off again the next morning, packed with our new items and riding refreshed mounts. I knew travelling the Acuties wouldn't be easy, but nothing could've prepared me for the crushing cold and relentlessly harsh landscapes awaiting us.

CHAPTER 27

I HAD NEVER seen snow. Winter never came to Terra. The higher we climbed, the colder the air became. My body wasn't used to the type of climate we rode into a little over a fortnight after purchasing our furs. I admit the white powder dusting the ground gave it a sort of clean beauty, but the clouds of steam swirling from our mouths and noses with each breath we let out had me feeling uneasy.

I poked Chel in the back from atop our horse. "Why do I feel like I'm a dragon?"

She snickered. "It's what happens when the air is really cold. Does it not get cold in Terra during the winter?"

"Not like this, no," I grumbled, pulling my fur cloak tighter around myself.

We traveled up a small road winding through the towering mountains the regents of other kingdoms took when they travelled to Ventosa for Noctis De Celestia. We stayed at inns along the way when we could, but there were nights when we had to make camp outside. Those nights were the worst. We built shelters with branches and logs to block out the wind, but the cold, snow-packed ground didn't make for a comfortable bed. I barely slept, spending most of my nights shivering against the bodies of the others. We began to run out of food and had to ration what little we did have left. I was cold, hungry and miserable. We all were, though no one spoke of it. We had agreed to this. I cursed Celestia a few times for sending me to the icy kingdom.

One crisp, clear morning, I dug into one of our sacks and pulled out the last of our dried berries. The dried meat we'd brought had gone first. The bread had got wet and turned moldy. I tossed the berries at Chel and pushed myself up.

"Where are you going?" she asked. Zephyra and Percifal were already out hunting, but they'd had little success so far.

"Fishing." I'd seen a lake just off the road the previous day. It was frozen over, but if I could make a hole, maybe I could catch a fish.

"Wait. I'm coming with you."

We plowed through the untouched, pristine white snow. Ice crystals sparkled in the sunlight beaming through the evergreen trees. By the time we reached the lake, the bottoms of our trousers were soaked.

"Let me go first," Chel said. "The ice could be thin. Let me make sure it's safe."

"Awe, are you protecting me, Lady Water?"

She rolled her eyes at me. "Don't be stupid. I can breathe underwater. You cannot."

"After you, my lady."

Chel stepped carefully onto the ice, testing its strength. When the ice held, she beckoned me over.

I joined her and, kneeling down on the ice, I took out my dagger and began chipping away at the white surface. The air burned my face as I hacked away; stopping only to swipe away the slush I'd created.

Chel watched with her hands on her hips. "I hope you know what you're doing."

"I don't, but the rodents Percifal's been catching aren't enough for the four of us."

I hacked and hacked, but the ice was too thick. I grunted in frustration and threw my dagger down. I sat back and breathed in the frozen air. Sweat coated my forehead. At least I was warm for once. It wouldn't last long.

"Perhaps you'd like some help with that," Chel taunted. "Move over." She crouched down beside me and placed a hand over the place I'd carved a dip in.

Realizing she planned to use her power, I scrambled backward. "Are you insane? What if the whole lake erupts through the ice?"

"Have some faith in me. I can control my power." She turned her focus back to the ice. The ice around her hand turned dark, and then water pushed through. She pulled more and more water up until a hole formed in the ice, bringing three fish up with it. Satisfied, she scooted back from the hole and smiled. "Have you ever even fished?"

A strangled sound caught in my through. "What kind of question is that? Of course I've fished. Terra has rivers and lakes."

"You've never seen snow before. Who knows what else you've never experienced?"

I narrowed my eyes at her. "I can be just as useful as everyone else, you know?" I turned and bent to gather the silvery fish.

"Uh, Seph," she warned as a whining sound filled the air and froze my muscles. "Sepheus, move!" Chel screamed. A crack shot down the ice beneath my feet.

I made to run, but it was too late.

The ice opened up underneath me, and I plunged into the icy water.

Nothing can describe the amount of shock I felt in that moment. My blood froze inside my veins. I couldn't breathe... couldn't move. My eyes were open, but I saw nothing but darkness. Endless, deadly darkness.

My whole life flashed inside my mind. My childhood full of bloodshed and a loveless father. The lonely nights I'd spent wondering if I'd ever have a friend. My failures at succeeding to make my father proud. Claudia. King Corbin. Queen Nicola. My witch grandmother.

And even when Blaise's face entered my mind, I felt nothing but despair and regret. I'd wasted my entire life, and now it was ending. Maybe it'd be a relief to be dead.

But one face hadn't yet flashed through my mind.

And there, through the water, Chel appeared, swimming franticly for me. She was going to save me... save me from this freezing water. Save me from myself.

I clawed at her as she dragged me upward. She struck me on the head and the world disappeared.

When I opened my eyes again, I had been laid out on the ice. Chel panted, her hair and clothes sopping wet. We both shivered uncontrollably.

She believed I was worth saving. She believed in *me*. I wouldn't die empty and alone. And so I reached out a shaking hand and cupped her cheek. "Th—th—thank you." Then I said the words I never thought

I'd say to anyone. "I—I think I'm s—starting to fall in love with you."

"Me too," she breathed. Tears pooled in her eyes and she slapped my hand away. "So don't die on me, you fool!"

My throat tightened and I looked away. No one had ever told me they loved me before. My own mother hadn't even thought I was worth her own life. What Chel had just given me... I blinked away the wetness in my eyes.

I was so cold. The initial shock began to wear off, and my teeth now chattered so hard I couldn't hear my own thoughts.

We slunk off the ice, treading back through the snow. We followed our tracks from earlier.

"Zephyra!" Chel bellowed.

We stumbled to our camp. Zephyra met us, taking in our state. "Oh my goddess, what happened?"

I'd begun drifting in and out of consciousness. I was *so* damned cold. I couldn't feel my hands or feet.

"He fell into the lake," I heard Chel say. "You need to use your power to warm him."

"I—I'm not sure if I can," Zephyra stuttered.

"Zephyra, *now.*" Chel's voice cracked on the last word. "He may die if you don't."

"What if I burn him from the inside out?"

I didn't hear Chel's answer. My heart pounded too loud, my ears rang in an endless note. Fools, we'd been fools to set foot on that lake. Icicles clung to my eye lashes as I tried to blink.

Whatever Chel had said must have been enough to convince Zephyra. The fire elemental took both of my hands in hers and looked into my eyes. "Sepheus, I'm going to try to warm you. If I kill you, I'm sorry. Do you accept?" It took me a moment to comprehend she wanted me to agree, so she repeated a little louder, "Do you accept?"

I nodded. "J—just d—do it."

Zephyra breathed in deeply and closed her eyes. Percifal brought over the blankets. He wrapped one around me and one around Chel.

Zephyra's hands warmed, the first sign her power was working. The warmth transferred to my own palms. Then, like liquid gold, the warmth spread, melting the ice in my veins. I felt colour return to my face. I breathed evenly once again. I stopped shivering as her fire magic warmed me from the inside out.

Sweat pooled on the back of my neck, and I pulled my hands away. "Enough. That's enough." I grinned at the very concerned fire elemental. "Thank you, Zephyra. You did it."

She returned my smile.

"You need to warm Chel now," Percifal said to her.

Indeed, I hadn't noticed Chel also shivered from where she watched. She may have been able to breathe underwater, but the cold air still affected her. And being wet in this climate wasn't safe. To my amazement, my clothing had completely dried from Zephyra's power. We should've been using her to warm us since we'd entered the Acuties. But after she was done warming Chel, I noticed the tiredness in her eyes, the way her back bent forward as she dragged her feet to stand with Percifal. It took a lot of control to hold her power back enough to keep it from burning us alive. Warming us for comfort wasn't worth draining her.

Percifal prepared the rabbit he'd caught for us to eat afterward. There wasn't much meat when split between the four of us, but it was more than the mouse he'd caught the night before. We'd lost all the fish when the ice broke and it wasn't worth the risk to try again, so we had to be grateful for any morsel of food we could get. Finding anything worth eating in the wintery land proved tough, and I supposed Percifal was still off his game since recovering from his wounds. Arrows would have been nice. We could've used them to hunt birds. Why had no one bought arrows instead of blades? Blaise would have. I shoved the thought away as I accepted my piece of meat.

After our skimpy meal, we packed up and left.

Frustration gnawed at me at having to ride with Chel after confessing my feelings to her. I wanted to show her exactly how I felt about her, but I couldn't do that with Zephyra and Percifal beside us. I ran my hand along her thigh and brushed my lips against the back of her neck. She leaned back into me before stopping my hand with her own.

"If I have to suffer, so do you," I whispered into her ear. Oh, it'd been a long time since I'd been able to take pleasure in a woman. Too long.

"You don't think I'm suffering too? What I wouldn't give to lose myself again."

"Did we miss something back there?" Zephyra put in, annoying me.

"Seph told me—" I clamped my hand over her mouth before she could finish her sentence.

Zephyra raised one eyebrow.

"We're both restless, is all." I smiled at Zephyra. Admitting I may have a heart to other people… I wasn't ready for that. Besides, keeping our desires a secret felt more intimate, more thrilling.

Chel tossed her hair over her shoulder, causing it to hit me in the face, surely on purpose. I simply ran my fingers through the silky strands and felt her relax. I chuckled, enjoying our little game.

We climbed higher up the mountains until the road came to a plateau, a sign we were getting nearer to the kingdom of air.

I slowed our horse so we fell back a little ways from Zephyra and Percifal. Just out of earshot. "I'll need to thank you properly for saving me," I murmured to Chel.

"I wasn't going to let you die," she said, still staring ahead. "We need you."

"Regardless."

She ducked her head to the side to peer at me. "Don't scare me again. I'm tired of losing people. I can't do it again."

"You won't lose me," I promised, and then added, "I'm a knight. I shouldn't need saving. I'll have to be more careful."

She nearly chocked at my words. "You're a *knight?*"

"It's quiet shocking, isn't it? I'm also a royal, though I don't actually consider myself one."

Now she twisted to stare at me. "Excuse me?"

I don't know why I felt the need to tell her my truth. I guess I needed someone alive to know before I died. My plunge into the lake had been a close call. So I confessed to her, "King Lelund was my father. My mother was his mistress."

"You're an heir of Terra? Does King Corbin know?"

I shook my head. "He doesn't, and I want to keep it that way. My father never claimed me before he died. I'm not legitimate, and I don't wish to be royal. Even being a prince is too much responsibility."

Chel shifted in the saddle and looked back through the horses ears. "Ironic you're currently responsible for saving all of Sarantoa then."

I let out a long breath. "It wasn't by choice. And after we're done banishing Vesirus and his demons back to Mnyama, I'd like to live a long, simple life."

"Nothing about life is simple, but don't worry. I'll take your secret to my grave."

I pushed our horse into a trot to catch up to the others and said, "Thank you."

We had to make camp for one more night. This time we spotted a deer through the snow covered trees. Zephyra used her fire to kill the animal. She cried about it after, but we ate well that night.

As we lay down to go to sleep beneath a pile of furs, the smell of rot drifted through the air. I tried to ignore it, believing it to be only my imagination. But an unsettling feeling crept over me as the wind stilled.

A loud screeching had us all scrambling to our feet.

"What was that?" Zephyra whispered.

As if in answer, a shadow darker than the night sky loomed through the snow covered trees. One of the Dark Lord's demons had found us.

"It must have tracked us by scent," I answered, calling to the spark of my magic, preparing to fight.

"Percifal, run," Chel begged.

Sword in hand, he hesitated.

"You have no magic to fight this thing with. Go!" Zephyra's words, or the desperation in them, had him bolting through the snow right as the shadow descended upon us. A shadow that didn't just block out the light, a shadow that *consumed* it.

I whipped a thick, twisted vine at the shapeless figure only to watch it disintegrate and fall to the snow in a useless heap of ash.

The shadow screeched, a blood curdling sound, and dove for Chel. Snow melted to form a wall of water between her and the demon.

The water did nothing to hold the shadow demon back. Chel cried out in pain as darkness touched her arm, clawing at the shadowy tendril that wouldn't let go.

With a roar, Zephyra produced a spear of flames. The shadow demon shrank back from the fire, releasing its hold on Chel. Though it didn't seem to burn, it feared the fire.

The demon turned on Zephyra, breaking up to swirl around her. Chel and I watched helplessly as it engulfed her and her flames in darkness. The fire elemental screamed in agony. Chel and I could do nothing but watch in horror as the demon swept Zephyra upward, still covering her in darkness.

My heart sank. We had lost and it hadn't even been to Vesirus himself.

"No!" Chel cried, fists clenched, tears streaming down her face.

I felt her pain as I watched the demon sweeping farther and farther away, taking Zephyra with it.

But then, a flash of light and an inhumane wail burst from the sky.

The shadow demon dispersed into a thousand pieces as fire erupted, shooting in a golden column from sky to earth.

Chel and I gaped at each other before bolting to the flames now smoldering around the charred space of forest.

Zephyra lay on her back with closed eyes. Percifal had beat us to her and kneeled on the blackened ground at her side. A few scratches peppered her arms and a long one crossed one of her cheeks, but she otherwise appeared untouched.

"Is she..." Chel began, afraid to ask.

"She's alive," Percifal confirmed, picking her up to carry her back to our camp.

Zephyra's eyes fluttered open as he set her down on the furs. "Did I kill it?" she asked in a roughened voice.

Percifal brushed her hair off her cheek. "I believe so. Are you all right?"

"I—don't know. When it touched me, I felt all the life being sucked from my body. But now..." She frowned. "I feel—empty."

"Try and light a fire," I suggested.

Zephyra sat up and reached for a stick. Percifal picked it up and handed it to her.

We waited, none of us moving, none of us breathing.

Zephyra's face crumpled as she dropped the piece of wood. "My magic... it's *gone.*"

"It can't be gone," Chel protested. "Surely you only need rest."

"I don't know," Zephyra mumbled. "But right now, I can't feel the spark that's usually dwelling within me. I have no magic to help us with."

Percifal wrapped his arms around her, holding her tight. "We'll figure this out."

"How?" I demanded, kicking a log we'd cut earlier for the fire to keep us warm through the night. "How are we going to figure this out?"

Zephyra began to cry. Percifal glared at me.

"We still go to Ventosa," Chel said. "Whatever happened to her power... maybe the air elemental can help."

"For goddess sake!" I roared. I stalked off through the trees. Fury swept over me. I needed to be alone. I unsheathed my sword and hacked at branches. How could we win this war when we could barely defeat *one* demon? And now we were short an elemental. The Dark Lord would damn us all to Mnyama, and Celestia wasn't going to save us. We fought in her war, and she wouldn't lift a damn finger to help us.

I returned to the camp after my arms had tired from taking out my frustration on fallen logs and branches. Zephyra and Percifal already slept, utterly exhausted.

Chel opened her eyes and watched me as I pulled some of the furs over my body. The emptiness in her gaze... I saw as much hope there as I felt.

To make matters worse, Percifal informed me the next morning both of our horses had broken their ties and bolted during the attack. I didn't blame them, but I still cursed as I trudged through the snow with a saddle pack strapped to my back.

Zephyra had tried to use her power again to no avail.

With exhausted bodies and dampened spirits, we arrived at Ventosa two days later as the sun gave up the sky to let the moon rule over the earth. I realized how the palace had gained its name when I spotted it across the long, narrow bridge. A layer of thick, silvery ice covered the Crystalline Palace. The moonlight reflected off the smooth walls, causing the whole palace to glow like something from Celestia's realm.

The kingdom had no walls, but anyone travelling to the palace had to transverse the deadly bridge leading between two snow covered mountains... their defence mechanism.

I swallowed hard as I peered down at the bridge covered with ice and snow. I wasn't usually afraid of heights, but this... this was daunting to say the least.

We stepped carefully onto the bridge and slowly began traversing our way across.

"This bridge may be a good idea for keeping enemies out," Percifal commented. "But what about letting your own subjects escape danger? This could also end up being a trap for those who dwell here."

"It's something we'll have to ask Queen Starella," Zephyra said, keeping her gaze straight ahead. None looked down for fear of falling.

When we were close to the end, I held my breath. One wrong move and we could lose our life. It wasn't worth the risk to rush.

Closer. Closer. Almost there.

I stepped off the bridge behind Chel and let a *whoosh* of air out of my mouth.

Once we were all on solid ground I looked at the giant palace before us. Of all the palaces of Sarantoa I'd seen so far, it was the most spectacular. The milky light of the moon glinted off the long, icy spires. Though ice covered the outside layer, white stone made up the building's jagged structure beneath it. Diamond cut glass filled each window, and the doors appeared to be made from pure, polished silver. I understood now, why people called Ventosa the kingdom of ice. And we were about to find out if the hearts inside were just as frozen.

CHAPTER 28

W E WERE MET by a group of guards wearing dark violet and white uniforms with two leaves and a diamond embroidered in silver upon the chest, Ventosa's official crest.

As the only legitimate royal, we let Zephyra do the talking. And she had the most polite manners. "Good day, sirs," she said with diplomacy, not a trace of the despair she felt about her missing magic. "We have come to speak with your queen."

"And who are you?" One of the fair-haired guards asked, peering down his sharp nose at her, sword in hand. I'd only seen such behaviour in courtiers before. Guards were usually humble. Dutiful... harsh when they needed to be, but humble.

"I am Lady Zephyra Caldura of Solis, and these are my allies. We are friends of Ventosa."

The stiff guard took in her state and scoffed. "You don't look like a Lady of Solis."

"It was a long journey, and your land isn't the easiest to trek," Zephyra said through clenched teeth, while still attempting to keep her tone pleasant.

I'd fight these guards to the death if they didn't let us into the palace after the nightmare we'd gone through to get there. I'd likely lose against so many, but I'd prefer death over leaving those wretched mountains empty handed.

After mumbling to his comrades, the guard turned back to us. "Fine. I'll take you inside. It will be at the queen's pleasure, whether she wishes to speak with you or not."

"Thank you." Zephyra's shoulders loosened.

We followed the guard up the steep stairway and through the silver doors of the palace, which were so shiny they could've been mistaken for mirrors.

Inside, the guard caught the arm of a maid scuttling by. "Find Hilda," he ordered the young woman dressed in a plain white dress. "We have company."

"Yes, of course, sir," she conceded and then hurried away.

The guard had sheathed his sword but kept his hand on the pommel the whole time we waited, his attention never faltering from us. More guards eyed us from their posts around the open and spacious main floor of the palace, almost as cold as outside. Every white tile on the floor was perfectly clean. How hard the servants at Ventosa must work to ensure not a speck of dirt could be seen.

Footsteps clopped rapidly across those tiles. A tall woman with wheat-blond hair and a strong, square jaw placed her hands on her wide hips; Hilda, the head handmaid if I had to guess. "My queen is finished holding court for the day, and she's not expecting any appointments. What is the meaning of this visit?" she demanded, as though she were reprimanding a child.

"Apologies we weren't able to send word ahead of our arrival," Zephyra said to the handmaid. "Our information is for the queen's ears only. We come as allies of Her Majesty to offer her important information."

Hilda tapped her foot on the polished floor. "Hmm, so you say. Well, you're in no state to be in the presence of Her Majesty. I'll have my maids attend you. After you've bathed and donned something more suitable, you may feast on tonight's left overs in the servants' quarters. After that, it's up to Queen Starella whether or not she wishes to meet with you on this eve." This woman had some nerve. I had to bite my tongue to keep from putting her in her place.

Zephyra pursed her lips in thought, and then she simply said, "All right, thank you, Hilda."

The woman gave her a stony look before hollering the names of four maids over her shoulder. The four maids, dressed in the same white uniform dresses, came running over, ready to follow her orders. "Take care of our new guests. Prepare them for an audience with the queen."

The maids curtsied in unison and mumbled, "Yes, Madam."

We were whisked away into bathing rooms; Percifal and I in one and the ladies in a separate one. Once we were dunked, soaped and scrubbed, we were shoved into stiff, clean clothing and escorted downstairs to the servants' quarters.

A few of the kitchen staff still lingered in the small dining room next to the kitchens, finishing their meal of left over food.

"Fetch these guests a plate. Hilda wants them fed," one of the maids, a middle-aged woman with dark blond hair, said to the cook sitting nearest. He shoved the last of his food into his mouth and did as the maid had asked.

The maid gestured for us to sit at the rectangular table. "Eat. Hilda will return shortly and inform you of the queen's decision." She left us to go continue whatever other duties she had.

The cook placed plates with scraps of roasted hen, bread and glazed carrots on the table for us. The room temperature food was the best I'd had since the last inn we'd stayed at.

As promised, Hilda returned shortly after our plates were scraped clean and we'd drained our cups of ice cold water. "Queen Starella will see you in the Lunar Room," she informed us. "Come with me."

We trailed her up a set of stairs to the main floor, and then up another longer, wider set near the back of the glittering white palace accented with hues of cool purple.

We were taken to a room at the top and led through a silver gilded door with moons etched upon its surface. Inside, a silver throne, with diamonds encrusted in the arms, sat on a dais. A mosaic spread out in a circular pattern from beneath it in colours of blue, purple and white. The crescent moon outside illuminated the room through the glass ceiling. Four guards stood attentive on each side of the throne, and upon the seat lined with white fur sat Queen Starella Pavanas. A white gold and diamond crown rested on her head, its points reaching for the moon above. The young queen stroked the pale-blond hair running down one of her shoulders in a long twist. Her white and silver gown put our garments to shame.

A man who was in his fourth or fifth decade and shared her features leaned against one side of the throne, resting his elbow on its back. His dark indigo gaze studied us as though we were vermin in *his* palace.

The queen's eyes, that same shade of indigo, held curiosity. "Tell me," she began. "Who are you, and why have you come to my kingdom?"

Zephyra cleared her throat and stepped forward, introducing us each one by one. When she was finished, she asked, "Have you heard of King Zaeden's plans to conquer all of Sarantoa?"

"Yes," the queen breathed before craning her head to look at the man behind her. "We've received word he's overthrown King Corbin in Terra." I stiffened at the sound of my king's name falling from her pale lips. She set her gaze back on us, placing her white-gloved hands on her thighs and leaning forward. "Is that why you're all here? To warn us?"

"We are, but that's not all," Zephyra continued. She raised her chin and I admired her bravado. "We've come to seek your aid in this war. You see, each one of us, not including Percifal, is an elemental from each of the other kingdoms. We believe the air elemental to be here in Ventosa." She didn't bother to reveal her own magic had deserted her. We agreed to find the air elemental first. We'd face the problem of her missing powers after.

Queen Starella's face turned an even paler shade of white, if that were possible. While Terra never saw winter, Ventosa never saw summer.

The man standing beside the throne dressed in white and blue finery stepped forward, placing a slender hand on her shoulder. "Magic is forbidden in our kingdom. We're sorry to disappoint you, but there's no elemental here."

Queen Starella set her jaw but didn't say anything.

"No one you know of," Chelela chimed in, shifting on her feet. "But perhaps the air elemental dwells here in secret. Or perhaps they do not know yet they hold air magic in their veins."

"No one in Ventosa has magic," the stone-faced man repeated. "Now, you've wasted enough of my queen's time. And you've confessed to having magic yourselves. We should have you all thrown in the dungeon."

Zephyra shook her head and stepped back. She looked like she was about to get sick.

"No," the winter queen stiffened. "No," she repeated quieter. "They are our guests. I will allow them to use our guest chambers here for as long as they like."

When the man beside her made to argue she raised her hand. "However, a guard will be posted at their doors. Should they try to use their magic here, they will be arrested."

"Thank you, Your Majesty," Zephyra bowed her head.

"Surely, Your Majesty, you must be able to help us," Chel pled. "King Zaeden is coming for Ventosa next, and he's bringing Vesirus with him."

The queen's hand trembled as she brought it up to fiddle with her hair. "I'm sorry, but my father tells the truth. The elemental you seek is not here."

A storm passed across Chel's face before she bowed and bit out, "Thank you, Your Majesty. Good luck to you and your kingdom when Vesirus tears you all apart." And then she stomped out of the Lunar Room.

I saw the fear shine in the queen's eyes before I followed Chel out.

"Guards, escort them to a guest chamber," I heard the queen's father order.

I grabbed Chel's elbow. "These people are nothing but condescending fools!" she snapped. "They aren't going to help us. Vesirus is going to win. Soon our realm will become a new Mnyama, and we'll all belong to the Dark Lord. I'd rather end my life now and join Celestia!"

I grabbed a hold of her hands. She tried to pull them away, but I held firm. "Chel... Chel! Don't say that. We'll figure this out."

A guard had exited the Lunar Room and waited close by. I didn't care if he heard. Let them all hear the fear in her heart. And damn them to Mnyama for not giving a shit.

"How? How are we to figure this out when we don't even have the air elemental, and Zephyra's magic is gone? It's *gone*, Sepheus!"

The guard shifted on his feet. I pressed my lips together, and then glanced at him. "Take us to our chamber." While I didn't care if others heard our conversation, it wasn't fair to Chel to have others witness her break down.

Keeping his eyes averted, the stoic guard led us back downstairs to a wing of the palace lined with identical doors.

He opened one door and said, "I'll be right out here. Should I feel suspicious about what's going on inside, I will not hesitate to enter."

We both ignored him, slamming the door in his face. Let him stand there all night, but if he tried to enter… I ran my palm over the hilt of my sword. I was in no mood to comply.

A hearth already burned at the back of the chamber. I used a flame to light a candle before continuing our conversation from where we'd left off. "We don't know that Zephyra's magic is truly gone."

"If it is, we're doomed."

"There's still you and I. We still have our magic."

She laughed bitterly at that. "Our powers were useless against the shadow demon. I highly doubt the two of us could stop Vesirus on our own."

I scrubbed my hands over my face. She was right. Of course she was right. My attempts to make her feel better weren't working.

Chel lay back onto the bed and stared at the ceiling. "We should enjoy what we have left of our lives. Soon, our spirits may be stuck in eternal torture."

I stretched out on my side and faced her, admired her. She looked gorgeous in the pale blue gown she'd been lent. I breathed in her scent. She smelled of fresh daisies and honey. I ran a finger along her bare arm. "If darkness is to win, if there's no hope… I'll gladly die by your side so we may both return to Celestia."

She twisted her head to peer at me and smiled, though there was no joy in her eyes, only sorrow. I couldn't keep my eyes off those perfect lips, not until my own softly claimed them. If our days were numbered, I wouldn't waste another moment. I closed my eyes and cupped her cheek, deepening our kiss.

My other hand roamed lower until it rested on her hip. Her breath caught, hunger flashed in her sapphire eyes, the sorrow wiped away.

And then someone knocked on the door.

We broke apart and sat up.

"Yes," Chel called, straightening her bodice.

Zephyra and Percifal entered our chamber. "I thought we should confer," Zephyra said, taking a seat on the dark blue lounger. Percifal leaned against the wall beside her and crossed his feet. His onyx hair had begun to grow back, but he hadn't bothered to shave.

"There's nothing to confer about," Chel replied.

"We still need to find the air elemental," Zephyra argued.

"How? And what does it matter now that you've lost your magic?" Chel put her head in her hands.

"Celestia said the air elemental is the key. Perhaps she'll know what to do about my magic."

"Have you felt anything?" I asked the fire elemental. "A spark?"

She looked away and said quietly. "I'm not sure."

"Have you tried to light a fire since we arrived here?" I pried.

"She's tried," Percifal answered for her.

The chamber went silent with hopelessness. Far be it for Celestia to place her bets on a bunch of mere mortals. We'd tried, and we'd failed. At least maybe the air elemental would never know of their failure.

Chel placed her hand on top of mine. "We're out of options. I'd like to remain here with Seph until it's time to return to Celestia. When Vesirus comes for Ventosa, we'll—"

"Cowards," Percifal didn't let her finish. "You're giving up? Taking your own lives? You don't deserve to return to Celestia if you do."

"Maybe Zephyra should pray to the goddess for a miracle." I wasn't jesting, not really. But Percifal whirled on me.

As he opened his mouth to defend his lover, a knock sounded.

The four of us stared at the door.

"Enter," Zephyra choked out. She took a deep breath and tucked her unbound hair behind her ears.

Time stopped as the woman of winter entered the guest chamber. She didn't have to knock. Every chamber, every *door* in this palace belonged to her. "I apologize for the way you were all treated earlier," Queen Starella started. "I shouldn't be here. If my father knew... well, I'm here anyway, so never mind that." She ran her fingers over her twisted rope of hair.

Chel put her chin in her hand and studied the queen. "Yes, why are you here? What have you to say to us?"

Zephyra shot her a look of warning, but the queen wasn't fazed by her rudeness. Or maybe she hadn't noticed for she kept her eyes on the burning candle. "My sister," the queen offered. "She may be able to help you."

"I'd wondered what had happened to Princess Auralina." Zephyra ducked her head, catching Queen Starella's attention. "Please don't take offence, but if I remember my lessons on royal ancestry correctly, your older sister should have been queen, not you."

Queen Starella's fingers stilled on her hair. "Yes, she should have. But Auralina has a sickness of the mind. At least, that's what my father tells people."

"And this isn't true?" Zephyra coaxed.

Chel leaned forward onto her elbows as we waited for the queen to answer.

Queen Starella blinked slowly, and then she sighed. "No, I don't believe it is. And if what you say is true—that Vesirus is coming for us—she might be our only hope. Oh, my father is going to kill me for this."

Chel reached forward and placed her hand on the queen's arm. A bold move, but Queen Starella looked at her with eyes full of sadness and regret. "Are you saying your sister has magic?" Chel seemed to realize herself and pulled back her hand and added, "Your Majesty."

"Yes," Queen Starella breathed as if she'd been holding the truth inside of herself her whole life.

I rose. "Take us to her."

"I—I—we'll have to be careful. There are guards watching the tower door."

"Aren't they *your* guards to command?" I questioned.

"They are, but half of them are loyal to my father. They may wish to alert him if they see us going into that tower."

"We'll disguise ourselves," Chel suggested. "As palace staff."

The queen's forehead wrinkled. "You don't look like you're from here. Especially you two." She gestured to Chel and Percifal.

"I have a better idea," Percifal offered. "You four go fetch Auralina. Leave the guards to me."

Zephyra opened her mouth to argue, but Percifal shook his head at her. She knew there'd be no talking him out of this. I understood his loyalty to our cause. He'd been raised to lead an army. He *needed* to be useful. I couldn't imagine how powerless he must have felt aligning himself with four elementals.

Queen Starella stared ahead, a distant look in her eyes, so still I began to wonder if she'd heard, but then she shook herself. "It may be the only way. I will threaten them with imprisonment if they disobey me. You can keep an eye on them while I take the others inside the tower. Fetch me at once if they try to leave their post."

"I'll do more than fetch you," Percifal mumbled lowly.

"Please don't hurt them. They are citizens of my kingdom."

Percifal's smile didn't meet his eyes. "I'll do my best, Your Majesty."

"What about you?" Zephyra asked the queen. "You said your father will kill you."

Queen Starella's eyes sparkled. "Let me worry about my father."

It was settled. I couldn't believe our luck. It turned out Zephyra didn't need to ask Celestia for a miracle. The goddess had already bestowed one upon us.

The young queen stepped closer to the door. We all stood as custom dictated. "I need to prepare. I will come back for you when it is time," she said.

We bowed to the Queen of Ventosa, and she left us to wait inside the toasty chamber.

Percifal poked at the fire while Chel paced the room. Zephyra sat quietly on a stool, probably going over what she planned to say to the air elemental.

I lazed casually on the bed with my boots off, watching the others with amusement. I had more patience than the other three. This was nothing compared to waiting for a suspect to crack after cutting, burning and torturing their mind and body. I could've waited all night, but the door opened. Everyone stopped what they were doing and stared at the queen.

"Come with me," Queen Starella whispered.

I pulled my boots back on and bowed to the queen on my way out the door. My lips curled up. Our journey hadn't been a complete failure. And soon, I could leave this frozen kingdom behind.

Queen Starella's silvery skirts swished as she led us down the palace corridors. I counted every corner we turned, memorizing each direction. I squinted, trying to see better in the dim light.

We came to the end of a corridor and stepped into a wider space, where the ceiling stretched higher. Two guards stood beside a door to an inner tower, leaning against the wall with their arms crossed. I studied their faces. One kept his blond beard long like his hair. The other had a scar which stood out starkly against his unshaven cheek.

They came to attention at the sight of their queen and bowed. "Your Majesty," the one with the beard said. "Is something amiss?"

Queen Starella stopped in front of him and met his eyes. "Yes, actually, something is amiss. Let me inside the tower to speak with my sister."

The guards both eyed us, shifting uncomfortably. "Are you sure, Your Majesty?" the bearded one questioned.

Anger flickered in her indigo gaze. "Yes, I'm sure. Hand me the keys."

"Of course. Apologies." The bearded guard fumbled for his ring of keys and surrendered them to her. His comrade watched the rest of us with keen interest. If one of them was going to betray Queen Starella to her father, I'd bet anything it'd be him.

The door swung open and the queen stepped forward. "I'm leaving this man," she indicated Percifal with a wave of her hand, "with you. If either of you try to leave or alert my father, he will fetch me and I'll have you thrown in the dungeon."

"Yes, Your Majesty," the bearded guard conceded. The guard with the scar simply bowed his head to her.

We climbed up the narrow, windy staircase inside the tower. We passed one floor with another door but kept going. Up, up, up.

We reached another door at the top. Queen Starella produced the key ring, searched for the correct key and unlocked the door.

I followed the others inside the largest bedchamber I'd ever seen. Though clean, the chamber was crowded. Numerous paintings of winter scenes, skyscapes and different animals covered the walls. A bed draped with ivory blankets had been placed in one corner. To one side, a lounger covered in dark purple material sat with a tall oak bookshelf beside it, filled with tons of books bound with leather. On the other side of the chamber, a square table held a chess board. Beautiful pieces of ebony and ivory rested on the board, waiting to be played. A lamp burned lowly at the back wall, which contained the only window in the chamber, a tiny, circular glass covered window; big enough only to fit one's face through.

And at that frost covered window, a young woman with hair so pale it appeared silver peered outside as though she could see through the ice to the world beyond, her shoulders perfectly straight beneath the fine, lavender lace gown. A queen without a crown.

As we all waited, staring at the one who'd brought us to the kingdom of ice and snow, Auralina Pavanas turned and set her clear amethyst eyes upon us and said in a crystal clear voice meant to command, "I've been waiting for you."

Find out how the story concludes in the final book of The Elemental Diaries.

Do you want a free novella? Sign up for my newsletter to receive The Mark of Motish, a prequel to The Elemental Diaries.
www.AndreaBLamoureux.com/newsletter

A MESSAGE FROM THE AUTHOR

I hope you enjoyed **Sepheus**. As an independent author I rely heavily on reviews. I love to hear what readers think about my stories. Even if you leave me a sentence about your favourite part, I'd be forever grateful.

If you want to keep updated about my books and know when I'm doing giveaways, subscribe to my newsletter at:

www.AndreaBLamoureux.com/Newsletter.

I will only send you mail when I have something to offer.

ALSO BY ANDREA B LAMOUREUX

The Elemental Diaries Series
Zephyra
Chelela
Sepheus
Auralina (Coming fall of 2019)

Elemental Diaries Side Stories*
The Mark of Motish

*Available for free to newsletter subscribers or for purchase on most ebook retailers. Visit www.AndreaBLamoureux.com to find out more info.

ACKNOWLEDGMENTS

As always, thank you times a million to my husband, Corey. My dream to write books would be a lot harder without you by my side.

Thanks again to Yvonne Less at Art 4 Artists for creating yet another amazing cover. I'm always so excited to see what you come up with when I bring you an idea.

To my editor, Kristine Schwartz from Schwartz Fiction Editing, thank you for helping me with polishing this story up. I know I can count on you, and for that, I am truly grateful.

Tami, thanks for making the pages beautiful. It's always a pleasure working with you.

Mom and Kevin, I am glad to have you two both in my corner. I can't thank you enough for all you have done for me.

This story wouldn't be the same without my beta readers. ChristianMichael Dutton, I appreciate all of the input you've given me. You've helped me create something I'm truly proud of. You are a master when it comes to critiquing. Ramona Miller, I am always excited to share my stories with you. Your thoughts as an avid reader mean so much to me.

To all of my advanced readers, thank you for being part of my team. I am so happy to share my stories with each and every one of you. I look forward to your thoughts each time I release a new book.

And to all of my readers, thank you so much for taking the time to read what I've created. Thank you for your reviews, for spreading the word about my books, and for all your support. I write these books to give you a break from reality. I hope I have succeeded in that quest.

ABOUT THE AUTHOR

Andrea lives in Alberta, Canada with her husband and two cats. As an only child she had to be creative growing up to keep herself occupied. Reading and writing have always been two of her favourite activities. She got her artistic side from her mother and her persistence from her father. She's always been a fan of fantasy themes and even dresses up in corsets sometimes.

Apart from reading and writing, she enjoys listening to her favourite music and horseback riding. She always tries to keep herself busy because she's a free spirit who gets restless easily.

If you'd like to find out when her next books are coming out you can find her online at

www.AndreaBLamoureux.com

Made in the USA
Coppell, TX
27 July 2020